Wrenched from the stag's side, I was cast like a doll to the ground. I slammed against the earth and pain coiled me into a knot. I groaned and spit blood. I saw the stag above me, his antlers etching a black pattern against the blue sky.

And then the antlers disappeared. Dazed, I watched as the stag's form shifted. There was a menacing hiss and a huge viper towered above me where the stag had been. Its head followed me, weaving back and forth, its black eyes glittering. As I crawled across the ground, the soulstring dragged him closer to me. I frantically tore at the soulstring on my wrist.

The viper's form faded and another took its place. An enormous black raven cawed harshly. His sharp talons raked the air and he lifted his beak, prepared to strike.

It's not real!

"Snyder is easily one of the best new voices in fantasy, capable of mixing a lyric style with a lean edge."

—Charles de Lint
author of *Yarrow*

SOULSTRING

MIDORI SNYDER

ACE BOOKS, NEW YORK

This book is an Ace original edition,
and has never been previously published.

SOULSTRING

An Ace Book / published by arrangement with
the author

PRINTING HISTORY
Ace edition / November 1987

ISBN: 0-441-77591-8

Ace Books are published by The Berkley Publishing Group,
200 Madison Avenue, New York, New York 10016.
The name "ACE" and the "A" logo
are trademarks belonging to Charter Communications, Inc.
PRINTED IN THE UNITED STATES OF AMERICA

10 9 8 7 6 5 4 3 2 1

With love, for Stephen

ONE

IT WAS A beautiful day, just on the cusp of summer to fall, when Severin of Thall arrived with his two brothers at Moravia Castle. The sky was a dense blue that seemed as solid as the inside of a teacup. Up from the fields came the dusty smells of wildflowers and sweet hay, cut and drying in the sun. I could smell loaves of bread baking in Cook's outdoor ovens, and the savories roasting on open spits for the noonday meal. Gazing idly out the window, as I often did, I watched the swallows darting for insects and, farther up in the open sky, I could just make out the fanned tail feathers and splayed wings of a hawk floating lazily on the warm updrafts.

I sat perched on the window of the sewing room in the high east tower, which overlooked the fields and nearby forest. In my lap rested a piece of embroidery, which I ignored for the moment as I stared out the window. The window seat was nestled in the crook of three large gabled windows that jutted out from the stone walls. The wide, clear panes were crowned with quatrefoils of blue and violet glass, which cast a cool light in the room. Scattered about the room were half-finished tapestries, embroideries stretched on frames, and lumpy piles of linens waiting to be mended. The sewing room was usually filled with serving women gossiping while they plied their needles to keep up with the endless demands of our household. But I was alone that day, which was just as well, for I was in no mood for company.

I hated to embroider and regarded it with the same enthusiasm one might have for counting hairs on a dog's head. I only did it to avoid my mother's stern lectures on the duties and responsibilities of Moravian noblewomen. On that day I was trying my best to embroider a manticore on a handkerchief and was making a woeful mess of it, too. I had poked my finger numerous times and it had bled, leaving a speckling of brown spots on the white linen. I had pulled the stitches too tightly, so the whole piece bunched and the design skewed to one side. The manticore had a lopsided grin that, rather than looking fearsome, was distinctly comical. And the backside of the piece was a snarled tangle of matted threads into which I could scarce push the needle.

From time to time, I stopped struggling with my needle and looked up to stare wishfully out the window at the fields and forest. I loved the sewing room because I could open the window and lean out, my shadow falling over the wall of gray stones. With the wind blowing sharp on my face, and my hair waving, I would imagine myself a bird poised for flight. Down from the tower I could feel myself swoop, catching the wind and lifting as I sped over the checkered fields, across the tops of the pines and into the thin blue line of the horizon beyond. I wanted to go anywhere, anywhere at all, as long as it was far away from Moravia Castle. Dreaming and yearning as I did then, I never accomplished much sewing in this room.

The sun was streaming over my shoulder, lighting up the dreadful job of needlework in my lap and making me feel very ill tempered. My black velvet dress was hot and the stiff lace collar scratched my neck. The stays of my bodice pressed tight over my waist and sweat trickled down between my breasts. I scratched irritably, stretched, and tried to blow cool air across my upper lip. My efforts did little to alter my discomfort so, in disgust, I finally gave up. Tossing the embroidery down on a bench, I stood and stared angrily around the room.

My sister Ilena's work was stretched on its frame before her empty chair. The piece was smooth and flat, the stitches neat and even. Along the edge of her chair, baskets of brightly colored silks waited in a row. On the bars of the frame, threads, needle case, and scissors hung in order. Ilena was a quiet young woman, well mannered and elegant—all the things I was not. Her skin was translucent and milk white; her shining black hair was worn swept high on her head with never a stray lock. Her gown was immaculate and well fitted; the maroon or gold silk of her inner sleeves dramatic against the sheen of black velvet. She was a perfect noblewoman, lovely and demure.

But the scene she had embroidered was ghastly and horrible; a scene that no doubt our father found thrilling. A dragon was eating some poor soul, cracking him open like a river crab and sucking out the meat. Ilena was skilled with the needle and she had captured the scene quite vividly, using red silks against the green of the dragon's scaled belly. I shuddered then, thinking of that bright room and my sister's head obediently bent over her work, embroidering gruesome tapestries to please Father. But then, we were all obliged to please Father or risk his terrible temper. I pleased him most by staying out his sight as much as possible, which suited us both quite well.

The piles of unfinished mending rebuked me for my disinterest in sewing. I ignored them and instead decided it was time to escape. I wanted to take off my stuffy dress with its itchy collar, put on something soft and colorful and take myself to the pond for a swim. If I hurried, I'd have just enough time to visit the pond and then return for the noon meal before anyone noticed I was missing. Maybe, I thought, growing more cheerful, I'd pick some flowers and make a summer's wreath for my head. Once picked the flowers would wilt quickly in the heat, but the idea of something green and flowering instead of dusty black velvet was too appealing to resist.

My mind made up, I resisted the urge to dash out of the room. Instead I poked a cautious nose out of the doorway and peered down the corridor. I would have to pass my mother's chambers and one long stretch near the gallery where I might be seen from the bailey. A servant, arms laden with dirty linens, crossed the bailey heading for the laundry house. I waited until he was gone and tiptoed into the corridor, holding my skirts tightly bunched in my hands so they wouldn't rustle.

The door to my mother's chambers was open and sunlight from a window cast a bright rectangle of light across the dark corridor. I froze at the edge of her doorway, waiting to be certain that I could pass unnoticed. Mother was talking to Ilena and she sounded, as usual, annoyed.

"No, no! You've made the sleeves too short again, Ilena," she complained. "He looks like a peasant's child who's outgrown his clothes. Your father won't like it at all. And this ruffle, it hides his face!"

Ilena gave a resigned sigh. "Mother, I can't help it if Vooris insists on growing faster than I can sew, and the ruffle isn't that bad . . . it just needs to be stiffened a bit. Here now, look, there's more fabric in the sleeves, I think I can lengthen them."

"Ow! You've pricked me, you idiot!" That was Vooris, petulant as ever. In the corridor I rolled my eyes. Next to Father, Vooris was the last person I wanted to see just now. "Ow! You've done it again. You're doing it on purpose!" he shrieked, his voice cracking. At fourteen years old his voice couldn't decide whether to stay high-pitched and almost girlish, or to drop into the lower tones of a man. I think it vexed him to no end that Zuul's voice had already deepened. Zuul was Father's page and Vooris's arch rival. Close in age, even in looks, it always seemed that Zuul was but a step ahead of Vooris and Vooris struggled to catch up.

"Now, Vooris, *dear*," Ilena was saying between her teeth, probably clenching pins in her mouth, "if you wouldn't fidget so it would be a lot easier."

"Enough!" he shouted. "I've had enough of this standing around listening to women's tittle-tattle abouts ruffs and getting skewered by pins. Get Zuul to do it. He's almost the same size."

"Almost is not the same. I think he's a bit taller," Mother clucked. "And besides, your father is needing him right now." She paused and I could hear Vooris grumble. "You want to look nice for your father, don't you?" Ah, I nodded outside the door, the usual threat.

Vooris grumbled more loudly.

"Stand still!" Ilena said exasperatedly.

"Go faster."

"I can't when you wiggle like a pig!"

"Better than looking like one. The way your nose turns up Ilena, you're the image of Cook's black sow—*ow!*"

"Sorry Vooris, an accident," Ilena replied tersely.

"Now Vooris, don't be such an ogre. Let your sister and me finish and I shall see to it that Cook prepares something special just for you." Mother was trying out her usual bribe in a soothing voice.

"Cold roast mutton, steamed potatoes with dill, honey carrots, and apple pudding with cream. I want it now, right now!" he insisted, and I heard him stamp his foot.

There was a pause and then Mother sighed heavily. She knew as well as I that Vooris wouldn't touch the food once it arrived. He only did it to annoy Cook and thereby pass his frustration on to someone else.

I heard the rustle of Mother's skirts as she made for the doorway. Pressing myself against the wall, I hoped the curve of the archway would hide me well enough. She bustled out, scowling, and turned away from me, heading in the direction of the main stairway. I waited until she was far enough ahead of me and then slipped past the open doorway. I caught a fleeting limpse of Vooris's slouched back, one arm held out, the fingers wiggling impatiently while Ilena pinned the sleeve in place. He tossed his head like a nervous horse and exhaled noisily. He was standing in a bright patch of yellow sunlight and his suit was of black velvet. I felt a dart of sympathy for him as I rushed past, already imagining my release from my own hot, sticky clothes.

Once in my room I threw off the velvet dress with its crushing bone stays and stood before the window, sucking in big grateful gulps of fresh air. My room was perched high above the kitchens and I could hear Cook banging pots and screaming angrily at the scullery maids. A rolling pin went flying into the courtyard and I saw a maid, arms wrapped protectively over her ducked head, fleeing across the yard to the well for more water. No doubt Cook had just received Vooris's request.

I reached into the closet and took out my favorite dress. It had a wide skirt of moss green and the green bodice had been embroidered with yellow flowers about the neckline. I pulled it on over my white linen undershift and rolled back the sleeves. I grabbed a straw hat with a wide brim and blue ribbons and slipped out of my room to the servants' stairway. My feet made a soft patter as I twisted down the winding spiral staircase, which opened out beside the kitchens.

I crossed the courtyard quickly and darted behind the

stables, hoping not to be seen by any of the stable hands, though at that hour I needn't have worried. Most had finished their morning chores and were off in the fields to help with the haying. I was startled suddenly by the harsh sound of Father's voice cursing the stableboy for not having his horse ready for his morning ride. I crouched behind the stone wall of the stable, waiting. The horse was brought and I heard Father pull himself up into the saddle with a short grunt. Then I heard the sharp snap of his riding crop and the horse bolted away, its hooves clattering on the paved stones of the courtyard. I exhaled heavily, relieved, and then hurried away down the muddy path that led to the fields, the ribbons of my hat fluttering gaily behind me.

"Humph!" I could imagine Father saying if he saw me now. "You look like a common goosegirl, not a noblewoman in the house of de'Stain Moravia. Your skin is as ugly as a brown toad."

I thrust my chin in the air angrily and stamped down the path. Maybe to him that was true, but it wasn't how I saw myself. Pale white skin is prized among Moravian nobility and I was a berry brown with a speckling of freckles over my nose and shoulders. My hair wasn't raven black but auburn, and under the summer sun it became streaked with strands of reddish blond. My eyes weren't the deep brown of my sister and brother but hazel, which changed to green when I was angry and gray when I was not. And if I dressed like a common goosegirl, so what? I thought angrily. Better to be common and enjoy oneself than be noble and miserable, I answered myself. That I had no idea what life was like for the common folk didn't matter; dressing like a goosegirl to please myself and irritate Father did.

Threading my way through the fields to the pond, I stopped a moment on the edge of Cook's herb garden, delighting in the rich fragrance of the herbs. I looked them over, trying to remember all the different names that Cook had taught me. There a bush of comfrey, its bristling leaves and delicate white flowers good for teas to soothe coughs. There was curled parsley, basil, purslane, and the feathery leaves of fennel to aid digestion while they flavored the food. Pennywort and raspberry in the far corner were for a woman's menses, and the different mints and columbines were made into tonics for the blood. Along the edges, Cook planted beebalm, the shaggy heads of blue and pink flowers attracting the bees to the garden and flavoring the honey in the hives nearby. Cook often brought me here to teach me the properties and uses of herbs. This garden, like cooking, was a passion of hers, and she boxed my ears if she thought I wasn't paying close enough attention to her instruction.

I continued past the garden and through the fields, surrounded by the dry, dusty scent of wheat. I arrived at the edge of the fields and shivered as I stepped from the sun-warm fields into the shaded woods. The color of the day changed from blue to pale green as above me arches of oak, maple, and linden formed a leafy canopy. I inhaled the musty fragrance of the forest and on my tongue it lingered like the taste of wild mushrooms. I was touched suddenly by the tangible memory of Cook and me hunting morels in the spring.

Cook was gruff and violent when angered. Her blue eyes would flash dangerously and her ham fists would fling pots or any other crockery that happened to be in her way when she was in a temper. But she could also be kind when it suited her. That spring, she had led me through the woods and showed me the secret location of a patch of wild morels. Picnic baskets under our arms, we had set out in the early morning and stopped at a shady spot in the woods. There beneath oaks, their bark still damp from the new running sap and the ground wet with dew, she pulled back the carpet of decaying leaves and showed me the brown honeycombed caps of the morels just breaking the soil. We picked some, being careful to leave behind some for the fall gathering. Then she showed me other plants that grew in the forest, wild cousins to the herbs tamed in her garden. We picked armfuls of green wild plants and added them to our picnic. Finding a circle of warm sunlight, we sat and ate. There was a salad of sheep sorrel and the tender shoots of dandelions. The watercress tasted crisp and tart on my tongue as I mixed it with slices of cheese and bread.

"Cook, who taught you about the woods?" I asked between hungry bites.

"Me dad," she answered. "He were a forester and a grand man. He could walk out into the forest in the morning with nothing and come home, his pockets stuffed with the green goodness from the woods. He said the woods talked to him if he were quiet enough and listened." She took another bite of bread and cheese and laughed lightly. "He told me that I didn't make much of a forester's daughter for all my love of chatter." Then she sniffed suddenly and her eyes grew pink and teary.

"Fathers don't think much of their daughters, do they?" I said bitterly.

"Bite yer tongue!" and she smacked me none too gently on the top of my head. "Me dad was a good man, nothing like the master, and he loved me well enough—" She stopped abruptly, her face stricken as she saw how her words hurt me.

My mouth went dry and food in my hand seemed no more desirable than clay. "Yes, well, I'm sure that's quite true. It's *my* father that doesn't love me much; but then, there's little besides himself that he does love." My face hardened into a mask as I shoved unwanted feelings of anger and loneliness into the farthest corner of my being. I would have liked to lay my head on Cook's generous bosom and weep, but I wouldn't allow myself to do that. I had learned long ago to hide my feelings and I refused to acknowledge my hurt.

Cook laid a heavy hand on my shoulder and spoke to my stiff neck. "You're a good child and there's much to love in you."

I said nothing, but sat staring out at the shifting patterns of light playing through the leaves. Cook waited, watching me. Then she sighed noisily and removed her hand from my shoulder.

I wanted to believe what she said was true. But it wouldn't have helped me much, even if I had believed her. Instead I silently repacked the picnic baskets and we returned home, the brightness of the day clouded by the talk of Father.

Standing on the path, I shrugged away the unwanted thoughts of Father. They had no place here. This was my retreat, my refuge from all that Father meant to me. Picking my way through the old path, my mood lightened at the sight of a stand of willows that marked the pond's edge. I approached slowly, allowing the peace and beauty of the place restore my happiness.

The sun glistened on the pond as dragonflies bobbed and danced with bright sparks over the water's smooth surface. Unable to restrain myself further, I undressed quickly, tossing my clothes to the side of the path. Then, kicking off my shoes, I ran to the water. Goose bumps were already pricking my arms I jumped into the pond. I dived deeply through its murky green water, letting the cold pass through me in one enormous shiver. Then I surfaced, rolled on my back, and spouted water like a lazy otter. I swam back and forth across the pond a few times and then floated on my back to watch the sunlight sparkling on my body like a gown of diamonds. As I floated my anger and frustration were washed away by the cool water. Here I could imagine that there was no such place as Moravia Castle and that I was anybody other than Magda de'Stain Moravia.

No one was a bit happy when I was born. Least of all Father. When the midwives told him I was a girl, he left the bedroom enraged, his face whiter than the maid's bleaching. He then unleashed his considerable fury on Moravia Castle, bringing down the newly built east wing and collapsing the sorcerer's tower into a heap of broken stone. Still not content with the smoking rubble, he then attacked the farms and village. Fields of wheat and oats withered and shriveled under his sorcerous anger. Milk curdled in the cows, the wool on sheep was scorched an ugly brown, and eggs cracked beneath the hens. It was Cook who told me about it and, knowing Father, I can well believe she spoke the truth.

There was a good reason for Father's disappointment. He is the sorcerer Gregor de'Stain Moravia, the thirteenth generation in a family of sorcerers. At one time the de'Stains served kings, but centuries have passed since any king was strong enough to dominate the quarrelsome princes who carve out their little domains in Moravia. Since there has been no other sorcerer family, the de'Stains have long held a unique position of power. Moravian princes tried to seduce the de'Stains with plots of conquest, hoping that with a sorcerer for an ally, they would be able to acquire the realm of a king. The de'Stains were a proud family, and though they might have dabbled in skullduggery when bored, they wanted never again to be servants to a king. It was kept secret that the sorcerer's talent did not extend beyond the ancient borders of our corner of Moravia. Thus the de'Stains were feared by their neighbors, lest the de'Stains might suddenly desire to expand their holdings, and at the same time, respected for the seeming security of life within our borders. Only a fool would have tried to conquer the house of de'Stain Moravia and its sorcerers.

For thirteen generations those of the house of de'Stain

Moravia lived comfortable lives. The sorcerer's talent provided a wellspring of power from which each generation of sorcerers did not hesitate to drink. My family has always been proud and obsessed with its lineage. And it has been greedy, insisting on measures to insure our family remained the sole possessors of the sorcerer's talent. It wasn't really difficult to achieve. For thirteen generations the sorcerer's talent passed into the blood of the firstborn, who was always male, which is probably why women in Moravia had very little to do with power. That is, until I, Magda de'Stain Moravia, had the impertinence to be the firstborn. For Father it must have been quite a shock. It must have seemed to him as if thirteen generations of de'Stain power lurched to a halt, stuck like the wheel of a cart in a muddy rut.

My mother wasn't happy either. It was the most important event of her life and I ruined it. This one act of producing the male heir to the house of de'Stain Moravia promised her a place of honor and security in Moravia; I am told she cried when I was presented to her and continued to search beneath my swaddling in hopes the midwives had been in error over my gender. Shunning me for ruining her future, she sent for a wet nurse to care for me.

It's hard for me to imagine any mother who, after the strenuous act of labor, shouldn't rejoice in her healthy firstborn baby. Or any father who, after gazing into the wide-eyed stare of the infant, shouldn't feel pride at the resemblance to be found there. Cook told me I was a pretty baby, big and noisy, with a halo of reddish curls. But I was a girl and my parents couldn't forgive me. I was named Magda, after my maternal grandmother—Father refused to name me after any of the women in his family, believing I had insulted them by not being male.

But this was only beginning of our family's misery.

My poor mother. To have suffered one shame was awful, but with the birth of my sister Ilena two years later, the second shame must have been unendurable. Father was livid, though he did restrain himself and only the farms suffered damage that time. He refused to speak to my mother or even to see her, convinced she had planned this catastrophe. I remember her then, huddled in the sewing room as she wept.

I, however, was delighted. With her black wisps of hair,

milky-blue eyes, and pink cheeks, I thought my sister was a lovely doll created especially for me.

I can't tell you why it happened, but Mother become pregnant again two years later. When I was a little older I had romantic fantasies about it; fantasies, mind you, that had nothing to do with the real lives of my parents, since they remained as cold and detached as ever to each other. I imagined my mother rushing to my father's study, her clothes in a wild disarray, her hair undone and billowing. She would hold a knife to her bosom, pleading with Father for one more chance. Impressed by the intensity of her passion, he would relent and take her in his arms. More likely, Father came to her and held the knife to her throat and demanded she give him a son. Either way it worked and my brother Vooris was born when I was five years old.

Father, normally cold and distant, was beside himself with joy. He held my brother constantly and to our astonished eyes delighted in making stupid faces until the baby laughed or gurgled. Then, with all seriousness, he would turn to my sister and me and announce that here at last was a child of the blood, vessel of the Moravian talent and our future destiny. My mother, quite simply, was relieved; no more would she have to suffer Father's cruel silences and withering glances. She had found grace and favor in Father's eyes.

But this domestic happiness was short-lived, for you see, I was furious. For five years Father had treated me and then my sister with complete disinterest. I didn't complain and neither did she. I assumed that was how it was between parents and children and I should not expect more. But seeing Father suddenly affectionate with my brother, doting on him, praising him, deeply wounded my pride and infuriated my child's sense of fairness. In my father's caresses of my younger brother I saw all the love that was denied me and in my mother's grateful expression all the pride that I didn't bring her. I didn't know how to relieve the torrent of emotion that filled my small body to bursting, the sadness, the jealousy, the terrible anger. One day at the noon meal, however, much to everyone's dismay, I discovered the family gift for releasing fury.

We were eating in the small dining hall off the main kitchen. The sun was shining through the two, ancient oriel windows that looked out over a garden. My plate was stained with a red patch of light from the rose trefoils in the window. Mother was fussing at Ilena and me with her usual commands of, "Sit up straight, Ilena! Don't slouch, and Magda stop biting your nails!" Vooris, who had been sleeping in the bassinet near Father's elbow, had been removed from the room after he soiled himself. The smell of it lingered faintly. Nonetheless, Father was pronouncing on Vooris's future as a sorcerer, while at the same time admonishing my mother to eat properly that she might be better able to nourish this prodigy on her noble milk. I was in a blacker mood than usual, having just been told that I could no longer play in the nursery, a place that had been my home since birth, because the noise might wake the baby. I decided then it was better to receive attention for being a dreadful child than to be ignored and shoved aside while my brother reaped the glory. Like a loaded cannon, I needed only tinder to ignite the fuse, which my mother unwittingly provided.

The maid was taking off the soup bowls in preparation for the next course when Mother snapped at me.

"Magda, stop playing with your knife. You're ripping the linens."

"Stop shouting at me!"

"Magda, you'll not speak to your mother in that tone!" Father glared at me from his chair at the head of the table.

"At least I talk to her. *You* never did until that—that *thing* came into the house." My face was hot, anger bubbling like porridge forgotten on the fire.

"How dare you speak of Vooris as a thing!"

"He is!" I retorted angrily. "A rotten stinking thing that looks like a pig."

"Go to your room immediately!" he commanded.

"I can't. You took it away from me!"

"Magda, I'm warning you," Father started to say, his voice dropping into a low growl.

"I don't care, I don't care! I hate all of you! I hate—"

I was staring hard at Father as I shouted and suddenly felt the air squeezed from my chest, my words strangled in my throat. He held my gaze, his pupils widening black as obsidian against his pale skin. I saw the yellow flame of power glow in his eyes, gleaming bright like the eyes of a cat reflecting torchlight. My head grew light as I struggled to breathe. From deep within me an echo sounded, booming in my ears and rising to answer the power Father forced on me. It reared up and threw itself through my body like a squall on a small pond. In my eyes a blue and silver flame flickered and then flashed to life like lightning. Father must have seen it, for he drew back, horrified. But he was too late to stop the flood of power that surged through my hands and erupted in the room.

Dimly I heard the sounds of crying and screaming but I couldn't understand them. Like the spout on Cook's teakettle that whistled with hot steam, fury forced its way through me with a reckless vengeance. I didn't know what was happening. Only instinct guided the power in its wild destruction. But I wasn't at all afraid. It was exciting as my emotions hurtled through me in a whirlwind maelstrom. I'm not certain how long I stayed like that, arms stretched out as the power rushed to my hands, but I remember the sense of lightness and wonderment as the power peaked and then receded, leaving me drained of all my anger.

I was surprised when I put down my arms at last and opened my eyes. Contrary to my own sense of peace and calm, the room was in utter shambles. Dishes had flown off the table and crashed into the walls, leaving streaks of green food stains on the tapestries. The floor sparkled brightly with bits of shattered glass. My mother was covered with sorrel soup; a few of the leaves stuck to her neck and she looked like some curious water sprite that had just surfaced from beneath a lily pad. My sister was wailing and waving her arms about, for the milk had spilled down the front of her new dress and ruined it. In the kitchen I could hear Cook screaming that "something" or "someone" had burned supper and she "didn't hold wit' no sorcerer types wot ruined good, honest food!" She came bursting into the room with her big spoons, prepared to do battle, followed by a handful of curious scullery maids, their mouths agape.

I must confess that I was very pleased with myself. Seeing the crashing mess I had made filled me with immense satisfaction. I began to laugh, hands cupped gleefully over my mouth, until I saw Father's face, which sobered me to a stone. At first his eyes were wide with surprise. His elegantly coiffed hair was a snarled tangle and his black doublet was splattered with wine and food. He was leaning back from the table, fingertips gripping the edge as if to keep from being toppled by a strong

wind. The look of surprise quickly vanished and his eyes narrowed to angry slits with a piercing gaze that rooted me to the
spot.

He stood up slowly, ignoring my sister's crying and my
mother's efforts to rescue pieces of broken china. He raised
his hands toward me and I cringed, suddenly cold and very
frightened. His face was white with rage, his lips thin and
bloodless as he murmured strange words. My mother looked
up from the floor and screamed, "No!" Around me the air was
charged with the feel of his icy magic. Unable to move or
resist, I stood there, frozen in a spreading red haze. Then the
sunlight from the window faded and, before my terrified eyes,
the room disappeared.

When I blinked next the world was dark and smelled musty
and dank. My heart pounded in my chest as I thought of the
stone crypts in which my ancestors were buried. I was afraid
to reach out in the dark and find the cold slab of a tomb wall.
But gradually I saw a slim thread of light, and then another
forced through a crack in a door. The musty odor held the
scent of old hay and dung and I knew that I was not buried
alive but removed to one of the sheds behind the stables. I
leaned my sweaty forehead against the wall of the shed and
heard chickens scratching the dirty and the snuffling of pigs at
the door of my prison.

I languished in that dark shed for a least five days, though
it might have been longer. Only Cook came to see me, to
bring me food and empty the chamber pot. She would shake
her head at me. "Por youngin'," she would mutter, and then
she would lock the door again. I was cold and miserable, to be
sure, and there were times when I cried very hard for the
comfort of my warm, dry bed. But I was also strangely happy.
I knew I had power, and the knowledge that thirteen generations of the great de'Stain talent flowed in my blood quickened the beating of my heart and consoled me. Sitting there in
the dark I tried to call up the power. Though I could sense it, it
remained frustratingly out of reach, as if I were trying to
scratch my nose with my elbow.

No matter, I told myself, Father will show you how to use
it again. I assumed that my punishment was for destroying the
dining hall. Once I was released, I knew father would forgive
my outburst—so like his own—and then praise me for inher-
iting the talent. He would cherish and love me just as he had

done my brother. I imagined us studying together, Father instructing me in the ways of statecraft and sorcery. With the walls of my shed as witness, I vowed fervently to work very hard so that Father would be proud of me.

"Come on, youngin', out." Cook came to get me when my punishment was done. She pulled me squinting like a mole into the light and, holding her nose, dragged me by one hand to the kitchen. "Ouf, girl, you stink so's I can hardly tell you from the slops. It's enough to turn me from my food. You'll not go in like this, that's for certain."

She reached down an empty bucket from a peg on the wall and filled it with hot water from the kettle. She tossed me a small brush and a bar of coarse soap. "'ere now, see that, you make use of that and I'll get you something clean to put on." Happily, I started scrubbing my face with the soap.

Washed, hair braided back, and wearing a clean dress, I went to the Great Hall for an audience with my parents. I was excited and eager, for Cook told me that it was true that I alone had inherited the de'Stain plower. My brother Vooris had not a speck of talent to him beyond the ordinary. With jealous satisfaction, I knew that Father would now welcome me into the communion of sorcerers. I would be loved at last.

The Great Hall was long and wide and my steps made a light tapping as I walked. I felt small and vulnerable and my confidence ebbed as I approached my parents. They were sitting rigid in their chairs and they regarded me with cold formality. My mother had aged and faded to a gray shadow beside my father. She spoke no words of greeting and her eyes darted everywhere, refusing to look at me. In her lap she twisted a handkerchief round and round. Father looked regal, the black velvet of his doublet stark against the stone of his carved chair. Around his neck a single chain of gold glittered, and in his hand he held the short ebony staff, the symbol of de'Stain power. His face was a powdered mask, his eyes unreadable black hollows.

I wanted to drop to my knees and beg forgiveness but I was afraid to move.

"Father," I began meekly. He stopped me with a sharp wave of his hand.

"Never," he whispered fiercely. "Never call me that again."

I was silent, my hopes fleeting with his spiteful words. He stood and I flinched, afraid of the staff he pointed at me.

"You are a curse, a demon. Because of you Moravia suffers. Because of you the house of de'Stain is dishonored."

Tears started in my eyes and my throat grew tight, unable to swallow. He stepped down and circled me, moving slowly, I was terrified, feeling his rage burn hot, then icy, on my skin. The hairs on my neck prickled as he passed behind me and I thought he meant to strike me.

"A mere girl, arrogant and willful." He came around and stood before me. "Was that your mother's plan, Tania?" Father spoke to Mother, his hard gaze still on me. "Everyone knows how she hated my father for not marrying her. Or perhaps it was your father. Everyone knows he resented being second choice."

"Gregor, please," she said softly, and I heard the handkerchief tear.

"An excellent plan, my dear. One I should congratulate you on. What better way to bring down the house of de'Stain than to bind the power to a girl. How did you do it?" He turned to her, the smile mocking and cruel.

She didn't answer but stared at her lap. Father turned back to me and the smile disappeared. He held up his staff and spoke harshly.

"You have power that is not rightfully yours. I can't take it from you, but I shall see to it that you never use it again."

The staff bloomed with yellow flame, striking me with the force of his power. It pierced my chest like a fiery lance and I screamed as the pain tore through me. The room whirled violently. I sank to the floor, my hands pressed against the searing pain in my chest. Then he withdrew his power, wrenching it away from my heart. I lay there breathing raggedly, unable to dispel the terror that my heart no longer beat. I listened and beneath my hand I heard the faint thump as if my heart were hidden behind a thick wall of impenetrable flesh. I looked up at him, shocked, and saw his face pale as chalk, tiny drops of sweat staining his forehead through the powder. His hand trembled as he lowered the staff; for an instant I saw pain reflected in his eyes. Mother had hidden her face behind her hands, unable to watch.

"You are alive, Magda, but only because I wish your

mother to know that her plan will not defeat me. The house of
de'Stain Moravia will survive in spite of you. But don't tempt
me further or I will kill you, as easily as I would snuff the
candle that burns me."

Do not ask me how I knew, but he lied. As children can
sometimes hear deception in a parent's voice, I could hear it in
his. I was alive because he couldn't kill me. I saw it in his
grim face, sweat streaking the powder on his cheeks like tears.
He trembled and I knew he shared my pain, just as surely as
we shared the gift of power. It was, however, small comfort to
me as I lay on the cold floor of the Great Hall feeling
wounded and crushed. Watching my parents leave, I felt the
wall of flesh around my heart harden to stone.

It should have been a secret. No one was ever to know that
I had inherited the sorcerer's talent. My father hoped to shield
my brother's deficiency until such time as my brother married
and sired a new heir. Father was convinced this future grand-
child would set right the breach of power in our lineage. The
de'Stain Moravia would again have a sorcerer to rule.

I was a thorn stabbing his side, for if word got out that I
had inherited the talent, there would be suitors from every
corner of Moravia ready to marry me in hopes of starting their
own lineage of sorcerers. As a wife I would be obliged to
honor my husband's family at the expense of my own. Thirteen generations of being the only sorcerers had increased the
resentment of our neighbors, and there were many who would
have leaped at the chance to see the supremacy of the
de'Stains challenged. Father refused the suggestion that I be
married off to some doddering old courtier too ancient to do
anything as vigorous as siring a son, for even a lowly stableboy can be substituted to father an heir beneath the failing
eyes of an old husband.

It wasn't the ambitions of other men that bothered Father.
It was me Father didn't trust. He was afraid of me, afraid of
what I might become, afraid that it threatened every plan and
scheme he designed for my brother's future and the success of
the de'Stain Moravia. He wanted me well within his reach,
where he could be certain that I wouldn't use the power that
was my birthright or pass it on to a child. He made me his
adversary, his rival for power. And while he feared me, he
neither valued nor respected me enough to want me to partici-
pate in his designs and one day succeed him. I was female and

that, it seemed, was enough to make me untrustworthy and weak, a dangerous vessel to hold magic.

But word got out. After all, servants don't care that much about family politics, and—to be truthful—my temper tantrum was rather spectacular. The story got whispered from mouth to ear behind cupped hands. From scullery maids and stableboys it flew to ladies' maids and pages. And from them, into the ears and ambitious hearts of Moravian nobles. At every hunt and court ball the story grew in portion until it was said I cracked the very foundations of Moravia Castle with my rage, which, in a manner of speaking, was true. Eventually there was even a comic version (how could it have been otherwise?) of my tantrum performed at the local hiring fairs by troupes of itinerant actors.

Father did his best to deny the rumors, claiming that they were nonsense and even malicious chatter. But the story persisted, and by the time I was eight, proposals of marriage were becoming frequent. Father ground his teeth and refused politely at first, stating my youth and his great affection for me as reasons for rejection.

Yet, when I was twelve Father surprised and shocked us all by announcing at a huntsmen's ball that I had indeed inherited —along with my brother Vooris, he was quick to add—the de'Stain talent for sorcery. Pairs of eyes glittered hungrily at me from around the room, and I felt suddenly naked. But, Father went on to say, I would be wed only to the man who could prove himself worthy enough of my gift. The room was silent as they waited to hear what he would ask of them. Three tasks, three challenges to a man's bravery must be passed before I would wed. The price for failure, death. A low murmur broke out among the guests, and here and there an angry voice was raised in protest. Father remained unperturbed and reached to take a glass of wine from the table. As he raised it, the guests quieted uneasily. The room ached with tension and hostility. Noblemen glanced at each other from behind hooded eyes, as if assessing the strengths and weaknesses of competitors.

"Honor or death!" Father reminded them, and drained his glass quickly. They could not refuse to drink to their own motto and, around the room, nobles drank as though the wine had turned bitter.

I watched Father uncertainly. He smiled at me coldly. At

his side Vooris, who was seven and already quite spoiled and bad tempered, stared moodily at the ground. Zuul stood at his elbow with a spiteful grin. Not for the first time I thought of Zuul as a twin to Vooris. Black haired and quick-tempered, Zuul seemed impatient to do Father's bidding. Always in Father's shadow, the page anticipated Father's every need. What is more, it seemed he enjoyed it. Zuul may have been the only one at Moravia Castle for whom pleasing Father was not an obligation, but a desire. As I watched them, eyeing the disgruntled nobles with satisfaction, I wondered why my father had made such an unexpected offering of me.

In the years that followed his pronouncement, I saw many eager suitors come and fail. At first I was flattered by the attention, mistaking it for love. But the men who came quickly cured me of that notion. They were younger versions of my father, brash and arrogant. At dinners they ogled me with a mixture of lust and ambition, which had nothing to do with me, but the talent I possessed. I withdrew into a shell, scarcely noticing the men who came to answer my father's challenge. As I became indifferent to them, gossip spread that I was a cruel and heartless young woman, enjoying the suffering of my suitors. It was hard for me to feel sorry for them. I didn't like them and none of them cared for me. Only desire to possess the de'Stain sorcery drove them to our doorstep. I could have told them that I had no sorcery to give them, that Father had hidden it from me, though few would have believed me. But the truth is I did nothing to save my suitors because they resembled Father. And it seemed each time one of them failed, I punished Father for the hurt he had caused me.

I rolled over in the pond, and dived once more into the depths. The water grew colder as I neared the muddy bottom. I held my breath as long as I could and then pushed off toward the surface, feeling the water part around my body. The skin on my fingers had turned white and wrinkled. My teeth were beginning to chatter. Reluctantly I pulled myself from the water and sat in the sun on a broad, flat rock. I lay back, the hard stone warming the skin of my shoulders and the sun shining on my face through an opening in the trees. I lay very still, except for the occasional shiver that trembled through me. Eyes closed, I concentrated on the little drops of water that tickled and itched as they dried on my skin. Arms stretched out over the sides of the rock, I dozed lightly in the sun.

Suddenly my eyes snapped open with alarm as I heard the sounds of people approaching. As quietly and quickly as I could, I slipped off the rock and back into the water. I swam to the opposite shore, hoping to reach my clothes before I was discovered. I could still hear them nearing as I collected my clothes from where I had tossed them on the bushes. Hunched over in the green shrubs, I dressed quickly, my clothes sticking to my wet skin. Whoever they were, they were arguing, and their voices grew more insistent as they neared. Men's voices. I groaned silently with annoyance. They had to be suitors, and that meant another tedious afternoon at a long lunch with father playing cat-and-mouse games. If they discovered me now, I thought nervously, they could just as easily decide that they needn't bother with the tasks, abduct me, and quickly "consummate" my marriage. Being abducted and raped was not the way I wished to be freed from Father and Moravia Castle. I held my dripping hair, tried not to move, and thanked whoever it was that watches over me that my clothes blended into the shrubbery.

I peeked through a gap in the hedge and saw them as they halted not far from my hiding place. They were three men on horseback and I stared at them intently. I didn't know them, nor could I recognize what house they came from by their dress. Moravia is not that big and I was certain that I knew most of her eligible nobles. But these were strangers and, studying their dress, I realized they weren't even Moravians. The de'Stains always wore black, but that was because my ancestors thought it the only appropriate color for a sorcerer's family to wear. The other nobles preferred a very gaudy style of dress, usually with brightly colored silks, heavy sleeves on the doublets, and padding at the shoulder. Their hose was often striped and their riding boots extended high to the knee with a wide cuff. Noblemen were usually clean shaven and they covered their faces with a light dusting of white powder. They wore their hair dressed in tight curls that rested below the shoulder and, when riding, were never without a wide-brimmed hat crowned with feathers.

But the men on horseback arguing with each other were dressed in a very simple fashion. For all its simplicity, it was, to my eye, still elegant. They wore jerkins of leather; not the coarse padded ones of our stable hands and smiths, but ones of supple leather, which had been tooled about the lacings with intricate patterns of interwoven braids and leaves. Their shirts were white linen, open at the throat and tied loosely at the cuffs. Brown woolen trousers were tucked into boots of stiff, black leather that gleamed with polish. Over their shoulders they wore woolen cloaks, woven in rust and brown and pinned at the throat with silver clasps. Even their saddles were of a simpler design, lacking a high horn and instead lying flat and smooth beneath the rider. Their horses were healthy-looking beasts, much larger than our breed, with big, sturdy chests and broad foreheads with small attentive ears pricked forward. One horse had a dappling of white spots across its brown rump, like a fawn's spring coloring. The horses wore little ornamentation, no headpieces decked with feathers and bells, but bridles of silver and bits decorated with a rose pattern at the cheek strap. They were steady animals, foraging patiently in the shrubs by the path while their riders argued.

I looked back at the men's faces and was immediately struck by how similar they all looked. Brothers, I thought; they must be brothers, for they shared the same square-cut jaw, dark eyes, and brown curly hair, cropped short at the neck. One was heavyset with a full beard streaked with white beneath a wide mouth. Dark brows furrowed over deep-set eyes into a frown. At his side a younger man fidgeted in the saddle, chewing on the edges of a small mustache. His gaze darted everywhere, as if he were searching through the thick underbrush. The third man leaned over and patiently stroked the neck of his horse. I caught a glimpse of even white teeth as he smiled at something another said. His profile was strong, the ridge of his nose straight. He righted himself smoothly over the saddle again and adjusted the folds of his cape. How odd, I wondered. Are they nobles? They came with no servants or pages to attend them. Yet even without a retinue they carried themselves proudly and with dignity. I stared, fascinated, concern for myself forgotten in my curiosity.

"Severin, is it possible that anyone can be so poor as to clear such a rude path, then? We must have missed the main entrance. Let's turn around and double back," the youngest-looking man declared.

"No, Nar. I tell you it's here. The other is a ruse. Keep following it and you'll wind up where you started and no closer to the entrance of the castle," the man, Severin, answered. Like Nar, he had a dark mustache and a new beard darkened his cheeks. He looked confident as he spoke, pointing out the small muddy path.

"It's nothing but a cattle path, this, for herd children to bring home cows. It's not a proper entrance to a castle like that one!" Nar exclaimed as he gestured to the high towers of Moravia Castle. From the pathway one could see rising airily over the treetops the gray stone towers with colored pennants waving from the turrets.

"Aye, I know." Severin nodded. "And I agree, it's a rude path we're following. But feel it with your own senses, Nar, and you'll see I am right. If we follow what 'appears' to be the path, we will be walking on our shadows before long."

I grimaced in my hiding place, for I knew this to be one of Father's nasty little tricks. The first task of any bridal party was to *arrive* at Moravia Castle. Father would keep suitors chasing a false path until they became tired, saddle sore, and very dirty. Father often tampered with the weather, making a heavy rain or freezing sleet so that suitors arrived cold, shaking with fever. Severin and his brothers were lucky, for the day was pleasant. Or could it be that Father was unaware they had arrived this far?

"Break the illusion, then? It's not that strong and there are three of us," spoke the heavier man.

"No," answered Severin, shaking his head. "I'm thinking this is a test. I say we play at being bewildered strangers who, with luck, have stumbled on the right path. I don't trust the power at work here. It's too . . ." He paused, thinking. "It's too unpredictable. Don't you feel it, Teren?" he said, turning to the heavier-set man.

Teren stopped his horse from wandering forward and I saw his face tense with concentration. His head swayed back and forth like a weather cock catching the wind; for a moment, it seemed his eyes came to rest on me. I hunched deeper in my hiding place, seeing the look of puzzlement cross his face.

"Hmm." He pursed his lips and squinted his eyes as if to see into a badly lit room. "You're right, Severin. Most times it's full of malice. Then it shifts and I can sense something different. But I can't put my mind to it," he said slowly.

"Right, then," said Severin with finality. "Until I understand it better, we take no chances."

"We started taking chances when we left Thall," Teren said curtly.

Severin remained silent, but I saw him frown. The horse jerked his head forward to nibble at the leaves of my bushes.

"Was there no other woman who might have served as wife, Severin, so that we didn't have to be here, wandering like blind beggars?" Teren asked.

"Did I ask you to come, then?"

"No, you didn't. But what man would have let his brother travel alone to make the bridal offer? I only ask, Severin, to be certain of why we're *here,* in this unwelcoming place."

Severin turned to his older brother. "The farseer said to come south, and south it is I've come."

"Aye, but—"

"Teren, tell me that you would marry without first knowing heart's ease?"

"Some do, Severin, waiting for time to make it happen."

"Have you, then?"

The older man didn't answer but shifted in his saddle, his face clouded with unspoken feelings.

"Just so," Severin replied evenly. "I know there's much that's wrong here, but even as we crossed the border, I knew it was right to come." He smiled then at Teren. "I promise you I'll not lose my wits. I say we go careful and cautious. We keep our strengths to ourselves and we play this game one move at a time. Is it agreed, then?" He looked over at Nar, who was hesitating, frowning at the muddy path as if it insulted him personally.

"Ach, all right," Nar finally conceded. "But I still think it rude coming up on the cow path to court your bride. It doesn't make me feel very dignified," the young man lamented.

Severin laughed, a deep warm laugh, slapping the other companionably on the shoulder. Severin's horse jerked his head upright, startled by the sound. "It was adventure you wanted, something more exciting than the farms at Thall, and yet it seems we can't escape the same old shit."

"It won't be the first time we've waded in shit, Nar. Just try not to slip in it, eh, little brother," Teren said, smiling at the younger man. "It'll spoil our image if we arrive reeking of the byre."

"If we are speaking of reeking, Teren, leave that wild garlic alone, then, until after we're safely on our way home. One 'good day' from you and the bride will wither away to nothing," Nar retorted.

Teren ignored Nar's outburst and turned to Severin. "I wonder that this cow path doesn't tell us something about your future bride?" He leaned forward in his saddle, eyes twinkling mischievously. "You'll be murmuring love songs in her ear and the young heifer will moo and give you a wet lick on the cheek."

"Perhaps," said Severin, smiling back, "but think of the milk I shall have, and the butter! Won't you be jealous, then!" They laughed loudly at that and then continued down the muddy path to Moravia Castle.

As soon as they left, I bolted through the woods and, running as fast as I could, took the shorter path through the farm fields to the castle. My mind was alive with curiosity. Where were they from? They had mentioned Thall, but I didn't know where that was and cursed my lack of education as I ran. We shared the same language but their accent was distinct, like a distant cousin. It lilted in a singsong fashion that was pleasant to hear, whereas our language was flatter and we spoke much faster. But there was something more, something hinted at. They had power. They had magical talent, at least enough to sense Father's enchantment. In spite of my long indifference to suitors, I was interested in Severin. Not as a husband, but as someone who might offer Father a true challenge at last. I wanted to be there when Father saw him arrive, for I was quite certain now that it was going to be something of a surprise.

I arrived at the path behind the stables just as Severin and his brothers were approaching the entrance of the back courtyard near the kitchens. The scullery maids, with dish cloths and pots still in their hands, came to stand at the doorway and gawk at these strange travelers who arrived by the back entrance. Teren smiled at them and shouted a friendly greeting, one bushy eyebrow raised inquiringly at the maids. They started giggling and darted back into the kitchen. Cook came out, her expression cross and her fists resting angrily on her wide hips. Even she looked surprised to see the trio but quickly recovered herself to shout at a stableboy sleeping on a bale of hay to take the lords' horses. She shouted at another one to fetch the master and be quick about it.

I was stuck hiding behind the stables for I dared not cross the open courtyard in my present dress and my hair a wet stringy mess. The stableboy held Severin's horse steady as he dismounted. He stared admiringly at the beautiful animal, patting his nose and smoothing down the arch of its sleek neck. He inquired after the horses' needs and Severin answered him in a low, pleasant voice. The stableboy was leading the horses away as Father arrived with Vooris and Zuul.

Father had dressed more hastily than usual and the fan collar of his black cape was crooked. Vooris stood next to him, his head down, ignoring Severin. He was kicking holes in the soil with his foot and raising little clouds of dust. Only when Father presented him did he raise his chin and point it arrogantly in Severin's direction. A lock of black hair fell over his eyes as he stood there looking sulky and disdainful. At Father's side, Zuul gazed keenly at Severin, studying him. Severin looked back and gave a polite smile.

Father announced in a smooth voice that their arrival had been expected and that they were to follow a servant to rooms where they might dress before the noonmeal. Huh! I snorted to myself. Maybe expected, but not quite so soon, eh Father? No chance to do a little mischief first, no pouring rain or hail? I enjoyed seeing Father put out, flustered by a situation not entirely under his control, and it increased my respect of the strangers.

When they finally left I flew across the courtyard and ducked into the safety of the kitchens. I could hear the clanging of Cook's pots as she prepared the usual feast to be given for suitors. I was glad I hadn't eaten yet that day, for I knew the meal would be long and that, as always, I would eat too much. Already the rich smells of food were making my mouth water and they followed me as I ran up the spiral stairs to my room to change.

I tried to dress quickly, slipping out of my green dress and looking for a new silk shift to wear beneath my black velvet dress. I found one that was still clean, a sharp yellow silk that I didn't much like because I thought it made me look like a fading buttercup. My velvet dress was wrinkled, having lain where I last tossed it in a crumpled heap. I tried smoothing it out with my hands. My hair was only partially dry from running home. I tried to comb it but my wet curls defied the comb. I gave up and stuffed it into a headdress, which I hoped would hide most of it until it had dried. I took one last look I the mirror and groaned. For once I wished that I could have had a few of my sister's graces. I turned away from the unkind glass and headed down the stairs before I was summoned.

I crossed the Great Hall quickly, trying to appear nonchalant, and took my place in the stone seats beside my parents. Father had recovered himself and his dress was impeccable. He was sitting stiff backed and regal in his black garb, his slim legs covered in black hose and crossed at the ankles. His fine, white hands rested on the carved arms of his chair. He seemed smaller to me since I had seen him standing next to Severin and his brothers. The rugged cut of their clothes made them seem more substantial than Father, whose cape couldn't hide his slimness, nor the narrow slope of his shoulders.

At his right hand sat Vooris, pulling irritably at the lace collar that hugged his neck and trying to scratch beneath the velvet doublet. It was actually rather nice looking, and I recognized my sister's needlework in the elegant gold stitching that quilted the front of the doublet. Though his hair had been curled, it had refused to stay curled; already locks of it were beginning to drop and hang in his face like bats. He imitated Father's arrogant expression, giving Severin disapproving looks from behind half-closed eyes.

My mother sat next to him, her face set in a perplexed frown as she regarded my headdress, for she knew I could abide nothing on my head. She was dressed in a shift of dove gray, matching her pale complexion and her graying hair, which she wore in a simple but severe braid about her crown. Her black velvet overdress looked dusty; I could never rid myself of the idea that my mother, who might have been young once and should still have been, simply woke one day old and tired and would remain that way for the rest of her life.

To the left of my empty seat, Ilena sat with a small, secretive smile playing about her lips. She, too, was looking at my dress. Then she daintily picked an invisible piece of lint off the brushed velvet of her skirts. I gritted my teeth when I saw her, for she was quite lovely. She had worn the maroon silk shift beneath her black dress, its wide sleeves lying across her lap. She had stitched a border of bright pink silk about the edges of her sleeves and bodice. That thin ribbon of color made her cheeks glow and accentuated the creamy white of her carefully powdered skin. She had dressed her hair with ropes of pearl and jet; as I took my seat next to her, I shriveled with embarrassment.

The strangers were ushered into the Great Hall by Zuul, who then took his place at Father's elbow. They looked much the same as when I had seen them in the woods. They seemed not to need extravagant clothing, or uncomfortable formal dress. Severin had shaved his light beard and the skin on his cheeks was a ruddy pink. They stood respectfully before Father, arms carried loosely at their sides as they waited for him to speak.

Teren and Nar settled their gaze on Ilena, who sat serenely, her eyes modestly downcast. I couldn't blame them; she was certainly more impressive than I. All the same I felt the blood flush on my cheeks. Severin looked at Ilena but his gaze didn't linger. To my astonishment he turned to me and nodded his head in a kind of acknowledgment, and then smiled. Teren and Nar looked away from Ilena to follow Severin's gaze. They were polite, but I saw the sudden look of question in their expression as they looked from Severin back to me. I was suddenly very nervous and shy, and only managed a thin smile.

Father stood. Throwing back one side of his cape in a pompous gesture, he presented me to Severin in a booming voice, which I realized was intended to make up for his small stature.

"Before you is the Lady Magda de'Stain Moravia, daughter of the sorcerer Gregor de'Stain Moravia. Within her blood flows the power of the de'Stains, for she is heiress to the talent of Moravian sorcery."

I wanted to roll my eyes at this, for as long as Father had his way, I was heir to nothing.

"Severin, of Thall," Severin replied and, nodding to his companions, added, "my brothers, Nar and Teren."

There was a moment of silence as we regarded each other expectantly. Father sniffed, and my spirits brightened; I knew that what Father had paused for wasn't going to come. It was usually at this point that potential bridegrooms, intimidated by my lineage, felt compelled to list every notable relative or ancestor in their line. It always seemed to take forever, and just when everyone was getting hungry. But Severin remained quiet, waiting for my father to continue the conversation.

I stole another glance at Severin and found him staring

back, his dark eyes shining, and a smile ready on his mouth. Suddenly amidst all that rigid court posturing, I with my silly headdress and trails of wet hair, I wanted to giggle foolishly. I repressed the urge to bawl like a heifer at Severin, just to see what he would do if he thought his joke might be true.

"I have come seeking the hand of Magda de'Stain Moravia in marriage," Severin announced quietly.

"And do you understand that there are three tasks to be fulfilled before you may rightfully claim my daughter's hand?" Father asked sternly.

"I do. I also understand that I have succeeded in passing the first task by arriving at Moravia Castle through an enchanted path. Or so the servants tell me," Severin said.

"Humph!" Father growled, stroking his waxy mustache as he frowned. "You may have succeeded at the first challenge, sir, but you shall not find the others so easily won. You are aware that should you fail any of the remaining two, you will forfeit your life?" He glowered importantly at Severin.

"Yes, I am," Severin replied calmly.

"Then, as custom requires, enter our hall and dine with us before the next tasks are put to you." Father gestured for us to take our leave and proceed to the dining hall.

As we entered the dining hall, Severin and his brothers stood respectfully to one side to allow us to pass by first. As I came close to him I fretted about the trails of damp hair hanging down my back, which he was sure to notice when I passed. I tried to turn sideways to avoid showing my back but was then obliged to stare directly into Severin's face. He looked amused and I quickly tried to look the other way as I scuttled by like a crab. I had never cared before what my suitors thought of me, and it was disconcerting to discover that I cared now.

TWO

THE FIRE WAS burning brightly in the great hearth, despite the fact that it was late summer. The logs crackled, casting showers of red sparks from the dry oak. Father liked to make suitors as uncomfortable as possible. Had it been winter, the fire would have been small and cheerless. Now it roared extravagantly and the room was warm and stuffy, the tall windows that usually opened out to the gardens closed and covered with dark velvet drapes. Only a small shaft of sunlight penetrated a crack in the curtain, its ray falling across the laid table. In its light, little dust motes danced over the dishes. I was beginning to sweat and itch in my dress and I longed to take off the stupid headdress.

Our table was long and spacious and set with white linen, my mother's crystal dishes, and ornate silver eating utensils. Candelabras had been prepared to give the room more light since the curtains were drawn. The beeswax candles smoked and gave the room an oily smell. We sat at our usual places: Father at the head of the table, Vooris seated to his right, and next to him my mother, dipping her fingers in the finger bowl and wiping the scented water off on a towel. I sat on my father's left and, beside me, a little farther down, sat Ilena, imitating mother and washing her hands in a dainty fashion. I wiggled my fingers in the cool water but would have preferred dunking my whole face, for it felt prickly, as if the greasy smoke rested on my cheeks.

Farther down, crowded into a cramped corner of the table, were seated Severin and his brothers. They weren't small men and the close seating arrangement saw them bumping elbows and legs as they sat down. Father often seated suitors at an uncomfortable and insulting disadvantage. The salt bowl was in the middle of the table, within easy reach of all of us, but they sat far below it. I didn't know whether or not it was an insult to be seated so far from the salt in Thall, but I could tell from their expressions that they didn't miss its meaning in Moravia. I watched as they exchanged glances, but Severin said nothing, remaining calm and gracious. They murmured thank-yous when the servants removed the finger bowls but neglected to give them a cloth on which to dry their hands.

Cook as usual had prepared a magnificent feast. There were a variety of stuffed fowls, perched on their platters as if about to fly; racks of lamb, decorated with cherries; poached salmons, which stared, glassy-eyed, amid beds of green herbs; creamed peas, glazed carrots, and carved potatoes; and a variety of gravies and sauces in silver dishes. On the heavy oak credenza were waiting the cakes, puddings, and custards that promised to burst the stays around my middle if I managed to eat that far through the meal. The wine steward arrived and, with a flourish, opened several dusty bottles of vintage Moravian red wine.

I watched Severin surreptitiously as the maid served the first course, a salad of tart greens sweetened with oil and parsley. He and his brothers took large helpings, including breaking off sizeable chunks of Cook's good white bread and covering it with solid lumps of butter.

"And how did you find the journey?" Father began, wiping the oil from his lips with a light touch of the napkin.

"Fair weather it was," Severin replied, "and it made for a pleasant journey. The forests we passed through were thick with pine and cedar. You are fortunate; Moravia is rich with wood."

"And Thall is poor?"

Severin caught the intended insult but shrugged it off.

"Aye, wood is scarce, but Thall has good meadowland and we border the sea. We do a fair trade in wool and horses."

"The sea?" Vooris blurted, and I stared at him, shocked to hear him sound so eager. Talking with Vooris was usually like kicking a stone. One got few responses and a lot of aches.

"Oh, aye. Gray and green it is, with high, rolling waves."

"Is it as salty as they say?"

"Salty enough to cure the fish before you've caught them," Severin teased, but Vooris continued to regard him with utmost seriousness. "Have you no river, then, to the sea?" he asked Father.

"No." Father replied sourly.

"Trade overland, is it?"

"No.

We do not feel the need for trade. What we need, we have here in Moravia."

"Ah." Severin nodded, and said nothing more, but his eyes studied the dreary room with its ancient drapes and greasy candle smoke.

The maid came to clear our dishes for the next course, stacking them carefully on her arm. She passed Severin and his brothers, her arms laden, and so didn't take their plates. They waited patiently for her to return. When she did, however, she ignored their salad plates and set new dishes. Severin slid his dirty plate to one side and smiled at the maid as she laid a new one.

We had Cook's barley soup, which was a thin broth of beef stock, little pearls of barley, and carrots carved to look like fall leaves. Nar had two bowlfuls. Beside him, Severin kept pace with three. Loaves of bread disappeared between their hands and the maid was sent scurrying into the kitchen for more.

Next was the salmon, surrounded by small trout that Cook had skinned and covered with a pink sauce. Once more, the three of them helped themselves to prodigious amounts of each.

"Your estates, they are large?" Father started in again, looking somewhere over Severin's head.

"There's fair enough for the farms and the livestock."

"And how many peasants on the land?"

"Your lordship?" Severin looked back, perplexed.

"Your peasants," Father insisted. "Who else works the land?"

"We work it ourselves."

"You're *farmers?*" Father asked with difficulty, choking on a piece of fish. Ilena had been giving sidelong glances to Nar, who was returning them with interest. At this bit of news, however, her head snapped around and she looked as mortified as Father. "Surely you don't expect me to have my daughter married to a common farmer."

You don't expect to see me married at all, I thought angrily. But I, too, was daunted by the prospects of being a farmer's wife. What did a farmer want with a sorcerer's daughter, I wondered suspiciously? Was I supposed to enchant the weather or wither a rival's cabbages in the field?

"Arlensdale is a fair farm," Severin answered. "There's my brothers and I, and twenty-odd others that work the land, including family and some that hire on for the season. Magda'll not have to work if she's of no mind for it.

Teren stared at his plate, a disapproving frown tightening the corners of his mouth. "With all respect, Thall has little use for titles. And naught was said about being titled before Severin's challenge was accepted."

"Indeed," Father replied calmly. He settled more comfortably in his chair and brushed away Teren's concern with a light wave of his hand. "Even a farmer has the right to try." It was clear that Father didn't think much of Severin's chances. He had already forgotten that Severin had succeeded at the first task. Or perhaps he believed their story, that it was luck.

The maid came around again to clear the dishes. She stopped at Severin's corner and looked questioningly at Father. There was quite a stack of dirty dishes gathering and scarce room to lay the clean ones. Father gave an impatient nod of his head and the maid, looking relieved, stacked them up and removed them from the table.

Then came the main course and the meal began in earnest. Never in my life had I seen anyone eat with such zeal as did Severin and his brothers. They eagerly helped themselves to large amounts of everything that came their way and were not in the least embarrassed when they required a second plate to hold their servings. Vooris snickered behind his hand as Nar stopped a servant who was trying to leave with a tray of lamb and took an additional helping, which he balanced carefully over a sea of peas and carrots. My mother looked appalled at this naked display of consumption, tsking every now and then in her napkin, and even Father stopped to stare, eyebrows arched primly, as the servants and platters of food collected in confusion around Severin and his brothers.

Father remarked dryly: "Your journey from Thall must have been long that you should have developed such appetites."

Severin looked up from his plate, a mild surprise crossing his face. "We'd not think of dishonoring this great feast with anything less than our best effort!" He smiled disarmingly at Father as he broke off a large piece of white bread and daubed in brown gravy. The maid had fetched Cook so that she could see for herself these strangers who ate enough for ten people. She hovered now in the doorway, watching Severin with pleasure. "Thall has good mutton, but this is a grand piece we're eating and I'm sure I've never had better." Cook crossed her arms proudly over her ample bosom and beamed at Severin from the doorway.

"Was that your horse, then, Master Vooris, that I saw in the stable? The white stallion?" Severin asked.

Vooris made no answer immediately but sat hunched sullenly over his plate. "Yes," he muttered.

"He's a fine animal. Do you race him, then?"

"No." He wrinkled his nose.

"Ah," said Severin mildly. "Perhaps you prefer the scholar's life, then. What do you study?"

Vooris paled and darted a fearful glance at Father. Father answered Severin's question with a curt reply: "We do not discuss the arcane teachings of Moravian sorcery. Power is best kept if the knowledge is not shared."

I felt a sliver of sympathy for Severin at that moment. We weren't a pleasant family to dine with even under the best of circumstances. Here it was, Severin having put his life in jeopardy, and we were unable to muster decent conversation. I was not allowed to speak at these dinners. Father feared I might somehow aid my suitors. Normally I didn't care. They had little to talk of besides themselves, the usual court gossip, petty politics, and the hunt. But Severin was different and I was intrigued. I found myself studying him, the firm line of his jaw, the broad cut of his shoulders. His hands were large, the fingers square and blunt, and the nails were short and clean. He was patient and methodical. I watched, fascinated, as he delicately and precisely carved the meat from the

chicken, never missing a bite and leaving behind a stack of
stripped pink bones. I was also impressed by his seeming lack
of arrogance. He was proud, I could sense that in his bearing
and in the way he spoke of Thall, but he never allowed himself to be baited by Father's insults, though Nar, I noticed,
turned several shades of red and white and stabbed his food
more vigorously than necessary. What does he *really* want? I
wondered. Severin caught me staring at him several times and
gazed back, a smile ready on his lips. Though I tried not to, I
blushed angrily. Turning away, I feigned disinterest. But
always, I was drawn back.

Dessert finally arrived and I was certain Severin was going
to slow his pace. The room had grown hot from the fire and
my face was flushed and sweating from the wine and the heat.
Only Father looked comfortable and untroubled. I suspect he
used sorcery to protect himself from the heat. I struggled to
put a spoonful of Cook's custard to my lips, because it was my
favorite dessert and, no matter how stuffed I felt, I couldn't
refuse. I suppressed a groan as I saw Teren and then Severin
take generous helpings of two different cakes smothered with
fresh cream and big bowls of the custard. Nar put aside the
custard but made up for it by adding a third wedge of cake and
the baked apples and cream. They seemed remarkably unaf-
fected by the large meal while I was becoming sluggish and
somnolent from overindulgence.

The maid cleared the last of the dessert dishes and brought
a marble tray with different cheeses and tart red Moravian
apples. The wine steward returned and opened several bottles
of heavy port. I shook my head weakly when the maid
brought the tray to me. All I wanted was to leave the table and
collapse somewhere cool where I could digest my meal in
peace. Even Ilena, who usually remained composed, was fid-
geting, trying to scratch her back against the hard wood of her
high-backed chair.

"If it please you, Lady Magda," Severin said in my direction, and I jumped, startled at being addressed directly, "I've
brought a gift that I hope will please you." Severin motioned
to Nar, who jarred Teren's arm as he stood, causing the port in
his glass to spill on the linen. Vooris started his obnoxious
snickering again and, had I been able to reach, I would have
kicked him soundly under the table. Teren didn't seem to be
embarrassed by the mishap. He stood and calmly walked to

the salt bowl. Mother reared back her head, regarding him as if he were an invader. He picked up the bowl and brought it back to his seat. With one hand he began spreading salt on the spilled wine, smiling up at mother.

"It'll take up the wine and keep it from staining," he explained. Then he set the salt bowl down in front of him and it suddenly appeared as if it was we who now sat below the salt.

Nar returned, carrying a small bundle, which he placed by my side. He sat down, taking care not to jostle his brother's arm again.

"It was made by Thall weavers," said Severin, speaking to me again. "Though it seems common, look closely at the pattern."

I opened the package, surprised at how light it felt in my hands. With the wrapper off, I saw it was a large and beautiful shawl done in a cream-colored wool. The borders were worked in flowers of pale rose with a trellis of green leaves. It was lovely and soft. I did as Severin bade me and looked closely at the tiny and careful stitches that had produced the beautiful work. I gasped when I noticed that the flowers of the shawl grew from tiny buds, opened into full blooms, and then faded, as if they were growing on the shawl itself. Ilena peered over my shoulder to look at what I had seen and gave a clap of delight when she saw the flowers continue to bloom and then die in a living pattern on my shawl. Like me, she ran amazed fingers delicately over the work, marveling at the silky texture and the skill that had brought the patterns to life.

"How is it done?" I asked, too astonished to remember that I was forbidden to speak. Father glared at me, but Ilena and I were too distracted with curiosity to care.

"'Tis a secret known to Thall weavers. One must join the clan and work for many years before weaving a living shawl such as this."

"What is the speciality of your family?" Father asked, his voice suddenly tense. I looked at Father and wondered for a moment if Severin hadn't made a mistake giving me this gift. Father had believed them farmers. But the shawl was made with magic. Thall magic. Father didn't like it and I could sense his suspicion.

"Horses," answered Severin. "My mother Theda is clan chief and her skill in husbandry has made our horses the finest in the markets."

"Your estate is ruled by your mother? A woman?" Father asked.

"She has the talent and the skill," answered Severin simply. "Arlensdale has prospered."

"And what of your father? What kind of man allows his wife to govern?"

I winced at Father's harshness. Severin took a deep breath, steadying himself, before responding. "My father died many years ago," he explained evenly, "but even when he lived it was my mother's skill that enabled us to prosper." Severin took a large gulp of the port. There was an edge in his voice when he spoke and I hoped Father would not push him too far.

To my relief Father made no reply. He ground his teeth, his white cheek jumping tensely with the movement, and toyed with the small cheese knife. He leaned back stiffly and Zuul bent forward to catch some whispered request. We all stared nervously at the page as he darted from the room.

"Now that we are done dining, I wish to delay no further but proceed with the second task," Father said coldly.

I was horrified and the food in my stomach lurched dangerously. It was a breach of custom. A suitor should have at least a night's rest to recover between each task. I cast Father an outraged look and he answered it with his own dark glare as if to say, it was as he thought: Severin was unusual enough to capture my interest. And there was the shawl. What other powers might this country farmer possess? I knew from Father's look he intended to waste no time guessing.

We waited until Zuul returned carrying three small caskets in his hands. Clearing away the remaining dishes around Severin's place, he placed the identical caskets in a neat row before him. A maid drew back the heavy drape from the window and I saw that evening had fallen. I was suddenly depressed as I saw that we had wasted a beautiful day sitting in a stuffy, closed room playing Father's cruel game. I wanted the day back; I wanted the shimmering pond where I first saw Severin riding on his horse, sunlight dappled on his shoulders. As I turned back to look at him, I wanted more than anything a chance for a normal courtship.

Father spoke: "One and only one of these caskets contains the key to Magda's dowry. You must choose correctly or accept the penalty of death."

Unfair! I screamed to myself. I knew the caskets to be

enchanted. Two of them were shrouded with inducement spells that seemed to shout, "Take me, me first!" But the third, the correct casket, had an aversion spell that forced the chooser to look away. If one's eyes stayed too long on the correct casket, one was besieged by nausea. Given the large meal we had just consumed, it would be impossible for Severin even to look at, much less choose, the correct casket.

Severin glanced at the caskets and then turned away to stare intently out the window, as if trying to catch a glimpse of something in the distance. He paid no more attention to the caskets before him. The room was quiet, just the whisper of the logs as they slipped in the grate and settled with a sigh. Father watched Severin, his face sharp and keen like a hawk. Even Vooris peered at Severin from beneath his tangled curls, and it seemed to me that he held his breath.

No one moved as the air bristled with the tension of waiting. Severin reached out swiftly and, still without looking, placed a hand firmly on one of the caskets. The spells dissolved, and Severin turned for the first time to look directly at the casket and draw it to himself. He opened it, and there, lying on a little bed of pink satin, was the key to my dowry. In truth it was a humble dowry, as Father never had any intention of seeing me off. Still, at that moment, it seemed to me as if Severin had opened the casket to reveal the key to my prison. He took out the key and, to my surprise, handed it not to Father, but to me. I was elated and wanted to throw my arms about him, happy that he had succeeded. Instead, I took the key as demurely as possible, remembering Father sitting at the head of the table.

Father stood, leaning forward on the long tapered fingers that rested on the table's edge. Behind him his shadow stretched on the wall like a leaping wolf.

"So it would seem, Severin of Thall, that you have had the luck to pass the second task."

A chilly draft entered the room and we sat unmoving in our chairs. I knew that voice. It came when Father's anger threatened to erupt violently; my own temper tantrum had been but a child's parody of his destructive abilities. My mother cringed in her seat, Vooris and Ilena stared, frightened, into their laps, and I held my breath, hoping that Father would not release the tempest he was gathering within. The cold gathered around the table like an uninvited guest. Severin and his brothers stood together slowly, shoulder to shoulder. Their movements were smooth yet alert to the threat in Father's voice.

"Tomorrow is the final task. If you fail, death will not be far behind. I can assure you it will not be quick."

"So I am warned. Until the morning, then," Severin replied evenly with a nod of his head.

"Do you hunt?" Father asked abruptly.

"When it's necessary."

"Good." Father's smile was feral, his teeth sharp points in the light. "We'll hunt the stag at first light! I'll have a stable-boy ready your horses." Then he sat down again and dismissed Severin with a curt wave of his hand.

"I bid you good evening, then," Severin replied, and the three of them inclined their heads in farewell.

When they had left, I rose, angry words gathering on my tongue. I wanted to leave before I was foolish enough to utter them. Father called to me as I was leaving.

"Magda," he said, stopping me with his icy voice, "may you also be assured that if this young man fails, you shall be by my side to witness the execution."

I swallowed hard. I had never witnessed an execution, preferring to flee to the pond where I could ignore the fate of my failed suitors. I refused to turn and acknowledge Father, but merely nodded my head and kept walking. Once in the corridor, I fled to my room, clutched tightly the key to my dowry in my hand.

THREE

I COULDN'T SLEEP that night but lay awake feeling confused and troubled. I stared at the clear sky, the stars winking like tiny gemstones, and watched as the moon traced silvery patterns across my coverlet. Father's contempt was a way of life that had infected us all. I had survived in spite of him, withdrawing into a lonely, solitary world of my own making. It was a world safe from the turmoil that came from needing and caring. I was strongest when I allowed no traces of compassion or longing to intrude on the world I inhabited. The suitors who had come before did very little to threaten my peace. They were an event to which I was a bystander; I remained untouched by their presence. But Severin was different. I could not ignore him. It was as if he had pounded on the walls of my world and, for the first time, I looked out. I saw him clearly, like the sharp green of a sapling growing out of scorched earth, and I was caught by the promise of a new life. A desperate wish rose in me; I didn't want Severin to fail the final task. I didn't want Severin to die.

The door to my world opened with a stiff creak of protest. As hope and longing welled in me, so did other, darker emotions push their way to the surface. I was struck by a troubling

sense of shame. My own coldness and indifference toward the
sad fates of my suitors had been as cruel as Father's contempt.
It was a bitter thought to swallow, but I couldn't push it away,
having discovered it. With grim determination I addressed it
instead. What should I do? I asked myself; but what could I
do, it was too late to make amends. But not too late to face the
truth. I suddenly needed to see with my own eyes what I had
shunned for so many years.

I slipped out of bed and shivered as my feet touched the
cold stone. Pigeons roosting on the windowsill startled awake,
rustling their feathers and cooing in annoyance. I grabbed a
black shawl, flung it over my shoulders to cover my nightgown, and put on soft slippers. I took a lit candle from a wall
sconce and held it aloft to light my way as I headed down the
darkened corridor.

Moravia Castle at night was dark and dreary, the corridors
poorly lit and chilly. My single candle cast thin, looming
shadows against the walls that disappeared into the crevices of
the ribbed ceiling. I thought at first that I would go alone to
the dungeons, but then I realized I wasn't sure how to get
there. Near the kitchens, I thought, perhaps under them, but I
didn't know where to find the entrance. I thought of searching
but hesitated at the idea, not wanting Father to find me wandering the halls in the middle of the night. At the top of the
back stairs I stopped and puzzled over what I should do.

Instead of going down the stairs alone, I turned right and
continued along the corridor to Vooris's room. I knew that he
had aided Father with the executions. Perhaps I could con-
vince him to tell me how to get there. It would mean putting
up with his surly disposition, but that seemed preferable to
wandering in the dark and maybe stumbling into Father.

I crept into the room and to his bed silent as a ghost. I saw
his shape, lying in the crumpled sheets, curled in a ball. I
thought him fast asleep, but as I approached I saw in the
moonlight that his eyes were wide open. Against his white
skin the pupils glittered jet black as they stared like a frightened hare caught in the silver light.

"Vooris?" I whispered softly. The body on the bed didn't
move, but I saw his eyelids flicker. "Vooris?" I repeated. "Are
you awake?"

"What's the matter, Magda?" came the sullen reply. "Eat

too much at the meal?" He turned to face me, Father's sneer on his lips.

I stepped back, irritated. Vooris straightened up in bed and rubbed his head. He swung his thin legs over the side of the bed and sat hunched on the edge.

"Bring the candle here," he commanded. Warily, I edged closer.

He took the candle from me and lit his own. In the yellow light of our small flames I was struck by how tired my brother looked. He held his head up to me; his hair, which usually hid his face, was pushed back, and I saw the dark rings that lined his eyes and the troubled set of his mouth. His face was heart shaped, and where youth should have filled it with fullness, he was thin and peaked, his chin a sharp point. Through the white nightshirt, open at the throat, I saw his chest, the collarbones raised in ridges beneath the shirt, his shoulders dropping and his slender arms huddled close to his body. His skin was milk white except for a purple bruise that spread on his shoulder and disappeared under the nightshirt. I pictured Father's hand on that shoulder and saw it press against the skin until it reddened and bruised. For the first time I realized my brother was slight; he seemed as breakable as a porcelain cup.

"Vooris, I need your help."

"Huh," he grunted and turned his head away. I gritted my teeth.

"Look, I don't want to argue—"

"Do you enjoy it?" he asked abruptly, interrupting me.

"Enjoy what?"

"The suitors. The tasks."

I shook my head. "Of course not. It's horrible."

He shrugged and scratched his cheek. "You know, every time one of your suitors is executed, I wonder, how does she manage it?"

"Manage what?"

"To remain indifferent. Teach me, so I can watch them killed and not be bothered by it; not have to suffer the nightmares that come afterwards."

I recoiled. "Don't blame me for their deaths. It's Father's idea. I've nothing to do with it!"

"Not even to feel pity?"

The words chilled me and I could give no answer. Vooris laughed harshly. "You're just like Father, aren't you? Without mercy or compassion. No, you never held the sword, or turned the rack, or laid a hand on the hot irons; but men died cursing you while you went your way, nose stuck in the air, ignoring the stink."

I trembled. "It's not my fault," I repeated stupidly.

"But you're still responsible!" he hissed. "It's because of you they come!"

"It's because of the sorcery they come," I shouted back.

"Why don't you do something to stop it?"

"Why don't you? You're the favorite."

"I don't have any talent, remember?"

"Neither do I!" I answered, frustrated.

"Huh!"

"It's true! Father hid it from me. I can't do any sorcery, not even to save my own life."

"Not now," he muttered to himself.

"What does that mean?" I asked sharply.

"Nothing," he said quickly. He stared at me, his expression a strange mixture of grief and jealousy. I thought for a moment he meant to tell me something. He hesitated, and when he spoke again, it was to change the subject.

"Why are you here, Magda?"

"I want to see the dungeons."

He cocked his head to one side, questioningly. "When?"

"Now."

"What's the hurry? They'll be there tomorrow."

Again I was silent. I didn't know how to tell him what I could scarce explain to myself. Before I could think of a suitable reply, Vooris suddenly grinned nastily.

"It's Severin, isn't it? Don't tell me you're stuck on the farmer?"

"Nothing of the kind," I retorted angrily.

"You're lying."

"You're an idiot."

He threw back his head and laughed. "Do you think I don't know that cow-eyed look? I've seen it often enough on Ilena's stupid face." My cheeks flushed angrily with indignation. Fuming, I turned away, ready to leave alone, but he stopped me.

"No, no, you're right," he said briskly. He crossed to the dressing table to collect his hose, which he slipped on beneath his nightshirt, and then pulled on black boots. "You should see the dungeons tonight. Better to be prepared when it comes your turn to watch the farmer executed." He fastened his black cape about his shoulders, throwing one side back with a flourish. "Are you ready?"

I hesitated, afraid. Vooris stared back at me, one eyebrow arched, mouth twisted in a tight, sardonic grin. He looked like Father and my fear was replaced with anger.

"Yes. Let's go," I said firmly.

We left his room and headed back the way I had come, down the corridor to the kitchen stairway. Vooris put out our candles, warning me that their light might arouse Father. We walked the tunneled corridor in near-darkness, only the weak flame of the occasional torch, spluttering in its soot-covered sconce, shedding a smoky light on the stone walls. At the top of the stairs Vooris stopped and listened, his head turning side to side.

"Did you know that Father can shape Zuul into a bird?" he whispered to me.

"Why?" I whispered back.

"To spy."

I peered over my shoulder into the darkness, fearful of the strange skittering sounds behind us.

"Come on, quickly," Vooris urged. We scrambled quietly down the stairs toward the kitchen.

Vooris led me through the kitchen to a door that I had not paid any attention to before on the side of the pantry. He took the torch to light our way down the stairs. As we passed through it I whispered to him, "I thought this led to the cellar."

"It does. The dungeon is below the cellar."

We walked through the cellar, our torch casting light on the piled sacks of grain and heaped root vegetables that would be wintered over. Mice chittered at our passing and I saw the flick of a tail as one disappeared behind a bag of grain. We arrived at a large double door of heavy oak banded with iron and built into the earthen wall. Vooris pulled at one of the iron rings in the middle of the door and it swung open with a groan. We scurried in like the mice and he shut the door behind us with a loud clang.

We were standing on a stone landing at the top of a set of wide stairs, which twisted down and out of sight. The torches burned with heavy smoke and soot had streaked the walls with black shadows. It smelled like a crypt; a cold, musty stone built into the low archways that was damp to the touch. As we started down the stairway it seemed to me that the stone wall breathed, slowly and almost perceptibly, its exhalation like weary sighs rank with the odor of decay.

The stairs twisted and turned, leading into other corridors that wove like a maze underneath the castle. I was hopelessly lost but Vooris led me on steadily, his torch flickering smokily. His mouth was pressed in a fine line, as if he feared to breathe. Despite the cool damp, he sweated, and from time to time he wiped his hands on his cape to keep the torch from slipping in his grasp.

We reached the last corridor and approached a doorway covered with a heavy iron grill. In front of it a guard sat, head slumped on his chest and snoring loudly as he slept. The front legs of the chair were tipped back to make the sleeper more comfortable. I stopped uncertaintly but Vooris strode firmly to the sleeping guard and kicked the chair with one foot. The guard tumbled onto the hard floor and landed with a surprised grunt. Then he woke, growling and cursing while he reached for his weapon.

"Is this how you guard the dungeons of Moravia, Rolvak?" Vooris demanded, standing with his legs apart, the torch held high in one hand and the other in a fist resting on his slim hip. He stuck out his lower lip. "I am sure that my father would not be pleased."

The guard quieted immediately and stood slowly. He was a huge man, his slab of a face topped with matted hair. He towered over Vooris and me like a roused bear, his head brushing against the low ceiling. At Vooris's words his face colored a mottled red and a white scar that cut across his forehead twitched nervously. But he kept silent, holding his halberd close to his barrel chest.

"Well, Rolvak? What have you to say for yourself?" Vooris taunted, throwing back his head to look up into the eyes of the big man.

Rolvak's hands grasped his halberd tighter and he swallowed a few times before he answered. "Nothing, young master. I must have dozed off on duty. It was wrong."

"Not good for the head of the guards to be caught sleeping, is it, Rolvak? Doesn't look good, does it?"

"No, young master," the man murmured, keeping his shaggy head bowed.

"Hmm, I wonder what Father would say?" He paused, head cocked arrogantly to one side as he regarded Rolvak. The guard shifted uncomfortably. "Well, I am not interested in that right now," Vooris said brightly. "The Lady Magda and I wish to visit the dungeons."

"Now, young master?" he gasped, surprised. "But you know it is forbidden to enter the dungeons without the master present. I can't let you pass."

"It is also forbidden to fall asleep on duty," Vooris retorted sharply. "I'll do you a favor, Rolvak. I'll say nothing to Lord Gregor of your conduct while on duty, and you will let us pass to the dungeons."

The guard continued to hesitate, weighing the consequences if either one of these acts were discovered.

"Come, come, Rolvak, we haven't got all night. It seems to me a small price to pay for a bit of discretion."

This time the guard didn't hesitate. Pulling a large skeleton key from the jangle of keys chained at his waist, he unlocked the grilled gate. He swung it open and stepped aside to let us pass.

"Remember, young master, don't stay long. It would do neither of us good if you was caught here now, and especially with her." He jabbed his thumb in my direction.

"Don't worry; just don't go back to sleep until after we have left," Vooris said. We stepped through the gate. I heard the guard grunt in reply and he sat down heavily on the chair again to wait for us.

"Welcome to my nursery," Vooris said nastily as we stepped into the large, dimly lit room. He gestured at all the instruments of torture that lined the room. "Let me show you Father's toys."

He took my arm and led me to where an iron maiden stood, shut and locked, cold eyes staring out of a metal mask. The features of the face resembled a woman, her expression empty and the contours of her body rounded like a cocoon. Arms were molded in the metal cross her chest, as if to hug closely the contents of her hollow body.

"Do you know what's inside, Magda? Spikes, long ones that pierce the body everywhere; except the head, so that the prisoner may feel for just a moment longer the pain of the blades as they enter." Vooris turned to me and smiled wickedly. "Shall we open it, Magda? I can't remember if there's anyone in it or not."

"No!" I shouted hoarsely, and shrank back, pulling away from his grip. "Please, Vooris, don't!"

The smile disappeared. "Don't worry, I won't. There's no one in there," he said, looking back at the iron maiden. "Father would never allow a body to stay long in the iron maiden for fear the blood would rust the spikes and ruin it."

I wanted to vomit; the rich, heavy food of our meal refused to settle in my stomach. I was cold and frightened, and we had only just arrived.

"Is it enough, Magda?" Vooris said, coming to stand close to me and stare at my sweating, pale face as I swallowed hard to keep the food in my stomach. "Shall we go now or do you want to see more?"

"More!" I said through clenched teeth. Vooris stared a moment longer at me, and then solemnly showed me the rest of room. We went from one hideous machine to another, Vooris explaining to me in a dull, flat voice how they worked; how bodies were pulled, severed, and broken in a slow process until death came at last as welcomed relief. When he finished there he led me to a small opening in the wall where bricks and stone stood piled neatly to one side. He explained that some of my suitors had died only after months of slow starvation from being walled in the tiny crevice, with an opening small enough so that they would not suffocate before they starved.

We stood before the empty niche and Vooris took my arm again. I could feel the delicate bones of his hand like that of a child who wakes fearful of the dark and seeks comfort.

"Come, there's only one more thing left to see." He led me through another low corridor to the edge of a deep underground well. I peered over the stone lip of the well but could see nothing but a black empty cavern. Even the light from our torch illuminated only a portion of the inner wall before it faded into complete blackness. I could smell the water; it was cold and sharp. Green moss grew along the walls of the well, fed by the moisture that seeped through the stones from below.

"A well?" I asked, puzzled.

"Yes, and very deep. I think it connects to a spring far beneath the ground, for it never smells rank but is always fresh like now. Father uses it to dispose of the bodies. They don't even have the benefit of proper funeral rites, but are dropped like rotten carcasses into the well."

We stood staring at the black abyss, neither of us talking. Absently, Vooris picked small stones from the mortar and tossed them into the well. They made a soft clinking sound as they hit the sides of the walls, and then the sound faded as the stones dropped deeper into the well. I strained to hear the splash but it never came, just a ghostly whisper as wind swept up out of the mouth of the well.

"Why is Father doing this?" I asked, numb with horror.

"Do you really want to know?"

"Yes! Why would anyone be so cruel?"

"What makes you think the others are less cruel?" he asked me.

"Who else could be this cruel?"

Vooris gave a short, humorless laugh. "Magda, you're so naive, aren't you? You don't know anything about politics in Moravia. It has a long history of cruelty. All those princes pushing and shoving for the right to be king. All those sorcerers intriguing for power. Where do you think Father learned it? Why do you think he brings me down here *but* to learn it? That's what it takes to be king in Moravia."

I stared at Vooris wide-eyed. "You? A king? Father's mad!"

"Thanks for the compliment."

"But the de'Stains have never been kings!"

"Because they were sorcerers. But Father has decided that since I am not a sorcerer, I will be a king. His ambition, like his cruelty, is no less than the others around him. But he has a weapon they don't. You." And he pointed a finger at me.

I frowned, confused.

"All of your suitors have wanted the same thing, Magda, a marriage of kingship and sorcery. All of them would have been my rivals in the play for greater power. Father has used you as bait, and he has culled them as they came, clearing a path for my ascension. Soon there will be no young ambitious men in Moravia to threaten me and I will gather the rest of the tired lot under a kingship."

"Oh, no," I groaned, aghast at how Father had used me and how I had allowed it to happen. Perhaps if I had not been indifferent, perhaps if I had resisted. I looked at Vooris, but his expression was unreadable in the faint light.

"The white stallion?" I asked, guessing for the first time the reason for the only white horse in a stable of black horses.

Vooris nodded. "A king's horse, naturally. Though the brute knows better than Father that I'm not the man for the job. He's already kicked me twice on my soon-to-be-kingly buttocks."

"Is that what you want? Kingship at such a price?"

"Getting kicked isn't so bad."

"No," I said with irritation. "Killing off my suitors."

"Others have paid for it with worse," he answered dully. Then, more softly, he whispered: "No, I don't want to be king. I've never wanted to be king. But how do you say no to Father?"

"You are his favorite—"

"I am his disappointment," he said bitterly.

"Better than his curse."

"Is it?" He looked up at me sharply. "He hates me for being weak and without sorcery, but he fears you."

"Why should he fear me? I can't do anything to him."

"Because—" Vooris stopped abruptly and again I saw him struggle to hold back the words that threatened to tumble from his lips. He glanced around the room, steadying himself, and when his gaze came to rest on me again, it seemed he had made a decision.

"I used to hate you. It was your fault for having the talent, your fault Father thought to make me a king, your fault that I watched suitors torn apart, your fault that I had nightmares. But worst of all was to know that it didn't even matter to you. That it never touched you, while I mourned in secret."

I stared at my brother's pale face and realized that I didn't know him at all. I had believed him a spoiled brat and now I discovered that beneath his sullen demeanor he had shouldered the burden of remorse that should have been mine.

"Vooris," I said weakly, "I'm sorry. I didn't think—"

"That's it, you didn't think! You never thought about anything but yourself!" Tears started to well in my eyes but I held them back. "But it's not your fault alone, is it? It's mine, too."

"It's Father's," I said sharply.

"It's all of ours."

For a moment Vooris was quiet, then he said brusquely: "Father means to kill you, Magda."

"Why'd he wait so long?" I replied, too bitter to feel fear.

"He's had to. He can't just kill you. Not yet, anyway. It has to do with the way the sorcery is inherited. You share your powers until you come of age. If Father tried to hurt you now, he would hurt himself."

Before me flashed the memory of Father's white face etched with pain as he struck at me in the Great Hall.

"Why not hire an assassin, someone else to do the job?"

"No, he'd still suffer with you. Whether he likes it or not, he must protect you. You've been as sheltered as a prize sow and you didn't even know it. Besides"—Vooris shrugged— "he's found another use for you right now. Wouldn't do to kill the bait, would it?"

"When does he plan to kill me?"

Vooris shook his head. "I don't know. I don't think even Father knows that. The sorcery in you will separate from Father's influence only when it's ready."

"And having no knowledge of it and no training, I would be helpless against him."

Vooris nodded slowly.

"Why have you told me? It's what you want, isn't it? To see me pay for the suitors' death with my own."

"I used to, but not anymore. I'm sick of seeing people killed," he answered wearily. I reached out, wanting to touch my brother, but he drew back, startled by the gesture.

"Come," he said gruffly. "We'd better get back."

We returned to the grilled gate and Rolvak stood quickly to let us out. As we passed through, Vooris reminded him: "Not a word about our being here."

"Yes, young master," the guard murmured, staring gloomily as we departed.

"Do you think he can be trusted?" I asked when we had gone a ways through the twisted corridors.

"Would you rather keep a secret with me or confess the truth to Father?"

"Until now I didn't know there was a difference."

"Do you think the same now?" he asked.

"No," I answered quickly. We stopped walking and I stared at the wisps of smoke trailing from his torch and disappearing into the turns of the corridor. "I wish things were different. I wish you had inherited the talent and not I."

"Don't wish that on me, Magda. If I had your power I'd probably be no different from Father. Better to wish me somewhere else. Escape, that's what I dream about. Running away from here and never having to see Moravia or Father again."

It was as if Vooris spoke of my own dreams, wishing myself a bird, flying away over the tops of the trees to the unknown lands that lay beyond. My mind snagged on Severin's description of Thall and I suddenly wished to see the wide meadowlands that led to a gray-green sea.

"Why Severin?" I asked, frowning. "I mean, he's got nothing to do with Father's plans. Why hasn't Father simply killed him?"

"Challenge, I expect. No one's come here before that has offered Father something as enticing as that."

"So he'll play it to the end?"

"More or less, just to see what Severin of Thall can do."

"What do you think Severin's chances are of winning tomorrow?" I asked.

"Better than most, I should say, given a fair contest." He turned to peer at me, head cocked to one side in the smoky light. "But it won't be fair. No matter what, Father won't lose," he said grimly.

"Should I warn Severin?"

"Think you can?"

"It's the least I can do."

He looked at me, skeptical. "It won't be easy. Father will be keeping a close watch. Your interest in Severin makes him more cautious."

"How does he know I'm interested in Severin?"

Vooris laughed at me. "You're not very good at dissembling, Magda. Look, you've never cared what you wore to these meals but today you arrive wearing a fancy headdress. Doesn't take much to guess why. Still," he added, "I'd have to agree with you. Severin is worthy of a second glance."

We stopped talking as we left the cellar and passed quietly through the kitchens. At the top of the stairs I stopped him. "Thank you," I whispered. Prompted by impulse, I hugged him. It was an awkward and clumsy gesture and I felt his shoulders stiffen in my arms. I held him anyway, refusing to let go until I felt him relax within my embrace and accept it. I was saddened that so simple a gesture should have been so hard for us. I released him and he turned, not meeting my eyes. He padded noiselessly down the corridor to his room and I saw the flicker of his sleeve, like a white moth against the wood, as he pushed opened his door and disappeared inside.

I stood there, brooding, and then made up my mind that I would warn Severin right then. I would tell him to leave tonight, and get as far away from Moravia as possible. I would tell him the truth of my hidden powers, that they were not worth the loss of his life. I shuddered to think of Severin dying in my father's dungeons, and of Vooris forced to watch.

Resolute and determined, I started down the corridor, hugging the shadowy walls as I went. Severin and his brothers had been quartered in rooms on the far side of the bailey, facing the main stairway to the Great Hall. My feet were cold as ice, but sweat dotted my face and my heart pounded as I held my breath and slipped past the carved doors that led to the antechambers of Father's tower. They were opened, moonlight streaming through the doors and falling on the corridor floor. There was no one to be seen but I felt the hairs of my neck raised with a cold whisper of air. I expected Father to appear at any moment, formed out of the shadows. I waited, trying to catch my shallow breath and go on.

I had taken but one small step when I was stopped by a soft, scuttling noise in the hall below me. I strained to make it out over the hammering of my heart in my chest. I heard the noise again and crept to the edge of the railing and peered down into the lower bailey. A bird was winging through the closed hall, wheeling and turning, its wings brushing against the walls as it turned. Just a bird, I tried to calm myself, a dove trapped inside and trying to find a way out. But I remembered Vooris whispering to me of Zuul, shaped to a bird; and I watched, alarmed, as the bird swept the Great Hall as if searching for something. It flew higher, just under the vaulted ceilings, and headed for my father's opened doors. I crouched lower, hiding myself completely in the shadow. The bird flew through the opened doors, but not before I had seen it was a sparrow hawk, its eyes glittering with yellow flame and its beak clicking excitedly.

It must have seen me! Father, I thought, terrified, he's going to warn Father! I abandoned my caution and fled to my rooms, my nightgown rustling noisily as I ran. Passing Father's open door I felt a chilling draft suck at my feet and pull my hair back. I gave a cry and urged my legs to run faster. I braced myself, expecting to feel a hand reach out and grab me from behind. Wings fluttered against my face and I screamed as I stumbled. A small bat tangled in my hair, hissing angrily. Desperately I shook my head and tried to brush it off. It released me and hovered nearby as I stood and then began to run again. The bat followed me, harassing me, tugging at my hair and swooping toward my face as I bolted down the corridor. From behind I heard the sounds of hollow laughter rumbling in the halls. I reached my door and slammed it shut on the flying bat. Alone I collapsed on the floor, trembling and drawing air in short, painful gasps. My heart was still pounding when I stood, legs shaking shaking and teeth chattering. I tottered into bed, pulling the covers up high about my chin. I stared at the door, fearful that it would open and reveal Father standing in its frame.

For a long time I lay awake watching the door. Gradually, as nothing happened and the terror ebbed, my thoughts returned to Severin. I hadn't succeeded in warning him, I thought disgustedly. As soon as I thought Father might catch me, I had scattered like a mouse and fled to my room. "No!" I whispered aloud to the silvery moonlight on my bed. "This won't do! Have a little courage, Magda," my voice said sternly. "You must do it. Severin must escape from Father. And what of yourself?" the voice asked, remembering Vooris's warning in the dungeons. A knot curled in my stomach. Later, I answered, pushing away the fear, I'll think on it later. For now Father couldn't hurt me and that was my strength. It was Severin and his brothers who needed my help.

FOUR

I ROSE EARLY in the morning, weary from my night's wandering, but excited with the barest fragments of a plan to help Severin and his brothers escape from Moravia Castle. The castle was quiet, most having joined the hunt in the gray hours of dawn. They wouldn't be returning for a while, so now was my chance to see Cook.

I knew she was fond of me, for even though we quarreled, she often defended me to Father in his blacker moods, speaking well of me while she shook her wooden spoons at him. She had no children of her own, so perhaps she had decided to dispatch her maternal needs on me. I think my tenuous status at Moravia Castle appealed to her fractious nature. She delighted in arguing with Father almost as much as she delighted in lecturing me. But I was grateful for the attention and admired Cook for her formidable courage. Only Cook, I thought, would help me now to plot against Father.

I found her near the ovens, leaning her great arms on a floured marble counter and, as usual, shouting at the kitchen boy to hurry up and be about his business. Locks of her fading red hair had escaped the white cap she wore when cooking and wet strands were clinging to her neck and forehead. Flour streaked her arms up to the elbows. From a brown bowl on the counter she pinched off bits of pale dough and patted them firmly between moist palms. Her fingers expertly twisted and curled the dough. I could see the shape of my favorite bilberry tarts taking place as if by magic beneath those big fingers.

"Cook?" I called nervously from the door. She stopped her tirades and turned to look at me, her broad, red face spread with a grin. She wiped her hands quickly on her apron and pushed back the brim of her cap, leaving flour on her forehead as she did.

"Look 'ere, youngin'." She motioned with floury fingers to the stack of tarts already prepared. "I've made yer favorite today in hopes that nice young man will win." Suddenly she frowned as she examined the stack. "'Ere, do you think I've made enough? He's a grand eater, that one. Never saw better since the days my husband were alive. Now there was a man could eat. You should've seen him—"

"Cook!" I stopped her, for I knew that once she started talking about her late husband, I'd never get a word in edgewise. She stopped and looked at me, eyebrows arched and her lips pressed together severely. I hesitated for a moment, worried that I had angered her. She waited, one toe tapping a warning on the tiled floor. I moved closer to her quickly so as not to have to shout my plan over the whole kitchen.

"Cook, listen," I started again near her ear. "Father means to kill Severin."

"Well, true enough, I suppose, if he don't pass the task," she answered matter-of-factly. Then she smiled at me and patted my cheek, leaving a light dusting of flour there. "But I've had one of me dreams, dearie, and I know he's the right one! Don't you fret now. Any man as can eat like that!"

"No," I said tensely, "you don't understand. Father is planning to kill Severin whether he wins or loses."

Cook's mouth gaped open slightly as she digested what I said and then her blue eyes narrowed and her cheeks pinked an angry red. "Why? Why should he do a thing like that? And to a lad like that, eh?"

"Father doesn't want to seen me married. He wants to keep my sorcery for himself, even if it means murdering Severin, as he has done to all the rest."

"No-good skinny-legged bastard," she muttered, grabbing

a pan and smacking it against her open palm. "I'll smash his ugly brains in if he tries it!"

"Help Severin escape instead," I said boldly.

She stared, shocked by the suggestion. "Well now," she mumbled, putting the pan on the counter and looking at me closely. "Who would have thought it?" She was quiet a moment, studying me, measuring the weight of my courage and the strength of my resolve to plot against Father. I didn't waver beneath the steely gaze, but stared back, my chin firmly set.

"Indeed," she said slowly, "and why not? High time, too. There's been too much death about this place." A twinge of sadness crossed her face, softening her course features. "Better you should be gettin' married and havin' babes. She cupped my chin in her hand and tilted my face back to look into my eyes. "Do you want Severin to win?"

"Yes, I do." I blushed, surprised by the admission.

"And if he won, would you go with him, to be married?"

"Perhaps, if that were possible, but—"

"Do you love him?"

My face flushed redder. "I don't know, Cook. I only know I don't want him to die."

She held me there a moment longer and then exhaled. "That's good enough for me! Right, I'll do it!" she declared, and I sighed with relief.

I started to sketch out my plan but she interrupted me with one of her own. "I'll have a stableboy bring round the horses and pack food for the journey," she said practically. "If Severin does fail the last task, your father'll want to take his time with the execution. I know him, he likes to have a big meal before he does the deed. I'll arrange to have Severin released from the stocks and brought here while the master's eating."

"How will you do that?" I asked skeptically. The guards were unpleasant men, made loyal by the fear of father's punishments.

Cook waved her hand as if my question were no more than a fly lighting on one of her cakes. "That head guard Rolvak, he's been on at me to marry him since my husband died. Wants someone as can take good care of that great stomach of his, I'll warrant." She stopped when she saw my face blanch at the mention of the big, burly guard. "Go on now, he's not that bad, a bit rough on the edges maybe, but I can smooth that out over time. 'Sides, I've been thinking it's about time for me to have another man about the place. Don't fret, he'll do it for me," she said confidently.

"And if Severin wins?" I asked hopefully, not yet ready to imagine Cook married to Rolvak.

"Get to his brothers and tell 'em to come and attend to their horses. I'll insist Severin's to come to the kitchen to taste a new dish; your father won't deny me that. I'll give yer father a dose of sleeping draft in his soup. That'll fix him for a time and we'll send Severin and the rest on their way. It won't be much, but it'll buy them a bit of time. There now," she said, satisfied, folding her arms under her bosom, "will it do for you?"

"Oh yes!" I answered, and because I was both excited and terrified, I flung my arms around her damp neck and hugged hard. "Thank you, Cook. Thank you for everything."

She tugged my arms loose from their hold. "Go on now, get away with you or folks will be wondering," she said brusquely, but her hand reached out to pat me on the head.

"Cook, supposing Father finds out you've helped me?" I asked, suddenly worried.

"Shush, he'll not find out. Don't worry about old Cook. I can take care of meself. Go on, get out of here and let me work now." She waved me away and turned back to the bilberry tarts, her lips pursed as she counted the stack.

I left the kitchen and went back to my room to prepare for the feast that would follow the morning's hunt. I dressed carefully, knowing that today would be the most difficult of the three tasks for Severin and that Father would be watching me. If I was to be of any help to Severin, I needed to attract as little attention to myself as possible and let Father believe that he had sufficiently frightened me last night. I put on a maroon silk shift with tight sleeves that flared into wide bell shapes at my fingertips. Over this I wore the heavy black velvet dress that I detested and buckled a gold chain around my waist. The sleeves of the dress were generous and lined with a lighter shade of maroon silk. I folded back the wide sleeves to just beneath my elbows, as I had seen Ilena wear them. I attached the black lace collar about the neckline of the bodice and adjusted it so that it fanned out around my face and neck in a stiff ruffle. I stopped before the mirror to arrange my hair, pulling the unruly curls back into a neat chignon that I dressed

with a pearl comb. I wiped off the little smudge of flour left
on my cheek by Cook and prayed silently that she would be
able to help me as she had promised. At the doorway I
stopped, feeling oddly faint. The hand resting on the cold
stone of the doorway was not as cold as the pit of fear in my
stomach. I took my hand away and straightened my shoulders.
Then, admonishing the butterflies in my stomach not to fly out
when I opened my mouth, I left, heading for the main courtyard.

I entered the main courtyard just as the hunting party returned in a burst of frenzied activity. The master of hounds
was leading the way, blowing on his horn to bring the hounds
to order, while they, bodies muddied and muzzles tipped with
blood, bayed noisily and ran in circles, still excited by the
fever of their hunt. Behind them came the nobles, shouting
and cheering to each other, their horses prancing and blowing
steam. Some of the riders were disheveled and muddy, the
result of being thrown during a jump; yet it didn't seem to
dampen their enthusiasm. They wheeled their horses to and
fro, boisterously slapping at the mud on their thighs. Servants
began offering trays of filled wineglasses and the mounted
huntsmen scooped them up, sloshing the wine over the servants as they toasted each other and wiped the mud off their
faces with sleeves daubed in the wine.

I saw my sister, Ilena, sitting astride her black bay, her
cheeks flushed rosy despite the dusting of white face powder.
Her riding suit was cut tight and high at the waist, pressing her
breasts upward into two appealing white mounds. A young
man with a florid face, blond ringlets, and very eager hands
was helping her down from the horse. They stopped a moment
by the horse and he whispered something in her ear, his fingertips tracing the edge of her bodice and brushing against the
curve of her breasts. She slapped his hand away playfully and
took a glass of wine. She answered him, her eyes shining
coyly over the rim of her wineglass.

I turned away and craned my neck trying to find Severin in
the flowing crowd. Instead I saw Father staring at me from
where he stood next to the master of hounds and feeding bits
of bloodied meat to his hounds. His mouth curved in a cool,
sardonic smile as he inclined his head, acknowledging me.
His black cape was thrown back and his white shirt was
opened at the collar, exposing his throat. Like the wings of a

crow, his hair hung in black waves and his eyes glittered, feverish with the joy of the hunt and the kill. His riding boots and black trousers were splattered with blood, and though I could sense the coiled tension in his body, his posture was relaxed, the bits of meat like bloody flowers dropping from the elegant hands. Behind him Zuul was leading away Father's horse; it was foaming at the mouth, white and pink where the hard bit had cut into the soft flesh. Zuul steadied the beast with a hand on its neck as it trembled, sweat gleaming on the silky black flanks marred by red stripes where the riding crop had opened the skin. I caught my breath, trapped by the aura of Father's power as he held my gaze. Around him the crowd streamed and flowed, but never touched him. I could sense the subtle presence of sorcery as the crowd moved through an elaborate dance in accordance with his designs. Despite my fear, I was awed by Father's skill.

His gaze released me as he shifted his attention to greet my mother and Vooris, who approached to congratulate him on the success of his hunt. He handed the red meat to Vooris, instructing him how to reward the hounds properly. Vooris grimaced as he touched the slick flesh and I saw him shrink back from the snapping jaws of the eager hounds.

I searched the crowd again and at last saw Severin and his brothers riding in slowly with the last of the hunting party. Behind them was the tangled carcass of a stag, gutted and tied to a pole that was carried on the shoulders of two servants. Severin's face was a frozen angry mask, his jaw clenched tight. Beside him, Nar was chewing on his mustache and he bristled sharply when a drunken rider lurched his horse across their path. Teren held himself aloof, frowning, dark brows knitting a line across his forehead as he stared straight ahead and ignored the raucous crowd. They moved slowly through the milling crowd, refusing the offered glasses of wine. As they dismounted I watched Severin cross to a water barrel. Dipping his hands into it, he washed his face.

The arrival of other noblemen and ladies in their carriages increased the confusion in the courtyard. Livery boys in bright silks and stableboys mingled with the guests to lead away the excited horses. Servants set up tables and began to lay out the delicacies of the hunt feast, Cook's finest achievements. Those nobles who been to the hunt jeered at their counterparts

who had just arrived, preferring their soft beds to the hard seat
of a saddle. Some, already drunk with the fast ride and the
wine, slapped the well-dressed backs, leaving dirty smudges.
The scent of rose water and cologne mixed heavily in the
dusty air with the pungent musk of horses and sweat.

While the de'Stains wore only black, no such restriction
existed for other Moravian nobles. They dressed with a flam-
boyant vengeance, each trying to outdo the other in a game of
courtly fashion. Green and bronze were the favorite colors just
then for men. Doublets were short and tight, revealing much
of the legs and buttocks. Their hose was striped or checkered
and, according to the whispered gossip, even padded to arouse
interest. The women were no less brilliantly dressed in shades
of blue ranging from azure to a deep midnight highlighted
with accents of pink and yellow silk. Gold laces and silk ribbons were used to tie on bodices. Sleeves were slashed to
expose little puffs of yellow silk. Some wore skirts that
stretched so wide and full they had trouble passing through the
crowd, while others wore several skirts layered in different
colors and pinned in bunches with jeweled pins of pearl and
topaz. By comparison I was dowdy as the dust swirled and
settled on my dreary black dress, robbing it of any distinct
color.

I tried to cross the busy courtyard, keeping my eye on
Severin and his brothers on the other side. I was stopped along
the way by different noblewomen who wished to engage me in
a particularly nasty kind of small talk that I was neither good
at nor enjoyed.

"My dear," called out Lady Katyana, catching my arm and
leaning forward so I was forced to stare at the enormous ame-
thyst pendant nestled at her neck, "what a sweet little chain
belt you're wearing. It's quite becoming and so charmingly
simple—like yourself." And she smiled thinly with rouged
lips. "How do you like the little bauble my Ivask gave me?"
she asked, and flashed the stone so I could see how beautifully
faceted it was and how expensive. "He had it specially made
for our coming wedding. Wasn't that thoughtful of him?"

"Yes," I replied, keeping my voice pleasant. "It reminds
me of the jewel I saw last year around Lady Mina's neck.
Why, it could almost be the same one." Lady Katyana's smile
faltered, for we both knew that Ivask had been bedding Lady
Mina last year and only the disclosure of her small and unim-

pressive dowry had ended the affair with haste. Lady Katyana
drew back haughtily and let go of my arm.

"Impossible!" she sniffed, but she searched the crowd for
Ivask and, when she spied him, set off in a flurry.

I feigned the part of a good host, smiling as I elbowed past
the guests, engaging in meaningless conversation and all the
while trying not to let my temper boil over. I knew what
Father was doing with this chaotic and bustling feast. A sorcerer can manipulate illusions; from the shadows he creates an
image of something that seems tangible and real enough but is
entirely without substance. That was the key to this final task.
With this swirling crowd and frenzied activity, Father put Severin at a disadvantage. Too many distractions, too many
shadows that would make Father's illusions impossible to
penetrate. Severin had a fair measure of talent; he had proved
that already last night. But with the feast and the fatigue of the
hunt, only one well trained in sorcery would be able to succeed in the final task.

Through a sudden gap in the crowd, I glimpsed Severin
again, standing across the courtyard, trapped by a nobleman
who, between pinches of snuff, was droning on about the
problems of his breedstock. Severin was letting him talk but
his face, rigid with unspoken anger, showed his concentration
was elsewhere. I decided it was easier to reach Teren and Nar
first and wove my way through the growing crowd to find
them. As I expected, they were standing by the serving tables
already sampling the array of dishes.

Teren forced a polite smile and bowed his head when he
saw me. "Good day, Lady Magda," he said, and Nar, with a
bilberry tart crammed in his mouth, did his best to imitate his
older brother. "Fine weather, isn't it?" Teren continued con-
versationally. I was much too nervous to care if it had been
snowing but I tried to reply as evenly.

"Yes, Moravia is lovely this time of year. Did you enjoy
the hunt?"

Teren's polite smile disappeared. "No!" he answered
shortly.

My eyes opened wide, surprised by his honest reply. "Why
not?" I asked, alarmed that Father had done some mischief on
the hunt.

"It's a terrible thing we've done."

"Don't you hunt in Thall?"

"Aye, we hunt, but not like this. Not for sport. We hunt when food is needed and then it is a quick, clean kill. This . . ." He paused, staring angrily at the revelry of the crowd. "This is without respect; to let the hounds run down the animal and then tear its throat. Fear and a slow death taint the meat." He shook his head disgustedly and I understood now the sour expression I had seen on Severin's face. "The stag is rare in Thall and admired for its strength and beauty. This hunt honored neither of us."

"I am afraid then you'll not like the main course," I said, pointing to where three servants laboring under a large and heavy silver platter were bringing in Cook's crowning achievement, the centerpiece of all hunt feasts.

Various meats had been cooked and then artfully shaped into one enormous sculpture in the likeness of a stag's head. The rack of horns and ears from the freshly killed stag had been added to the centerpiece, making it appear lifelike, the head thrust up and the mouth opened as if caught at the moment of death. Around the base of the platter, blood sausages and onions swam in a spicy, black liquid. The nobles roared their approval and dipped pieces of freshly cut bread in the sauce that stained the white grain crimson. They toasted themselves, downing their wine in single drafts; and then, as servants scurried to refill the glasses, they toasted my father for providing the successful hunt and feast.

Teren scowled and turned his face away.

"It's crude!" blurted Nar. "Only a beast would—"

Teren stopped his younger brother with a sharp look and the young man fell quiet, though he continued to shake his head angrily, offended by the sight. They stood tense and wary in my presence, waiting, I thought, for me to leave.

"You don't like me, do you?" I asked Teren.

He regarded me carefully. "It's this place I don't like."

"Will you trust me, at least?" I asked uncertainly, for he hadn't really answered my question.

He raised a single black eyebrow. "Why?"

Ilena and the man with yellow curls sauntered toward our table. The man bumped into Nar's side, causing him to spill his wine. Nar turned sharply.

"Watch it, good man."

The nobleman looked through us with bleary eyes and gave a nasty smirk. Then, wrinkling his nose and sniffing loudly,

he turned to Ilena. "What's that stink? It smells like pig shit!"
Ilena giggled behind her hand.

Nar's hand went to his short sword, and, just as swiftly, the
man reached for the hilt of his rapier, his eyes suddenly eager.

Teren grabbed his brother's arm. Yanking Nar backward,
he placed himself solidly in front of his brother. "Pig shit,
then?" he asked pleasantly. Pointing to a muddy stain on the
man's hose, he added, "Perhaps it's there on your leg. Shall I
fetch you a servant, then, to wash it off?"

The nobleman refused to look where Teren pointed, but
kept his eyes fixed on Teren's face and his hand on the hilt of
his sword. Teren shrugged and turned away from him.

"May I show you some of the gardens?" I asked lamely,
trying to find an excuse that would take us away from the
table.

"Indeed," Teren answered. He nudged Nar with his
shoulder but the younger man refused to move. "Come away,"
Teren whispered fiercely. "He's not worth it."

"I'll decide that, won't I?"

"And get us both killed in the doing. He's baiting you,
trying to give a good show for his companion. Don't be the
fool."

"I'm not a fool."

"Aye, you're not. So come away then."

Nar's brown eyes flashed defiantly at Teren, but he released his grip on his sword and turned his back to the nobleman. Still bristling with anger, he followed Teren and me
away from the table, along the edges of the crowd and to the
gardens.

"I am worried for Severin's life," I said, pretending to admire the lilies and roses in the garden.

"Severin believes he will succeed," replied Teren.

I looked at them nervously. "Under other circumstances I'd
be happy to hear that. But it doesn't change what I said. Severin's life is in danger. I am certain my father will kill Severin, even if he succeeds in completing the final task."

They both looked out to the crowd, scanning the faces for a
glimpse of Severin. They saw him, still engaged by the nobleman discussing breeding. Teren turned back to me, his gaze
boring into me.

"I've not liked this business from the start," he said curtly.

"Severin should've stayed home to marry. Come Nar, look to your sword."

"No, wait," I pleaded, and put a hand on his arm to stop him. "Please, it's important not to arouse Father's suspicions. He can be deadly when angered."

"We're not afraid of your father," Nar said sharply.

"I'm sure you're not. But you don't know my father. He's not discriminating in his anger. Others could be hurt if you move against him openly. Please, listen to me, I have a plan."

"Do we trust her, then?" Nar asked his older brother.

Teren's eyes seemed to lose focus as he stared at me silently. My body tingled and a slight shiver dotted my spine.

"Aye," he nodded, his eyes regaining a clear stare. "She speaks the truth."

Relieved they would listen, I quickly told them of Cook's plan. Neither of them liked it. I could tell by the way Nar fidgeted like a cat waiting to pounce, and Teren's glance never straying from Severin as he listened. There was a moment of silence when I finished as the two brothers looked at each other, deciding.

"We'd be like hares on the run," said Nar moodily.

"Aye," Teren agreed. "But I've no wish to see others harmed. And neither would Severin." Turning to me he nodded. "Nar and I will take the horses to the cook and we'll wait for Severin. But," he added sternly, "we'll not wait long. Be quick or we'll see to our brother's life in our own way."

"Agreed!" I said, trying to sound more confident than I felt.

We parted and I returned to the crowd, hoping for a chance to warn Severin. My back prickled and I became aware that I was being watched. I turned sharply and saw a group of men, among them the nobleman who had dallied with Ilena, clustered near the stag's head. They were staring at me and their expressions held a strange mixture of hostility and desire. I could sense the undercurrent of Father's handiwork; another step in the dance that he wove with me, like the hunted stag, as the centerpiece. Against their wills they would be attracted and, ignoring the warnings of their families, they would offer themselves in a challenge they had no hope of winning. Vooris's future would become more secure with each new death. They raised pieces of bloodied bread and wineglasses toward me in a mocking salute. Father's spell played on their ambitions for power, though it could not disguise the truth that they didn't think much of me. I hurried away from the hungry stares and the coarse laughter that followed their salute.

I found Severin at last, cornered by the Lady Almea, who was tapping him seductively on the chest with her fan. She was not old by Moravian standards but she had been widowed twice and was considered something of a risk. As she leaned close to Severin, smiling invitingly at him, I wondered if she wasn't offering him her own proposal. Unaccountably, I became irritated with her. In the morning sun Severin's brown hair gleamed chestnut, his cheeks ruddy with health amidst the pallid faces of the noblemen, bleached white with powder. He turned his head, looking flustered, and caught me staring. I waved and he flashed a smile of relief. He bowed politely to Lady Almea and left to meet me. She looked at me furiously and lifted her head indignantly before moving away. As I watched Severin approach, I felt a pang of emotion stab my chest and I chided myself for the weakness.

Severin had just reached me and taken my hand when Father's voice boomed out over the milling crowd.

"We shall begin the final task. Bring the suitor to the stables."

"Severin," I said urgently and held on to his hand. I was suddenly struck by how small my hand was in his palm. His large hand was warm and the calluses that lined the palm dry to the touch. I was standing very close to him and was distracted by the nearness of his face to mine. I noticed a small scar that cut through the edge of one eyebrow and the green flecks of color that lightened his brown eyes. His mustache had a speckling of white, and over his ears grew soft curls of fine red hair. The smell of leather and horses permeated his skin. Despite my chiding, my heart began to pound and the blood rushed to my face with a furious pink glow. "Severin," I tried again to speak, "I must warn you—"

He stopped me, drawing me closer still.

"Are you worried, then?" he asked curiously, a smile lifting the corners of his mouth.

"Yes, my father—"

"I'll not fail, you know. Not now that I know it matters to you."

"Thank you, but—"

Zuul suddenly appeared at my side and prevented my

speaking further. "Excuse me, Lady Magda, but his lordship has requested the suitor come to the stables."

I freed my hand, but not before Severin gave it a final reassuring squeeze. I turned to Zuul and felt the fear of last night return. His hair was cut longer than an ordinary page's and groomed almost like that of a young noble. He was well dressed in a black livery, with piping of gold worked along the seams; a doublet like the one Vooris had been fitted for only yesterday. I saw how similar to Vooris he seemed in appearance and yet how different I knew them to be. Vooris was Father's son, but Zuul was his man, for in his eyes the yellow flame flickered, like the eyes of the hawk.

Father's hand seemed to spin the world tighter and tighter about me. I stumbled, swept up in a sudden vertigo. Only with difficulty did I straighten myself and follow the others to witness Severin's final task.

The crowd of nobles stood in a large semicircle around the kennels, which were alive with my father's hunting hounds. They barked and yelped and threw themselves against the gates. All alike, with burnt-orange spots against white, they appeared as a whirling blur of color and noise. Father and Severin stood to one side of the kennel, near the gate's opening. Father shouted at the hounds and kicked the doors.

"Quiet, hounds!" he commanded. They cowered, quiet except for panting and the vigorous thumping of their tails on the dusty ground.

Father looked out at the crowd and smiled. "As you can see, my esteemed guests and suitor," he said with a nod over his shoulder in Severin's direction, "the finest hunting hounds in Moravia. See the gleam in their eyes and the shine on their coats. Eager brutes, ready to wake the dead with their howls." At this a few of the hounds began to whine shrilly and yelp.

The nobles raised their glasses in salute to Father's hounds, for their bloodline was indeed the best in Moravia. On many a hunt one could hear them giving voice far in the distance. That they were quite savage and would just as easily bring down a peasant child in their path as a stag added to their reputation for fierceness. Only Father truly controlled them, and, on occasion, I had seen him vent his anger by allowing his hounds to destroy whatever strayed in their path.

Father moved to the gate, calling the hounds by name in a smooth, low voice. Then, swiftly, Father released the gate and the hounds rushed forward through the crowd of nobles. There was screaming and shouting as the hounds burrowed between legs, tripping servants and nobles alike, snatching at silk skirts and fallen hats. They crashed into tables and upset platters of carefully prepared food. The master of hounds blew his hunting horn, trying to call them back from the swirling pandemonium. I pressed myself against the stable walls and heard the horses, excited by the loose hounds, whinny nervously and paw with their hooves on the stable floor. Father was laughing, enjoying the chaotic scene enormously. Behind him I saw Severin, unshaken by the hounds but his face tensed angrily. Then Father clapped his hands together and called loudly to the pack.

"Hie! Hounds, down now, enough! Sit!" His voice was edged with the sound of sorcery and the hounds obeyed a once. Untangling themselves from the crowd, they lined up before Father, panting eagerly. The crowd struggled to reassemble itself. Servants with linen towels rushed to wipe off food that had stained silk sleeves and skirts as it had been dashed to the ground in the melee. The crowd was humming with angry murmurs when Father spoke again, commanding their attention.

"Dear friends, forgive my little prank," he began in a more conciliatory voice. "It was necessary to demonstrate the difficulty of this task. Only one of the hounds that have just besieged you is real." Many in the crowd gasped and others shook their heads in admiring nods. "Your final task, Severin of Thall, is to choose the real hound from the illusions," he said, and he stepped away from the line of panting hounds to let Severin closer.

Severin looked at my father with a grim expression and then faced the hounds. He didn't hesitate, but walked along the line of waiting hounds, examining each hound where it sat rooted to the spot by Father's command. Though they could not move from their place, the hounds snarled and snapped aggressively at Severin as he passed. When he reached the end of the line he returned slowly to his place beside Father. Noblemen, ladies, and even servants gathered in small knots whispering and craning their necks to see Severin. Enmeshed in the crowd, I, too, watched, my hands twisting nervously at the gold chain on my belt.

Severin smiled and calmly, bending down on one knee,

called out to the line of hounds. "Here, boy, come here now to me." He stretched out a hand. My heart sank, afraid for Severin. The hound wouldn't come to Severin; only Father's command could release it. The hounds barked and howled as one hound began to grovel toward Severin, dragging its tail between its legs. Its yellow eyes rolled fearfully and it approached Severin, whimpering like a pup.

"That's it, good boy," Severin called encouragingly to the cowed beast. "Come here to me." Severin laid his hand gently on the spotted head and began to massage its ears affectionately. The hound capitulated to Severin's touch, rolling over on the ground and exposing its white belly. The line of snarling hounds vanished and the true hound remained prostrate at Severin's feet.

The crowd broke into delighted applause. They raised their glasses, calling for more wine with which to salute Severin for the feat of mastering a Moravian hound. Severin looked up from the dog and, seeing my frightened, astonished face, burst out laughing. It was true, I couldn't believe it. Until that moment, I had not thought it possible that Severin would win. I wanted to shriek with glee and dance on the tables with the same wild energy of the hounds. And yet I was so stunned that I could do no more than stand there and stare stupidly.

I might have stayed like that indefinitely if it weren't for the people who came to congratulate me on my pending nuptials. I suspected they were less interested in my happiness than pleased that Father had lost to what they deemed was an uncouth stranger. With satisfaction they insulted Father by displaying an enthusiastic response to Severin's success. Even my mother kissed me lightly on the cheek and told me she was happy for me. I started to speak, to answer the well-wishers who had gathered around me, when Father drew close and the words died in my mouth. He took my arm in a taloned grip. His face was deathly white and his black eyes sparked with malice. I found courage in Severin's success and faced Father, frightened but refusing to be intimidated.

"So, Magda. A man has succeeded at last. Congratulations, daughter, and may you both enjoy long life." The hand squeezed tighter and my fingers were denied blood.

"I hope we shall, Father," I replied. His hand continued to grip painfully as we stared at each other, and then abruptly, he was gone, swallowed by the stream of well-wishers. Pale and scared, I looked for Severin. He saw me and his smile disappeared. He pushed through the crowd, scarcely acknowledging the others slapping him on the back and calling to him. He reached out and pulled me toward him. He held me and I closed my eyes and leaned against his chest. The cold terror of Father's words faded in the secure warmth of his embrace. I inhaled deeply, happy I could breath again, could hope again beyond the unspoken threat in father's words.

"Thank you," I whispered gratefully, stepping free from his embrace.

He rested a hand on my shoulder, and peered into my face, concerned.

"Now it's I who worries about you. Are you all right, then?"

"Yes. Yes, thank you," I replied, suddenly self-conscious. And then, aware of the others still lingering to offer their congratulations, I led Severin away to a quiet spot where we might talk in private.

"You can't stay here, Severin. You must leave immediately."

"And miss the wedding?" he teased.

"There'll be no wedding. Father will kill you first."

"Is that any way to treat a son-in-law?" he said lightly, though his expression was serious and small lines appeared at the corners of his eyes.

"Please, you must go now," I said urgently.

"Aye," he nodded. "I'm thinking the same thing. Your father's not happy, is he? I've released his hold on you and he's no one to hide behind."

I stared at him, surprised. "When did you know it was my father and not I who demanded the suitors to be tested?"

"The first time I saw you, smelling like the summer fields and your hair dripping wet beneath your headdress." He paused and covered my hand with his. "You're not like your father, Magda, any fool with eyes can see that. Any man with sense would feel it."

"What do you really want, Severin?"

"To be happy. And you, Magda? What do you want?"

We were standing close to the stable wall. Shade from a cloud drifted over us as Severin hooked his arm around my waist. A small gust of wind blew strands of hair across my face and neck. Gently Severin brushed them away and rested his fingers lightly against my cheek. Then it seemed to me that Moravia did not exist, that nothing existed but this one moment as Severin bent his head to kiss me. Our noses were just touching when a noisy "Ahem!" at Severin's elbow stopped us. So close to my face, Severin smiled and sighed wistfully and I giggled, suddenly embarrassed.

"Beggin' your pardon, lordship, but Cook wants you in the kitchen. She says she's got something special wot she thinks you should try."

"Can't it wait?" Severin asked.

At the mention of Cook, I snapped out of my daze and immediately turned Severin around saying, "No, no, of course you must go, Severin. Cook will be hurt if you don't go."

Severin started to protest, but I insisted, steering him by the arm in the direction of the kitchens. As we reached the Great Hall, I could hear the musicians warming up and knew that soon the dancing would begin. I saw Ilena again, standing beside the man with the yellow ringlets, her arm resting on his. Though she held herself demurely, her face had lost its coyness and was openly flirtatious. A corner of me watched, amazed, for I had never known my quiet sister to hold much interest in the affairs of the court. Yet she looked comfortable among the throng of nobles, as if she had waited for this moment to arrive.

I let go of Severin's arm and said for the benefit of anyone who might be listening, "Go now to see Cook and I will join you presently at lunch." Not very original and a bit formal, but then it was the best I could muster at the moment. Severin looked puzzled as he contemplated my odd behavior.

"As you wish, my lady." Then he bent to kiss my out-stretched hand.

The dance music began and couples took their positions on the floor. I heard Ilena laugh, a high tinkling sound, as her partner whirled her around in the first movement. I wanted to hurry out of there before anyone asked me to dance. But as I turned to flee, I collided with Vooris, who grabbed my arm and waist and swung me onto the floor.

"I don't want to dance." I glared at Vooris as we were swept along the growing circle of partners.

"Shut up and listen," he snapped. "Where else can I talk to you without Zuul at my shoulder?"

I quieted down and allowed Vooris to dance me over to the

far edge of the Great Hall. It was yet another surprise for me as Vooris proved to be a graceful and accomplished dancer. I hadn't thought my morose brother to have so light and nimble a step.

"Father's poisoned the wine," he said bluntly.

"Has he, then?" I answered.

Vooris cocked his head back and smirked. "Starting to sound like Severin already, Magda."

"I was only joking!" I retorted. Vooris swung me around so swiftly I nearly stumbled. But he held me firmly at the waist and didn't allow my feet to betray me.

"Odd that you should find such news so funny."

"Let's just say I'm my father's daughter," I answered, thinking of the sleeping draft Cook was putting in Father's soup, no doubt just as Father's steward was poisoning the wine in the cellar.

"I'd rather not," Vooris said. "What are you planning?"

"Nothing," I answered. I was panting lightly, out of breath from the dancing, though Vooris showed no signs of being affected.

"Well, whatever nothing is, you've not much time left to do it."

"Then get me out of here," I gasped, breathing hard to keep up with the dance.

Vooris spun me around easily, our circles drifting us closer to the stairs of the Great Hall.

"What about you, Magda?" he asked. "Father won't be too pleased if more of his plans go astray."

"I haven't thought about it yet."

"You'd best start."

"I thought I was safe for now, that he couldn't hurt me without hurting himself!"

"He could torture you with illusions and never touch your body." Vooris tightened his grip on my waist and I stared at him, frightened. "Flee," he whispered. "Escape with Severin."

Numbly I nodded back in agreement.

We were almost at the stairs when Vooris whispered: "Good luck, Magda."

"Thank you," I murmured, bowing lightly as he released me, our dance finished. He returned the gesture with a bow of his own, delivered with his usual arrogance. Then he turned away from me and headed back into the crowd of dancers.

Alone once again, I fought to calm the rapid beating of my heart and tried to think. The rhythm of the dancing music clattered noisily in my head and the bright colors of the dancers as they swirled past made it impossible to concentrate. Only one thought penetrated the noise and confusion: I had to get away. I had to flee. Picking up my skirts, I started running up the stairway.

"Magda!" Mother's sharp tone stopped me on the marble step. "Where are you going? It is impolite to leave your guests so soon."

I turned and gave her a wan smile, passing a hand over my forehead. "I'm sorry, I'm just feeling a bit faint. It must be the excitement." This was Mother's favorite excuse for escaping dull gatherings.

"Oh, of course. Do lie down and rest. I'll send a servant to fetch you when the meal is served. Perhaps you can tidy yourself as well." She waved her lace handkerchief in my direction. "See if you can do something about your hair. It looks unkempt."

"Yes, Mother," I replied dutifully, smoothing back the stray locks to no effect. She tsked to herself and then rejoined the crowd in the Great Hall.

As soon as she was out of sight, I rushed wildly up the stairs to my room. If only they haven't left, I prayed feverishly. Quickly, I changed into more suitable riding clothes and then swept out of my room and down the spiral staircase to the kitchen. My thoughts raced faster than my feet, thinking of Vooris's warning. I had never really considered fleeing Moravia. There was nowhere I could imagine going where Father might not find me and bring me back. Yet suddenly it seemed there was no choice but to run, since to remain was a certain death. And what of Severin? I asked myself. Could I be certain that I was not leaving the kettle for the fire?

I arrived at the kitchen and saw Severin and his brothers standing beside their horses in the empty courtyard.

"Whist!" Cook hissed to catch my attention and shook her arm for me to hurry. "Get a move on, girl. You mustn't wait much longer. I've sent a servant to tell your father you're resting and will be down later."

"Are they waiting for me?" I asked, surprised.

"No," said Cook angrily, "they're waitin' for snow! Don't be thick, girl, of course they're waitin' for you!" And she bustled me faster toward the courtyard.

I saw now that Severin held the reigns of a fourth horse, a small, comfortable-looking mare. Tied to Teren's saddle horn were Cook's food parcels wrapped with red string. The horses stamped their feet, shaking their heads, impatient to be off.

"You've come, then." Severin smiled at me, relieved, and took my hand. "I wasn't sure you would."

"Neither was I," I replied, a bit dazed. He laughed and prepared to help me on my horse.

"Going so soon?" asked an oily voice behind me. "And not even a proper farewell?"

I whirled around and saw, standing in the kitchen archway, the man with the blond ringlets, his hand resting on the hilt of his sword.

"What I do is none of your concern!" I said haughtily.

"Perhaps not mine, but surely Lord Gregor would not approve of his precious daughter running off with a stinking farmer." He moved menacingly toward Severin, drawing his rapier from its scabbard with a chilling hiss.

"Leave me alone," I demanded.

"No. I won't see a farmer take what Moravian nobles have died trying to win. I will have it; you and the sorcerer's power." He swished the blade back and forth, cutting the air with deadly strokes.

I raised my hands as if I intended sorcery, hoping to scare him with the bluff. He hesitated, his gaze shifting back and forth between me and Severin. Severin grabbed my arm and pulled me out of the way.

"Don't do it, Magda," he said gruffly, and drew his short sword. "Teren, look to the horses, have them ready," he ordered over his shoulder. Nar appeared at Severin's side but Severin stopped him. "No. The fight is mine."

Severin moved forward to meet the man, his body crouched, the sword held out to the side. The man nodded his head and flicked his blade, inviting Severin to approach closer. Then he lunged quickly, the point of his sword aimed for Severin's heart. Severin straightened to meet the blade. He blocked the lunge with a downward swing of his sword and shifted forward to attack the man. The man moved swiftly, throwing his body to the side and bringing his sword up. The swords clashed with a sheering sound as steel scraped against steel. They drew apart and prepared for another assault. The blond-haired man sweated and licked his lips. Severin's body bristled, ready for the attack. The blond-haired man charged with furious thrusts, the sword darting from side to side. Severin was pushed back to the wall, blocking each rapidly delivered blow. At my side Nar tensed and drew his weapon.

A sudden clang stopped the man in midswing, his sword high in the air. He stumbled back, staring confusedly at Severin. Another clang and his eyes crossed and then turned up in his head. He fell to his knees, the sword slipping from his grip and clattering on the kitchen floor. Without a word he dropped forward, his head hitting the stone floor with a smack.

Behind him, one hand holding one of Cook's black pans and the other over her mouth in a horrified gesture, stood my sister. Ilena knelt on the floor beside the unconscious man and cradled his bruised head in her lap.

"Now see what you made me do, Magda?" she said angrily. "I didn't want to have to hit him. I just hope I haven't killed him."

"Ilena, thank you," I started.

"Don't think I did it for you!" she snapped at me harshly. "I could care less what happens to you." I stared wide-eyed as if she were a complete stranger wearing my sister's face. "I want to get married!" she shouted at me, her elegant visage twisted with frustration. "I want to get away from this horrid place and from Father. But I can't until you, my elder sister, are properly married off. And while I wait, every decent nobleman in Moravia marches to his death on account of you. I hate you."

She was right, of course. I had never considered what life was like for her, just as I had not considered Vooris's life. She had her own dreams, and I stood in the way of them, never realizing. "Ilena, I'm sorry," I fumbled, trying to make amends too late.

"Just go away, Magda. Once you're gone, I'll be free."

Severin tugged at my arm.

"Come, Magda, we must go before others come looking." I went reluctantly to my horse and let Severin lift me into the saddle. I leaned to give Cook a kiss farewell, but she'd have none of it.

"Go on now, you've no time for that!" she said, waving her arms at us. She sniffed loudly and wiped a hand across her eyes. "Go on now and promise me you'll have lots of babies!"

We were already moving through the open gate when I tried to wave farewell to Ilena. She stared back at me, motionless, her face wooden. She watched me pass through the gate and then bowed her head once more over the blond man, stroking his temples.

I gave a last look at the gray stones of Moravia Castle and then turned my face to the open fields. I spurred my horse to a gallop and the rushing wind whistled past my face. We galloped on the old path, through the yellow fields, then into the woods and past the pond where I had first seen Severin and his brothers. Before me Severin led the way, his body pressed tight against the back of his horse. I followed him, leaning over the neck of my mare as we dashed through the woods. Teren and Nar rode behind me and the thunder of the horses' hooves pounded a rhythm in my ears. "Flee, Magda, flee!" it urged, and I did. Bracing myself against the mare, my head ducked in her streaming mane, I followed Severin of Thall and fled Moravia.

FIVE

IT WAS NOONDAY when we set out galloping away from Moravia Castle, and, though the sun was shining brightly, we rarely saw it from the shadowy trail that led through the woods. The pine and cedar forests around the castle had been cleared centuries ago and there now grew a gentle forest of oak, maple, and birch. Here and there the bristled branch of a pine brushed my head, but for the most part, the trail was clear and passable. These were Father's hunting grounds, and they seemed to me no more than a huge cultivated garden. There were few fallen trees to be seen and the thick underbrush had been cleared away to allow the speedy passage of riders. I had never ventured beyond these borders and was surprised when we plunged into a dense wilderness of spruce, fir, and white pines, their overlapping branches brushing at our thighs and shoulders and all but obliterating the narrow trail we followed. Occasionally, the trees thinned, and through the gaps I spied other castles and fields, which lay like little islands set among the deep green.

For the first time, too, I saw the peasants' homes tucked away in the forest; hovels of graying wood, leaning forlornly beneath the trees. Moss grew like green thatch on the rooftops. Around the mean shelters scraggly gardens competed with the stones for dominion over the rocky soil. Near one hut we saw a child dressed in a ragged shirt that barely covered his belly. He squatted by an open hearth poking sticks in the ashes of a smoky fire. He raised his dirty face to us, his eyes tearing from the smoke, and then scampered, frightened, into the hut. From the doorway a woman's face, frail and worn, peeked out. The child clutched at her torn skirts, hiding his face.

"Why are they so frightened of us?" I asked Severin.

We passed the side of the hut and saw a small red hind hanging up, its throat slit.

"There's your answer, then," whispered Severin back to me. "Husband's poached the deer, I'll wager. What's the punishment in Moravia for poaching?"

"Death by quartering," I said glumly.

"Hardly fair, is it?" grumbled Nar. "There's not been much to eat for a while, from the looks of that child."

"You'll not see that in Thall," said Teren. "There's few who would not help to feed another when times were hard. "Wait!" he called to Severin, and began untying the red string from one of the food packages Cook had given him. Silently he took the package and walked to the open hearth. Inside the doorway, the child shrank back. The woman held up a large club of gnarled wood, prepared to protect herself and her child from the intruder. Teren said nothing, but gently laid the package near the hearth and returned to his horse. Then we turned our horses and headed deeper into the woods. I looked back, curious, and saw the woman slip out and snatch the package. She held it to her nose, sniffed, and then, clutching it to her breast, hurried back into the hut.

It was twilight before Severin agreed to stop to eat a meal and rest the horses. I slid off my horse, exhausted and bow-legged. I was not a very accomplished rider and lacked coordination on a horse. A day of bumping and banging against the saddle filled my buttocks and thighs with excruciating pain. The skin on the inside of my thighs felt chafed and raw. Severin saw me as I tried discreetly to rub the stiffness from my backside.

"Here now." He grinned. "I've got something for that. Nar, have you the salve handy?" he called to his brother.

Nar nodded in reply and fetched a small pot from his saddlebag.

"Here, Lady Magda—"

"Just Magda. Please, just call me Magda."

He nodded again thoughtfully. "It's salve for your muscles. It'll help to ease the stiffness."

"Thank you," I said, feeling embarrassed. "I don't ride much I'm afraid."

"Don't worry on it," he said with a light smile. "There's no one who's ridden who hasn't gotten plenty sore one time or another. Why do you think I've carried the salve with me from Thall, then?"

I thanked him again and then went a little ways into the woods to be alone. I opened the pot and rubbed a dab of the clear ointment between my fingers. It smelled sweet and spicy and my fingertips began to grow warm. Looking about to check I wasn't being watched, I hiked my skirts around my waist. It was awkward holding the skirts in one hand and smearing the salve on my thighs with the other, but I managed. My legs instantly began to tingle with a welcomed relief. I wasn't quite so wobbly when I returned to the camp, though Severin gave me his arm and helped me to sit on a round, flat boulder, which was mercifully still.

"I'm sorry to push us so hard, but we must get as far away from Moravia Castle as soon as possible. Magda, how far can your father use his power?"

I frowned. "To the border, but no farther."

"That's a fair distance already," said Teren grimly.

"Aye," mused Severin, "all the more reason to push ahead quickly. We'll make this short, then."

"Haven't we stopped for the night?" I asked, aghast at the prospect of getting back on a horse so soon.

"No. We've stoped to eat, and then we'll ride till moonrise." Severin looked at me worriedly. "Will you be all right, then?"

"Yes, of course," I answered quickly, determined not to appear weak. "Really," I insisted. "I could ride all night if I had to!" I lied cheerfully.

"We may have to," Severin muttered at the ground. I tried not to look horrified by the prospect.

Nar spread the food that Cook had prepared on the ground and cut thick slices of bread and cold beef. I was so hungry after the long ride that the simple dark bread and cold meat tasted like a feast. She had also packed some bilberry tarts, which we devoured, not leaving even a crumb big enough to feed a vole. There were small rounds of hard cheese, some dried fruits, and small cakes, which Severin suggested we each carry portions of in our pockets. I huddled in my black cloak, feeling the evening chill settle around my shoulders. Then we mounted our horses again and I tried to ignore the soreness in my thighs and the pain that creaked along my spine.

I was thankful at least that we rode at a slower pace, Severin leading the way through the quiet woods. I moved as if in a dream, the trees night shadows, the sound of the horses' hooves muffled by the fallen leaves and the constant jogging motion of my horse's gait swaying like a cradle. I breathed in the sharp odor of pine resin and sometimes, when a cool breeze drew down our path, I smelled the musty fragrance of decaying leaves. Ahead of me I could scarcely see Severin. The brown cloak he wore blended with the dark shadows and only the soft clinking of his horse's bridle reassured me that he was there. No one spoke; we rode in silence through the woods until, at last, a round, golden harvest moon appeared over the tops of the trees and Severin halted his horse.

I slid from the saddle wearily and, though my legs trembled, I followed Severin as he led his horse to a small outcropping of rock colored silver by the moonlight. My hands ached as I fumbled awkwadly with the straps of the mare's saddle.

"Sit, Magda," Nar said gently to me in the dark. "We can do this in our sleep."

"Often have," chuckled Teren. "Nar, do you remember summer fair, then? Riding all day, dancing most of the night with the lasses—"

"Was it dancing you were doing, then?" Nar interrupted. "Ouch!" he cried as a saddlebag landed on his head.

"We rode home in the late dark," Teren continued, "hoping to arrive and get the horses unsaddled afore Mother woke."

"And did you?" I asked.

"No," Nar snorted. "She was waiting for us by the barn with a look that would sour the milk when she saw how drunk we were. We paid for that one, all right!"

"Did we?" asked Teren distractedly. "I don't remember that part."

"How could you, then?" Nar shot back. "After bidding her 'good morning' you fell off your saddle, cracked open your head, and had to be carried into the house. I, on the other hand, was made to go out riding again, rounding up the wild ponies for no good reason other than Mother said she wanted to have a look at them. My head was screaming with pain and I couldn't walk for two days because of the skin I'd worn off my rear end! You know, as an older brother, Teren, you cut a poor figure of moderation."

"Did I sit on your chest, then, and force the drink down? Seems to me I stopped you afore you made a fool of yourself with that lass from Brissan's farms. Remember her, do you? She had the rosy cheeks and the brute of a boyfriend?"

"I remember!" answered Nar impatiently. "You asked their pardon by confessing I was a virgin and too eager to show good sense."

"He might have killed you otherwise."

"Not before I died from the insult of it! Do you recall the look she gave me? Pitying and motherly. It was awful."

"So was the smirk on her boyfriend's face, which you offered to remove for him afore I pulled you away."

"I could've managed it, you know," insisted Nar.

"Oh aye, you and what clan? You were too drunk, weren't you, to notice how big he was?"

"I was drunk enough to see two of him and it still didn't scare me!"

"Well, the one of you would never have made it against either two of them, so don't say I don't look after you."

I sat on the rocks, enjoying their banter. Even with their arguing it was restful to listen to the sound of their voices, the lilt of their speech rising and falling like music. Severin came and sat beside me. In the moonlight his face appeared hollow eyed.

"Are you all right, then?" he asked.

"Yes," I answered, touched that he should care. "Please, Severin, let me help you at least prepare the food."

"Too late," answered Nar cheerfully. "I've got it here already. We'll have something hot in a moment."

"Use the flint and tinder," Severin said quickly. "We can't afford to waste our strength."

Nar nodded in agreement and soon, from between his hands, I saw the flint spark and ignite the tinder. He blew on it gently and it burst into a little yellow flame. Before long, he had built a comfortable fire, which warmed our camp and brightened my heart considerably. He put a small black pot on the fire and filled it with water from a skin. When it boiled, he added a handful of herbs that he plucked from a pouch at his waist. Seeing me watching him, he smiled back, the light playing merrily in his eyes.

"A bit of Thall tea to give your spirits a boost and replenish the blood. It's a specialty of our grandda's." Then he poured some of it into a mug and handed it to me.

I wrapped my aching fingers around the steaming cup, letting the warmth chase away the chill. I bent my head to drink and the light fragrance tickled my nose. I sipped it carefully, delighted to find it sweet and soothing. It seemed to bring the warmth of the fire to the very center of my body, melting the ache in my joints and bringing the blood to my cheeks.

"It's wonderful!" I exclaimed as I glanced up from my cup to thank Nar. He was sitting beside Teren on the other side of the fire, pouring the tea into the other three mugs. Severin joined them, taking his mug with a murmur of thanks as he sat down. I stared quietly, shocked by their haggard expressions in the firelight. Their voices in the dark had sounded cheerful and easy, but seeing them now, heads bowed and shoulders hunched forward, I realized they were exhausted.

Severin caught my anxious stare. Blowing cool air over his own mug of tea, he tried to ease my worries. "We look worse than we feel," he said lightly. "We've been holding a cloaking spell to hide us while we rode."

"Cloaking spell?" I asked, confused. My concern shifted to alarm and my hand tightened around the mug of tea. "Are you really farmers or sorcerers?"

"No, no . . . it's not like that!" All three of them spoke at once, shaking their heads at me, but I stared at them warily, wondering what I had chosen by fleeting Moravia with strangers.

"Magda, *everyone* in Thall has a magical talent," Severin explained hurriedly.

"Everyone?"

"Aye, everyone. You're born with it. Magic is in the soil we plow, it's part of the air we breathe and the water we drink.

It is a gift from the land. Each person carries a portion of Thall's magic within him. It's renewed and replenished by the land as needed. Here we don't have the land to sustain us, so each time we work magic, like the cloaking spell, we lose strength. But don't worry, we'll fare better after we've had a drink of this tea."

"Why, what's in it?" I asked suspiciously.

"Tea," he shrugged. "Our grandda makes it. His talent is as a healer, and he blends the herbs from his own garden into tea. The herbs have magical properties as well as healing ones. I've known hunters in Thall, injured in the wood and lain helpless many nights who survived with nothing but a tea such as this. Come now, tell me you don't feel better then, having drunk some of it?"

It was true. I did feel better; the twisting ache along my spine was fading. My shoulders had relaxed and my legs stopped trembling.

"Do you all have special talents?" I asked, intrigued by the magic of Thall, so different from Moravia.

"Aye," Nar answered me. "There are some things that all can do, such as handling fire, shifting wood, or holding the cloaking spell. But after that, the magic comes through each person in its own way."

"What's your talent?" I asked Severin.

"Animals," he said proudly. "I have a sense for them. I get it from my mother, Theda. She has only to look at a pairing of horses to know just what the foal will be, good traits and bad. It's her talent that's made our horses the best. I work with horses mostly, but my talent includes all animals."

"That's how you knew the real hound, isn't it?" I said, suddenly understanding how Severin had been able to call Father's hound.

"I sensed the hound's fear, the fear of punishment if it moved. I convinced it that I'd not hurt it, that I'd protect it. Love is a stronger master to serve than fear, so the hound came to me."

"But how did you guess the right casket? Why didn't the aversion spell make you ill and turn you away?"

Teren tossed his head back and burst out laughing. His shoulders shook and he had to set his mug down to keep from spilling the tea. As his side Nar slapped his thigh and joined in laughing with his brother. I stared at Severin, surprised and puzzled by their outburst, and he looked back at me with a sheepish grin.

"I like to eat," he started, and I couldn't help but laugh myself at so simple a truth.

Severin scratched his head, smiling good-naturedly at the three of us, and waiting until we had quieted down.

"Every cook in Thall learns an aversion spell. How else, then, can they protect food, set out to cool, from little children that wish to sneak a taste? It isn't a hard spell to break, just needs a bit of concentration and a quick hand. The trick is never look directly at it, but keep it in the corner of your eye. Then you snatch it"—he reached his arm miming the act of stealing the forbidden food—"before the spell has a chance to make you sick. It's just a matter of timing. I was very good at it."

Severin's explanation brought fresh peals of laughter from me. It amused me to think that Father, in his arrogance, had selected a task that was child's play in Thall. It gave me hope that Father might underestimate Severin's skills again. Perhaps we had a chance at escape after all.

"And you, Nar, do you have a special talent?" I asked the younger man.

"Aye, one for trouble," quipped Teren.

"Only when you're around, Teren," he retorted. "Seems to follow you, it does."

"Nar has a talent for healing, like our grandda," Severin explained before his brothers could begin arguing again.

"Children mostly," Nar said, returning his attention to me. "I like them, you see, and I can sense an illness coming on long before Grandda. I've helped at birthings, lending the child strength to be born sound and healthy. And I've been at dyings when all I could do was shelter them from fear and offer comfort."

"An important gift," I said, impressed by Nar's skill.

"Aye, it is," agreed Teren, cuffing the younger man affectionately.

"What's your talent?" I asked Teren. He looked back at me and I could feel the weight of his measured stare. It made me uncomfortable and I bristled.

"A traveler," he answered. He leaned forward and picked up the cheese from the ground. Holding it braced against his chest, he cut a thick slice.

"Where do you travel?" I asked, not understanding.

He pointed to his head. "Inside," he said, his mouth full of cheese. "I help those who are lost in here. There is a man who withdraws in grief at the death of his wife, or a child who hides a secret that twists and turns her life into a nightmare. They become lost in themselves. So that's where I travel. To find them at the root of their pain and heal it if I can."

"You all make me feel quite useless," I said humbly. "There is only one kind of talent in Moravia, and as you've seen, that's a power better done without."

"But Magda," Severin said, leaning forward to cut bread and meat, "you're more powerful than any of us. Don't you know that, then?" He handed me the food.

I shook my head disbelievingly. "It's not true."

"But it is. In Thall magic comes from the land and is renewed each day. We need the land to sustain our magic."

"The same is true with Father. His power does not extend beyond the border."

"Perhaps because the magic of Thall does not permit it. We passed a wall when we entered Moravia, though we couldn't tell whether it meant to keep us out, or to keep something within. Look, Magda, Thall is a country of little magics, ordinary people with gifts to lead ordinary lives. It is a feast of magic shared among many. But you, after your father, hold all the magic of Moravia. It has passed from the land into your blood. You are the source."

I bit into the food hungrily, thinking it was time to confess my shortcomings.

"It may be that Moravia's magic flows in my blood, but I can't use it," I spoke bitterly. "Oh, I've tried often enough, but I can't make it come to me. I did it once, when I was a child, but that was more by chance. My father was furious that his daughter, not his son, had inherited the family talent. He did something to hide my power from me. I know it's there, but I can't use it." They looked at me with odd expressions and I tensed. This is it, I thought. They've discovered they came to Moravia and won a bride who has no magic.

"Do you know anything of farming?" Teren asked suddenly.

"No," I answered.

"Nothing about crops, or keeping animals?"

"No."

"Housework, then. Can you sew or cook, do anything useful?"

"No," I said, getting angry.

"That's enough, Teren," Severin said sharply. Severin faced me. "He's having you on, you know, Magda. Don't let him push you." Turning to his brother, Severin spoke. "Useful, is it? And where were you when we did the foaling this spring? Your back, was it, that gave you trouble then?"

"And then there was haying," Nar added, grinning wickedly. "His arm, I think."

"Elbow," Severin corrected him. "Seems a mysterious ailment that Grandda couldn't heal. Had to rest it, you know. And remember when we had to fetch supplies in Thistledown? A sudden fever kept you home and neatly tucked in bed while Nar and I sloughed the whole day in a cold rain."

"All right, enough." Teren raised his hands in defense. "You've made your point." To me he pointed a finger. "What your father has done, hiding your magic, is vile. But I'll tell you this Magda, don't come to Thall feeling sorry for yourself. Whether you've magic talent or not, Mother will ask you the same questions, and if you think you're useless, so will she."

"I'm not afraid of work," I replied defensively.

He nodded his head and then stood, stretching his arms high over his head. "That's good, then, for you'll see plenty of it in Thall." He rubbed his hand over his face, smoothing down his beard. "Come Nar, we'll check the horses and then bed down."

Nar gave me an encouraging smile. "I'll say good night then." He rose and followed his brother a distance into the shadows. I heard them murmuring to each other as they continued to argue softly while they quieted the horses and prepared for bed.

Severin watched them, his face a little sad. Then he turned back to me, his smile gentle. "Pay him no mind, Magda. He only thinks I need protecting. Besides, it wasn't Moravian sorcery or whether you can cook and clean that brought me here."

"Then tell me, Severin," I asked, "why me? Why with all the women there must be in Thall, why did you choose to come here and face the tasks?"

Severin sighed and took my hand. "Well, it's hard to explain exactly," he said. "In Thall there is something called 'heart's ease.' Those who have it say it's a feeling of rightness, a kind of binding of the heart when you meet and fall in love. The land doing matchmaking, my mother always said. Anyway, most won't marry unless there is a feeling of heart's ease."

"What if you don't feel heart's ease?"

"Some marry without it, hoping that with time, they can make it happen. Some ignore it completely, and marry for other reasons. And some, they sit and wait and wait on it."

"Like Teren?" I whispered.

"Aye," Severin answered, smiling sadly in the direction of his brother's reclining form. "He's waited long to feel it and still it's not come."

"And you, Severin? Have you been waiting, too?"

He shook his head. "No. I've felt it most of my life. That's not the usual way of it, you know. It comes after you've met someone, not before. But for me, it's always been different. Ever since I can remember I've felt heart's ease, not for someone I knew, but someone I had yet to find. It was frustrating and many a night I lay awake thinking on it. For the most part, I lived with it, but time was getting to where it started to drive me near mad. The longing got so fierce I couldn't settle down. I spooked the horses and Mother got impatient. She packed me off to my aunt, who's a farseer." Severin chuckled, remembering. "You know, I used to think Mother did it as a punishment. Aunt Livia is a bit wild. Lives in a cave and keeps goats. For days after I smelled of her peat fires and wild garlic. She cast the knucklebones and gave me a reading."

"She told your future?" I asked, incredulous. Not even Father could do that.

"No." He shook his head. "She could only tell me what was, what I couldn't see for myself. She said that what I sought wasn't in Thall. To find heart's ease I needed to seek in the south. It wasn't much to go on, but it settled my mind. I returned home and decided that when the season ended and my work was done, I'd ride south."

"But how——" I started to interrupt. Severin held up a hand to stop me.

"How did I know to come to Moravia?"

I nodded back at him, noting how the firelight sparked on

his hair. We were sitting close together, his leg resting warmly against mine.

"Before the season was over, I went to summer fair."

"The same one as Teren and Nar?" I asked accusingly.

His smile flashed brightly. "Aye, the very same. Mother set me to mucking the byres. Not easy to do when you're drunk, you know. I kept slipping on muck and stabbing myself in the foot with the rake. But I only went to summer fair to dance and see the actors," he said quickly. "Courting lasses was more Nar's interest than mine."

"Did the 'lasses' know that?" I teased, sounding unconvinced.

He held his hands up in a gesture of self-defense. "Truly, I only went to see the plays. And I saw a very funny play about a girl who couldn't keep her temper. It's a grand scene, you know. She flys into a rage, destroys the family dinner, and tosses all the dishes!"

Now it was my turn to be embarrassed. That awful play, I couldn't believe that it had made its way to Thall.

"It was great sport to see and I can tell you that it's a favorite in Thall; performed every year it is at summer fair to enthusiastic crowds!" Severin continued lightly. "Children aren't allowed to have tantrums in Thall. If you get angry or threatening, your parents send you out to chop wood, or pick out field rocks until you've calmed down again. Every child in Thall learns early that magic and a temper make bad companions. An unruly child won't be tolerated, for he'd become dangerous to himself and to others. And yet, all of us, I think, long for a chance, just once mind you, to let our fury go. Better than a storm off the sea, eh? The pleasure of smashing everything into the walls. That's why the play's so popular at summer fair, for it touches the deepest wish of every Thallian to be a child unbridled." He hesitated, then asked, "Was it fun, then, Magda?"

I groaned and hid my flushed face in my hands, absolutely mortified that my tantrum should have been Severin's introduction to me. "I don't remember. It happened so long ago," I tried lamely. I peeked over my fingers to see if Severin believed me and saw from his smirk that he did not. "Well, I guess it was rather amusing." I started to laugh. "You should have seen the room!" And at that, Severin laughed with me. But when I remembered what followed, my laughter died and

I grew quiet. "You should have seen my father," I said soberly. "I would have much rather chopped wood and plowed fields than face him." I shuddered, remembering the flash of pain that seared my chest, and the cold stone of the floor in the Great Hall. Severin's hand squeezed mine and I looked up at him, thrusting the memory away.

"How did you know the play was about me?"

"I was curious and I asked who wrote it." Severin prodded the campfire, adding another log. "They told me about you. 'What's become of her?' I asked, and they told me about the tasks and the suitors who tried to win you for marriage."

"And from that you decided to come?"

"I had no doubts. It just felt right and I knew it was you I was seeking."

"Your brothers aren't as convinced as you. Teren would have been happier had you not come at all."

"Aye, I know that. But then he's not feeling what I'm feeling, is he?" I looked at Severin, gazing back at me tenderly from tired eyes. His skin was burnished a reddish gold from the firelight. "I knew when I saw you I'd not been wrong to come. It's what I'd searched for, it's what I'd felt missing here," he said, tapping his chest with his fingertips.

At Severin's words I blushed, shy. I felt awkward, and my careful defenses scattered. Emotions I had long kept hidden began tumbling toward freedom. I was afraid, mistrustful of the rapid pulse that surged beneath my skin, and confused by the happiness at this declaration of love. I wrestled with my emotions, trying to gain the upper hand again. "But Severin," I responded briskly, "supposing I had been a cow . . . what if Teren had been right?"

"Now, how did you know—" He stopped short, surprised. "Never mind." He laughed and shook his head again. "I always sensed we'd been watched coming into Moravia Castle, but I didn't realize it had been by you. Well now, if you had been a cow I'd have done what any farmer does when judging livestock." He put his hands gently around my face. "Here now, let's have a look at your teeth, then. You can tell a good cow by her teeth," he teased.

As I started to laugh and protest, he leaned down and kissed me on my open mouth. It was a gentle kiss, yet it startled me and I stopped talking. His face near mine, he put his arms around me, drew me close, and we kissed again. I answered his embrace this time, tentatively, my arms reaching shyly about his shoulders. At first I thought only of the feel of his mouth, his lips surprisingly soft and the mustache tickling my upper lip. I closed my eyes and pressed into the solid weight of his shoulders.

I heard it then, in the beating of Severin's heart, a sound so clear and pure that it reached out and found me across the walls of stone flesh that had covered my heart. The sound grew as it resonated, the echo beating louder and louder against the stone. A gasp tore from my lips as the walls burst with a wrenching pain. The stone crumbled and through the pain a sense, like a caged wildness, escaped. It ripped through me like an angry river tearing across an open plain. I could taste it, metallic and bitter as ash. It reeked of the forest with the dark aromas of humus, pine, and bone. Behind tightly shut eyes, I saw it flash a searing blue like a streak of lightning.

I clung to Severin as I would a branch hanging over the edge of a waterfall. The wildness continued to rush through me, leaping in angry torrents until every hollow of my being seemed flooded with its power. It reached a peak and then sighed, turned and slowed, moving easily through me. I inhaled deeply with a long ragged sigh as I felt its rushing flow abate. It settled in my veins and a cool breeze drew across my cheeks.

"Magda?" Severin whispered.

I opened my eyes and saw him peering at me, brow pulled in a frown across his forehead. My hands were clutching his shoulders, the fingers digging into the thick wool of his cape.

"Severin, if that's heart's ease I don't think I will survive being kissed again."

"What happened, then?" he asked confused.

"I don't know," I replied, still breathless. "It was strange and frightening. That's all I can say."

He nodded silently, his face serious. He drew up the collar of my cloak and settled it snugly around my shoulders. Then, gently, he brushed away a lock of hair. "It's time you slept, Magda. The day tomorrow will be longer than this one. Stay within the circle and you'll sleep safe." He pointed near my leg and I saw the faint markings of a white circle that traveled around our campsight. He started to stand, but I stopped him. I couldn't bear the look of disappointment on his face.

"Severin, do you still feel heart's ease?"

"Stronger than ever." He smiled ruefully. "But I'll not force it on you, Magda. You're free to do as you wish." He turned to leave.

"Wait, Severin. Would you kiss me again?" I asked. He turned back, head tilted to one side.

"And could I refuse, then?" he answered, and bent to kiss me.

I braced myself, waiting for the violent storm to take me. But it didn't happen. Instead I heard the sound of Severin's heart, beating steadily. My own heart slowed and matched it, beat for beat. I wanted to cry then as a sweet sadness enveloped me. Warmth followed sadness, a warmth as inviting as the sun heating the newly turned soil in spring. Warmth was followed by a sense of peace, comforting and embracing. My awkwardness faded and I felt contentment. I laid my head on Severin's shoulder and gazed into the fire.

"Heart's ease?" I asked, not needing the answer.

"Aye," he said. He put his arm around me protectively. "Look!" He pointed to the moon, white and full above us. "It's what we call the 'Mother's Moon.'"

"Why?" I asked and then saw the obvious. "Because it's round like a pregnant woman?"

"That's part of it. The full moon's a fertile power, isn't it? We plant the root crops then, potatoes, turnips, and the like. All those that grow in the ground unseen. Couples marry during Mother's Moon for the same reason. 'Maids to motherhood full soon if bedded are on Mother's Moon,'" he recited.

"Isn't that like a farmer!" I rolled my eyes. "Plants his fields and then comes home to plant his wife."

"Not bad work, that!" Severin laughed at me. I laughed, too, and looked down at myself, wondering what I would look like if my belly grew as round as the Mother's Moon.

"What do you call the other moons?"

"When there's no moon in the sky, we call it 'Maid's Moon.'"

"Not a fertile time?" I interrupted.

"Not for the lack of trying, I expect." Severin chuckled. "That's when we hold the big parties and dances. A couple might slip away then unnoticed in the dark."

"Then I doubt one stays a maid for long during 'Maid's Moon.' And when the moon is waxing and waning, what then?"

"Ah, when all you see is a sliver of the moon hanging in the sky we call it 'Hag's Tooth,' for the old hag who'd only one tooth in her head. There's a good tale about her. She used her tooth as a sword to cut down the men who came to marry her daughters."

"What happened?" I asked, uncomfortable at the subject.

"Hero came, didn't he? Outwitted the old crone and rescued the daughters." I was silent. Severin gave my arm a squeeze. "It does happen, you know."

"In the tales," I said glumly. Father would know by now that I had fled with Severin. What would he do next? I wondered. I didn't want to think about it, but I couldn't stop the worried thoughts that crowded in. Was Cook all right? Were Vooris and Ilena? Staring at the leaping flames, I thought of my brother and sister sadly. I hadn't known them really until it was too late.

"Do your brothers always fight?" I asked Severin softly.

He gave a low laugh. "Always. Like old hens they are. It's no good trying to get them to stop, you know. Mother tried for years and gave up. Truth is, I think they enjoy it."

"My brother and I fought often. But we didn't enjoy it. It only kept us apart."

Severin was silent a moment. "I'm sorry for that. Teren and Nar may fight, but they'll always stand together if need be."

I thought about that and then recalled that Vooris had stood by me when he warned me about Father. Even Ilena in her own way had helped me to escape. I was angry and hurt that Father should have kept us apart. If he could have loved us for what we were, I thought, and not what he wanted us to be, our lives might have been different. Only Zuul was exactly as Father wished, and only Zuul was truly loved.

"Tell me about Thall," I asked, wanting to push away my sad thoughts.

Severin started talking, his voice low and soothing in the quiet night. I listened as he told me stories of his childhood and of the rolling fields of Thall. The moon shimmered like a silver liquid in my half-closed eyes and I drifted slowly into sleep, lulled by the gentle sound of Severin whispering in my ear.

SIX

I WOKE TO a cold rain that seemed to ooze up from the muddy ground even as it seeped down through the trees. Dampness clung to my clothes and I shivered, wrapping my cloak tighter to keep the warmth within my garments. It didn't help. As I adjusted my cloak the dank cold penetrated easily. A draft caught under my shift and chilled me to the bone. I tried to warm myself by rubbing my arms and shoulders briskly, but it was to no avail. My teeth began to chatter and I hunched my shoulders, my arms crossed tightly across my chest. The thick fog swirled against my face, leaving droplets on my eyelashes to trickle down my cheeks and off the tip of my nose. My breathed steamed as I exhaled warm air and I coughed, inhaling the mist with its rank odor. It tasted sour on my tongue, like stagnant water. I heard Severin's voice and crept through the fog to find him.

He was seated next to his brothers around a small sputtering fire. Nar was brewing tea, cursing the stifling smoke that hung in the close, moist air. Their faces carried grim expressions and even Nar's welcoming smile was guarded as he stared up at me through the falling drizzle.

"Severin," I asked, "what's wrong?

He looked up at the sky. "It's this fog and rain," he answered. "Not natural, is it?"

I sat down beside him and took a mug of tea. I held my face close to the rim of the mug and inhaled the tea's sweet fragrance, relieved as it replaced the musty stink of the fog. I should have known. The fog was one of Father's gambits played out on suitors. For the first time I was able to appreciate how truly miserable it must have been for those who struggled through it.

"It's Father," I said.

"Aye. He's looking for us. I felt his presence come searching in the night."

I looked up, startled. Severin's hair was wet and raindrops dripped slowly to his shoulders. The steam from his breath had gathered small beads of water on his mustache and beard. He looked pale and tired, but he managed a smile of encouragement. "He's not found us, then. The cloaking spell still hides us. But he's making it more difficult. He's using the fog to confuse and weaken us. We must ride close together. In this fog we'll not find each other again if we are separated."

"I see," I answered quietly. A dart of fear prickled my spine as I stared at the gloom. Father was in the fog, searching. The mist held the same fetid odor of the twisted corridors in Father's dungeon. I blinked away a water droplet and then saw myself, standing at the entrance of the dungeon, the fog rolling up from beneath, thick and gray, obscuring the stairs. In the fog Father watched, waiting for me to take a blind step over the edge of the top stair and tumble down. I turned my head stiffly, looking out at the fog pressing in around our tiny campfire. I perched dangerously close to the edge, terrified to move lest I fall.

"Come," urged Severin's voice. "We must go."

I didn't move; couldn't move.

"Come," he urged more gently.

Still I remained seated, my hands gripping the stone seat. "I'll fall," I whispered.

Teren came around and knelt beside me. His hands cupped my face and I stared back with wide eyes.

"Here, take my hand." I heard his voice but his lips never moved. I reached out and felt him grasp my hand. Gently he drew me back, guiding me away from the edge. "That's it,"

Teren coaxed, and I felt my terror recede as we moved farther away from the stairs.

He dropped his hands and rocked back on his heels. I blinked and the sensation of vertigo vanished. "An illusion," he said, answering the puzzled look on my face, "sent to scare, no doubt."

"It seemed so real! I was sure I would fall if I moved. Thank you," I said gratefully.

Teren shrugged, almost embarrassed. "Shall we go, then?"

I nodded and squared my shoulders. "I'm ready," I answered. I handed Nar my empty mug and stood, ignoring the trembling in my hands. I patted my pocket, feeling for the pot of salve. From my other pocket I took out a handful of dry fruit and a cake. The cake was stale but tasty and I ate it quickly as I followed Severin to the horses.

The mare whinnied nervously as I pulled myself up into the saddle. Severin held her head steady, claming her with soft words.

"The mare's frightened by the fog," he explained. "Try to give her a bit of reassurance if you can."

Fine, I thought, if I've any reassurance left. But I leaned over and stroked her neck, my hands leaving dark tracks in the wet hide. The mare bobbed her head, but then settled down, content to grind her teeth on the bit.

"Stay close," Severin reminded us, and he led the way through the dense fog.

I kept the rump of Severin's horse in my vision, the mare's nose nearly bumping it as we moved. It was the best I could do, for I couldn't see Severin at all through the grayness. When I looked behind me, I could just make out the head of Teren's horse, and sometimes Teren's face emerging like a ghost from the fog. Around us was a muffled silence except for the steady patter of water as it dripped through the roof of the forest.

A gnarled tree appeared suddenly between the boughs of spruce and pine, its branches cutting through the mist. The blackened bark was slick with dripping water. As I neared it, the mare shied, pulling sharply against the reigns. The branches leaned out, and the wet leaves slashed across my face. I bent my head to the horse's neck to escape their grasp. A twig became entangled in my hair, yanking my head backwards. I shrieked with pain and reached up to break the twig and free myself.

Severin reigned in sharply and the mare crowded into his horse.

"What's happened?" he called.

"A branch caught in my hair," I replied. "I'm all right," I lied, trying not to panic in the suffocating closeness of the mist.

"Are you sure, then?"

"Yes," I said desperately. "Please, let's just get through this fog."

Severin started riding again and I leaned over, frantically whispering words of comfort to my frightened mare as well as to myself as she followed close behind.

It was hard to tell how long we rode through the mist. My clothes were soaked, weighted down with cold water. My hair lay plastered to my head and neck, the drops of water dripping down my neck and under my shift. I could scarce hold the reins for my hands were numb with cold. I rode hunched in my saddle, teeth chatering, looking down at the bobbing space between the mare's ears. If I looked up any higher, rain fell into my eyes and blinded me.

"It's growing lighter," Severin called back. "The mist is lifting a bit."

I glanced up, afraid to believe it at first. But I saw Severin's back clearly, and then his head, wet and shaggy. He looked at the sky pensively.

"Seems we're getting a reprieve, then."

From behind me I heard Teren shout back. "God's for a fire! Anything to get warm and dry again. And food, Severin, we need to eat to keep this up!"

"Aye, soon," Severin returned. "Let's first make good use of the break in the mist to hurry ourselves."

Teren grumbled his assent and we nudged our horses, urging them to move faster.

Suddenly, a high-pitched scream pierced the muffled silence of the fog. The mare's hind legs bunched with fear and she wheeled around. A wild pig burst through the thick underbrush and darted between the mare's prancing legs. It squealed shrilly, its stiff tail upright and its tusks jabbing the air from an upraised snout. I struggled to stay on the mare's back as she reared to avoid the dashing beast. The pig continued to shriek in angry surprise and careened off the path, disappearing through the underbrush. Behind me Teren and Nar cheered with wild delight.

"Come on Nar! We'll have fresh meat tonight!" Teren's voice boomed excitedly.

They kicked their horses, jerking the reins in the direction of the running pig. Their horses bolted from the path in pursuit. As they raced past, I saw their faces, fixed intently on the pig, oblivious to anything else.

"We'll be back shortly, Severin. This won't take long!" Teren bellowed as they rode by in a frenzy.

"*No!*" shouted Severin, standing in his saddle to grab at his passing brothers. "No! Come back! *The pig's not real!*"

But it was too late. They never heard him, entranced by the sight and noise of the fleeing pig. We lost sight of them as soon as they left the path and plunged into the mist. We could heard the sounds of their joyous shouts answered by the frightened squeals of the pig.

Severin cursed and continued to yell in vain after his brothers, but they never answered. I brought the mare close to Severin's side.

"What's happened, Severin?" I asked. He stopped shouting and slumped over his saddle. He ran a tired hand through his wet hair, and his dark eyes, streaked with violet beneath, stared dully into the mist.

"They'll never catch it," he answered glumly. "The pig wasn't real. Just another illusion. Your father's got them now, you know. They'll follow the pig, round and round, never catching it and never realizing they've lost us. Teren was the strongest one of us holding the cloaking spell together. I don't know how long I can protect us without his help."

I said nothing, but stared angrily, as did Severin, at the empty mist. Father was toying with us like a cat that holds its prey between its paws, sporting with it before it finally kills.

"They shouldn't have come, you know. But they insisted," Severin said softly, staring out at the thickening fog.

"Severin, I'm sorry."

He shook his head. "Teren's usually got a good head on him. There's always a chance he'll figure it out before your father decides he's done with them." He paused and then looked at me. "I'll hope on that. But for us, we must hurry even more. Your father's distracted now but it'll go harder when he returns to us."

I felt the anger grow into rage. I wanted Father's power. I wanted to hurt him, make him suffer for the hurt he had caused others. Thunder rumbled above us, sounding like a deep-throated laugh. I looked up sharply and saw a jagged flash of blue lightning pierce the fog. It cast an eerie light across a wall of yellow-gray clouds. After another crash of thunder, the sky opened with heavy rain, drenching us anew in icy water.

We kicked our horses and continued riding, heads bent beneath the pouring rain.

It rained on and off throughout the day. When it wasn't raining, we were shrouded by the fog. It seemed as if we rode at the bottom of an impenetrable gray sea and I felt I couldn't catch my breath for the thickness of the air. I looked up, hoping to see the sky above us, but the mist obscured all sense of openness. Drops of water collected on my upturned face and trickled down my cheeks like cold tears.

Time was suspended in the mist, the day never losing the same gray hue of early morning. When darkness came, it settled gradually, like ink seeping through the fog. Weary and cold, we finally stopped, unable to go farther. Severin slid exhausted from his horse. I saw him weave unsteadily, and then he stopped himself with a hand braced against the withers of his horse. I went as quickly as I could to his side and wrapped an arm around his waist. He leaned heavily on my shoulder and my legs nearly buckled under the extra weight. His face in the dying light was ghostly, and though his brow was flushed with sweat, his hands were cold and clammy.

"Severin," I said with alarm, "are you all right?"

He paused a moment before answering. "I'm fine," he said hoarsely, "just weak. I need to eat and I need a fire for warmth. Help me to get over there, where those trees overhang. It'll make a decent shelter from the rain."

We stumbled around the thick shrubs of the forest floor until we arrived at the spot Severin had indicated. There was a clearing between three large pine trees nearly high enough to stand under. The lower branches intertwined and formed a canopy under which the fallen pine needles had remained fairly dry and soft. It was a welcomed shelter. Pitch from the trees gave off a tart fragrance that was refreshing after the hours spent in the dank, musty fog. Severin sat, his knees drawn up and his back leaning against one of the trees. His head drooping on his chest, he breathed heavily.

I returned to the horses, wrestled their saddles off, and tied them to a branch. I patted the mare's rump reassuringly and left her foraging among the bushes. I fetched what there was of our meager supplies and headed back to the trees. It was not completely dark and when I approached Severin in the dim light, his face seemed suddenly altered. His head leaned to one side, and his jaw was slack. His eyes were shut. Against the luminous pallor of his skin, they deepened like the hollows of a skull. I panicked, terrified that Severin was dead, having died in that moment, exhausted and alone under the trees.

"Severin!" I shouted, dropping the supplies. I started running, my skirts catching and tearing on the underbrush. His eyes snapped open and his head jerked up as he struggled to get to his feet. Already his hand reached for the short sword at his hip.

"Magda?" he called back, his voice raw.

I reached him breathless, swallowing hard and unable to speak. Shaking my head, I stayed the hand that held the sword and pushed him back down against the tree to rest. He stared at me wildly, his free hand gripping my arm as I eased him back into a sitting position.

"What is it?" he demanded sharply.

I sat on my knees beside him and passed my hand over my face in relief.

"Nothing, I—I—just got frightened," I stammered. "When I saw you sitting here alone, you looked so . . . pale . . . like a corpse," I whispered. "I was afraid my father. . ." My voice cracked and I began to cry before I could finish my explanation. As the tears came, I hid my face in my hands, overwhelmed by fatigue and terror. I heard Severin's jagged sigh as he shared my weariness and understood the reason for my weeping. He pulled me down on his chest and held me while I cried. He stroked my hair and back, and when my sobs had lessened, he wiped the tears away and kissed me, kissed me hard so that I would know he was far from dead.

"Magda, can you use a flint and tinder to start a fire?" he asked me when I had recovered from my tears.

"No."

"Here," said Severin, helping me sit up. He reached under

his shirt and pulled out a little leather box, a trefoil tooled on
its surface. It hung around his neck on a cord. He pulled it off
and handed it to me. I opened it and out tumbled a small
stone, a fish hook, a needle and thread, and a small wad of
cloth. He took the stone and placed it in my palm.

"It is important you learn, then. If we're separated"—I
shivered at the words—"you'll need to know how to start a
fire to survive. Here now, let me teach you."

First he instructed me to gather dry and broken branches
and stack them near our camp. While I did, Severin collected
small twigs, and with a knife, shaved bits of dried bark from
the tree. He made a small bed of the dry pine needles, bark
shavings, and tiny twigs. He took a larger stone he had found
and, holding it steady amidst the nest of tinder, struck it with
the flint. Tiny sparks jumped from the stone to the dry tinder.
He repeated it several times until the tinder began to smoke.
Hands cupped protectively around the tinder, he blew gently
on the smoke until it burst into a bright yellow flame. He
continued to blow carefully on the flame, feeding it kindling
until the fire was well established. Then he showed me how to
stack the wood on the coals so it would burn properly without
smoking.

When the fire was at last burning comfortably, I went to
regather the supplies I had dropped and then returned to the
camp. I took from Severin's bag the little black pot and filled
it with water from a skin. I added some dried fruit from my
pocket to the water and stirred it. I thought wistfully of Cook's
cold beef and dark bread but knew that what remained of them
was tied to Teren's saddle.

"Here," said Severin as he pulled out a pouch of tea. "Add
some of this, then, it'll give us strength."

We sat waiting for the tea, warming our aching hands over
the fire. It crackled noisily as pine cones sparked and burst
into blue-green flames. When the tea was done boiling, I
poured it into two mugs and handed one to Severin. We drank
it, breathing grateful sighs of relief as the tea revived our
spirits.

"How far is it to Thall?" I asked.

"Hard to say for certain." Severin pursed his lips and took
a cup of tea. "Your father's twisting the path and I can't tell if
we're headed straight or back and forth across Moravia. I've
kept us to the true path, but the road keeps shifting. It took

half a month's journey coming, but it might take twice as long returning."

"I see," I mumbled, discouraged at the thought of a month-long journey through the trees and the cold fog. And Father, somewhere, still waiting for us. An owl hooted on a branch and I jumped, spilling hot tea.

"Zuul!" I hissed.

"No," Severin answered, eyes gazing upward at the trees. "A true owl out hunting dinner."

"Hunting?" I asked incredulous. "How can it see prey in this weather?"

"That's what she's wondering!" He chuckled softly. The tea had lessened the gaunt look of his cheeks and the firelight reddened his features. His grin was infectious.

"What is it?" I asked, a smile rising to my own lips.

"She's none too happy, is she? Muttering something about 'bones not worth vomiting.' Funny thing is, there's a wood mouse not far from her sitting very still and trying to make out like it's not there at all."

"Like us," I said softly.

"Aye, like us." Severin nodded. He took another sip of tea and then reached into his cloak and brought out a cake. Breaking it in two, he handed me half. "Magda," he said seriously, "if we're separated, go to Thall. My family will take you in and help you."

"How can I get there?" I asked in a small voice. "You said yourself the path twists and turns. I can't see through my father's spells. As for the woods"—I shrugged, staring around me at the shadowy trees—"I don't know much about surviving out here."

"There are two ways to guide you," Severin said practically. "If this fog continues, remember not to look up for the path, but down at your feet. If you look up, the path will appear to waver in the wrong direction and you'll get lost. Concentrate on the ground just in front of you and you'll be able to stay with the true path. The second way is to use a star pattern if the fog lifts and you can see the night sky again."

"And so I'm either with my nose in the air or down at my feet! I'll probably drop over the side of a cliff from not looking where I'm going," I said peevishly.

"I didn't say it was easy," Severin answered evenly. "But I know you can do it if you have to. Here, I'll give you my kit."

He placed the cord with the leather box around my neck.
"There's flint for the fire, a bit of dry tinder, and other things
you might find useful."

"What about you? Won't you need it?"

He waved my question away. "It makes me feel better
knowing you've some protection for yourself."

I brooded a moment, holding his gift. No one had ever
asked anything of me before. As Teren had shown me, my life
at the castle was so sheltered that I was scarcely prepared to
do anything; too noble for common tasks, too unworthy for
noble ones. I had never faced a challenge and I had no confidence that I could succeed.

"Severin," I pleaded. "I don't know if I could do it."

He touched my cheek lightly. "You can, you know. You
must."

His gaze steadied me and I gave a resigned sigh. "All
right," I answered miserably. "Which stars should I look for?"

He gave my shoulder an encouraging squeeze. Taking up a
small twig, he scratched a pattern in the dirt. "Do you recognize this pattern, then?" he asked. I looked over his shoulder
to see what he had drawn. At first it was just lines traced in
the dirt between circles representing stars. Then I remembered
something from the old astronomy maps I had seen molding in
the library. There the lines had connected to form a dragon
blowing fire across the northwest sky.

"Yes, I do know it," I said excitedly, "it's the 'dragon' and
its lights up in the north during fall. Is that right?"

"Name's different, we call it the 'plow.' What else can you
expect from farmers?" He shrugged and smiled. "See, this star
here represents the blade, and here are the handles. At this
time of year Thall rests just below the blade's star. Use that
star at night, then, to get your bearings. As long as you move
toward it, you'll come to Thall."

"And once I arrive? What then?"

"Ask anyone you meet for help to get to Arlensdale. Most
in Thall will help a stranger, so you've no need to fear ask-
ing."

"Severin," I said, trying to keep the tremble out of my
voice, "if something happens to you, I am not so sure I want
to go on alone."

He turned to face me and took me firmly by the shoulders,
his dark eyes intense. "Don't give up, Magda. Your life is

worth more than that. Believe in your own strength. *I do,*" he said, and then he kissed me before I could disagree. "Besides," he said softly, close to my face, "I talk only of maybes. I've no intention of leaving you. I'll fight anyone and anything that tries to separate us."

I put my arms around his shoulders and hugged him, burying my face in his neck. Well, I told myself, hushing the nagging of my self-doubts, I'll do it if I have to. I'll try at least.

"Do you know how beautiful you are?" he said, tilting my head back.

I blushed under his frank gaze. "I've never met anyone like you."

"Not many farmers at court, are there?"

"That's not what I meant."

"What did you mean, then?"

"I've never met anyone I cared about, except Cook."

"Well, then, I'm in good company." He laughed. His nose brushed against my cheek and we kissed. It was a kiss that warmed me to the core, and though it was neither hurried nor rushed, my heart beat faster.

I curled close to him like a cat and lay my head on his shoulder. His chin rested against the top of my head. "I've something to give you," he said. I felt him reach into a pocket in his leather jerkin. "Here, hold out your hand." I did and felt him put a thin strand into it.

"What is it?" I asked curiously.

"A soulstring."

"It's beautiful," I exclaimed, holding the strand up to the light. It was a fine chain of gold, the links woven into a glimmering braid. In the fire's light it shone like a thread of flame.

"Would you hear the story of the first soulstring, then?" he asked.

"Yes, I'd like that," I answered, staring at the twisting strand of gold.

"I don't tell it as well as some, but I'll do my best." He cleared his throat and started his tale.

"Once in the ancient days, there lived a man named Gest and a woman named Mara. They were much in love and lived together happily. They had a neat stone house that looked down at the edge of the sea. Gest was a large man, tall and

big, with a chest like the prow of a boat, black haired and
black eyed. He was a fisherman and every day he rode the
waves in his boat, traveling the gray-green sea to call the
shoals of fish into his nets. Mara was a small woman, fingers
slender as thread, and long fine hair the color of flax. She was
a weaver and knew the secret craft of twisting life into the
threads. Gest built their stone house with windows facing the
sea, that Mara might be inspired by the shifting colors of the
waters. She wove them into her tapestries; silver fishes that
leaped in the blue waves and white birds that dived into patterns of foam. You could hear her working, the steady pounding of the treadles while Gest sang to its rhythm and repaired
his nets for the next day's catch.

"One day while Gest was at sea, Mara looked from her
loom and saw the colors of the day changing; dark, heavy
clouds matted the sky and turned the sea to an angry slate. She
feared for Gest, afraid he'd not return home before the storm
unleashed itself. She left her loom and went to wait by the
shore. She stared out across the horizon hoping for a sight of
his boat. The rain began to fall and the wind pushed the waves
higher on the shore to lash the rocks. Still she waited in the
driving rain, clutching her shawl tighter about her head. And
then she saw his boat. Its mainsail was torn and it limped
toward shore like an injured bird. She watched as Gest strove
to keep the boat abreast of the growing waves. And then she
saw the one terrible wave that turned the little boat like a top
and crashed over its prow, breaking the mast and flinging Gest
into the sea. 'Gest!' she screamed, but the wind tore away her
words. She waded into the sea, desperate to reach him, but
her wet skirts weighed her down and the waves drove her to
shore again. She saw his head bobbing in the water, his arms
trying to keep himself afloat.

"There was nowhere to turn for help. If she went to the
village, it would be too late. She had to find a way to save him
herself. She must use the gifts she had. She pulled three
strands of her flax-colored hair and wove them into a braid.
She called upon her weaver's gift to give the strand a life.
Tying a key to one end, she cast it into the sea and charged it
to find Gest. She held the other end wrapped tight around her
hand. The frail rope of hair grew and stretched across the open
sea. When it found Gest, floundering, his head near under the
water, it wrapped itself around his waist. Mara felt the tug and

began, slowly, to haul Gest ashore. As she worked, pulling his weight hand over hand, she thought only of their shared love. Into the string she gave every joy, every hardship, and every act of love that she had shared with Gest. The fragile rope held like a thread of iron, for such was the strength of Mara's love for Gest, and his for her. At last she pulled him into the shallow waters. Helping him to stand, she gave him her shoulder for support and they stumbled home in the rain.

"Mara's thread of hair was the first soulstring. Since that time, there is always the gifting of a soulstring at a wedding. It reminds us of the power of love, and as the love between a husband and wife deepens, so is the power of the soulstring strengthened."

Severin finished speaking and I stared, mesmerized by the fragile string gleaming in my hand. It seemed to hum with a life of its own, warming the hollow of my palm. I looked at Severin, moved by such a precious gift.

"Thank you," I said solemly. "I shall wear it always."

Severin laughed softly. "I'll hope you do more than that, Magda. Here, let me show you." And he plucked the soulstring from my hand.

My hand felt suddenly cold without the soulstring and I cried out at its parting.

"We're a practical people, you know. All our magic must be useful. The soulstring is a symbol of love and commitment. But it's also a tool, and a handy one at that." He held up the soulstring to the light for me to see. "Watch!" he said. "I've only to think of a need for it and it will change to suit that need. A ribbon, then, to bind back wayward curls . . ."

The thin gold chain broadened between his fingers to become a flat ribbon like the ones that had decorated my hat.

". . . or perhaps a strand of wool to mend a broken warp thread . . ."

The broad ribbon changed to a length of wool thread that spun to the ground until Severin commanded it to stop.

". . . and maybe," Severin said at my astonished face, "swaddling to tie a babe to your back . . ." And the soulstring changed again into a strip of soft, white cloth.

"Oh, Severin!" I said. "It's wonderful. But will it work for me?" I asked worriedly. "I'm not a woman of Thall. Are you sure I can call the magic from it?"

"Aye. The magic is there because of the love we share, not

our separate magical talents. A soulstring won't work when there's no love between a couple and a broken soulstring is the sign of a marriage that is dissolved." He handed me back the soulstring and I took it, eager to feel its comforting warmth in my hand. "Try it, then, and you'll see."

I held the chain aloft and concentrated. I could feel the subtle shifting of power as the string vibrated and grew warmer in my hand. The texture changed between my fingers and I saw it reshape itself from a chain of gold to a skein of embroidery silk. "It worked!" I blurted out, surprised and happy with my success.

"Good. Try it again, then," Severin said. "Think of something you might never expect from a thread."

I concentrated and once more felt the warming hum of magic as it transformed in my hand. My arm dropped from the weight of holding a heavy iron chair sturdy enough to restrain a bull. I wished it back again to its original form and watched as the edges of blackened iron faded into the fine gold strand.

"Here now, let me show you how to wear it on your wrist so that it's always handy."

I handed him the soulstring and he tied it around my wrist, fixing it with an odd knot.

"We call it a lover's knot, for it ties up tight and true"—he pulled one of the free ends—"and just as easily comes undone." The loop dissolved into a single strand again. He demonstrated the trick of tying and loosening the knot several times until I was sure I understood. "Give me your wrist, then, and I'll tie it on for you."

When he was done, he leaned back and, taking both of my hands in his, spoke in a solemn voice:

"I'm sorry, Magda, that this isn't Thall. For if it were, we'd have family and friends to share this moment. There'd be the wedding feast, a toast of health, and then hours of dancing and music. It is as much as we deserve. Instead we are here, in this cold rain hiding like mice in the woods." He looked up at the stately pine trees that formed our shelter and smiled ruefully. "We've no one but the trees to witness this moment and to wish us good health and long life. Yet, I will ask you this: I would give to you a soulstring and ask if you would be my wife?"

I looked from Severin's face to the soulstring on my wrist, sparkling in the firelight. It hummed with a promise, a promise of love and magic. It settled over me like a second skin, secure and comforting. Then I hesitated, old fears rearing with ugly thoughts. I was afraid to love, afraid to be hurt. And I felt unworthy of Severin's love, shamed by the needless deaths of so many other suitors. What right had I to happiness? But when I looked back into Severin's face and felt the soulstring on my wrist like a caress, I knew that I never wanted to be without his love or the soulstring.

"Yes," I squeaked in a little voice, and then more firmly, "yes, I would be your wife."

We embraced, holding each other tightly, that nothing might ever part us. And as we kissed, I drew my cloak about his shoulders and he drew his about mine, and we lay down by the dying fire. His head nestled in my neck and I lay my cheek against his smoke-scented hair. His lips brushed lightly against the hollows of my throat. I closed my eyes and, behind the lids, the flames continued to dance eagerly. Severin untied the lacings of my bodice and slid his hands inside my undone dress. His hands cupped my breasts gently and I felt the breath catch in my throat. I pulled his shirt free and slid my hands around his back, surprised by the warm smoothness of his skin beneath my palms. We both sighed deeply, marveling in the pleasure of discovering each other. As our intimacy grew, so did the lover's knot of embrace entangle tight and true.

I cried out, not in pain but from an ache at once sweet and sharp. I held Severin fiercely, locked in my arms, as his body flexed, every thread of muscle tensed. I heard him answer, a long, low growl, his cheek pressed against mine. I clung to his shoulders and my back arched to meet him. The dark wildness returned. It uncoiled and surged within me, pressing against the boundaries of my skin. The prison of my flesh yielded and I became one with the forest. I grew branches, green boughs that swept the forest floors. Sap bubbled in my veins and dried to hard amber. I was the soil, decaying and teeming with a multitude of life: morels springing up from the carpet of dry needles, the wood orchid unraveling with translucent petals from the trunk of a shattered tree. I curled deep, whiskers brushing against the sides of a burrow, and I perched on the bough, feathers ruffled by the cold, eyes gleaming yellow. The wildness reached out farther yet beyond the forest and I knew something else I had never seen before: high roll-

ing hills of gorse and heather and gray stones. I heard the bleat
of sheep and the mournful call of a loon. I smelled the sharp
tang of the sea and I tasted salt. The wildness spread outward,
smooth and peaceful as a river flowing into a delta. I sighed
deeply and opened my eyes.

Severin smiled down at me and kissed me gently. His lips
tasted of salt. I touched them with my fingertips in wonder.
Severin brushed away the damp hair at my temples and
stroked my cheek. He shifted his body to lie on his side and
drew me close to the crook of his arm. The fire was a small
string of gray-orange coals. I was warm lying close to Severin, the rough wool of our cloaks holding the heat of our
bodies. I lay a hand on his chest to hear the quiet beat of his
heart and felt my own pulse with the same slowing rhythm.

We lay there quietly, almost dozing, in the fading glow of
the fire. Reluctantly, I roused myself and stirred the coals with
a stick. I added more wood and watched, satisfied, as the fire
blazed up again, the wood crackling and popping with sparks.
I straightened the bodice of my dress, pulling the shift smooth
and retying the laces. My hair was in a tangled mess and I
tried to repin it with the few remaining pins I hadn't lost while
riding. Severin watched me, his face serene and happy.

"Severin, do you think your family will approve of me as
your wife?"

"Yes, once they know you as I do."

"Even your mother, Theda?

"Mother's a hard one, there's truth in that. But she's fair
and won't judge harshly without cause."

I chided myself for cowardice. Severin had faced Father's
challenges; surely I could face Severin's mother. But I wondered how I might be judged and what would happen if I was
found wanting.

"What happened to your father?" I asked. "How did he
die?"

"Plague. A sailor brought it with him on one of the trading
boats. He died in a harbor inn. The healers of Thall had never
seen this plague before, and didn't know how to cure it. Soon
after his death, the innkeeper, his wife, and children were
struck down. The other guests fled in terror, then, not realizing they took it with them, spreading it over Thall. It killed
over half of the people in Arlensdale, not even sparing those
that lived high in the hills."

"But that's horrible," I exclaimed.

"Aye. It was a grim time. And odd it was the way some took sick and died before the next day, while others survived or weren't even touched. There was no way of knowing who would get it. Teren and I were children and Nar still a baby when it struck Arlensdale. Mother had her hands full caring for us, for we'd all become ill in the same day. For a week she hovered over us day and night, spooning water into our parched mouths and holding us as the fever burned. Father was up in the hills, helping Grandda to give comfort to the sick and bury the dead.

"We'd passed the worst of it, my brothers and I, and were recovering when Mother got word that Father had taken ill. She rode up to the hills as fast as she could, but it was too late. He had died just before she arrived. They buried him up there and she buried her soulstring with him."

"She never remarried?" I asked.

Severin shook his head. "At first I think she felt it was her fault somehow; that he had died while she didn't even become ill. Later then, she became accustomed to being clan mistress and head of Arlensdale. Work chased grief and power replaced the helplessness of longing. Both mother and father, she steeled herself to the tasks of running the farm and raising sons."

"Did you miss your father?"

Severin frowned and scratched his head. "I hardly knew him. But I did miss not having a father. Mother wouldn't share Arlensdale with anyone, not even for our sakes. She wanted it to herself, you see, a memory of Father that couldn't be taken away from her. Odd, that." He smiled into the fire.

"What?"

"Well, it's like your father, isn't it? The need for power, even if it hurts others." He looked up and smiled at the stricken expression on my face. "Don't fret, Magda, she's not really like your father. Imposing, perhaps, a little selfish in her own way, but not unkind beneath all that."

"What do we tell her about Teren and Nar?"

He shrugged and exhaled, puffing his cheeks. "Don't know yet. They're still alive, I'm certain of it. I'd know if they were dead." He laughed to reassure me. "If I know those two they've figured it out by now and are working on giving your

father a splitting headache, not to mention the shakes and a
toothache if they can manage it. I'd almost feel sorry for him,
you know, for meddling with them and getting them angry."

And because I wanted to be reassured they were safe, I
laughed with Severin and believed him. I fed the fire once
more and then cleared away the mugs and repacked the little
black pot. We lay down nestled side by side. Severin's arm
draped over my shoulder, my back hugged close to his chest. I
watched the fire burning a bright orange, my eyes too tired to
shut easily. Severin's breath was warm on the nape of my
neck. He breathed slowly, steadily, and before long, my lids
grew heavy and closed. I feel asleep dreaming of the herb
garden I would plant in Thall. It would be like Cook's,
scented and blooming; a place for fat yellow bees to hum
pleasantly while I nodded off to sleep in the hot afternoon sun.

I slept deeply and continued to dream. But the threads of
my dream frayed and were rewoven with bleaker colors. The
garden was stripped of life. Plants withered and died at my
touch, their leaves turning brown and crumpled. The sun was
gone and I was lost amidst a desolate landscape. I turned in
my sleep, searching for Severin, but I couldn't find him. I
heard him call my name and I tried to rouse myself from the
heavy sleep. Something terrible held me. I couldn't see it but I
felt it wrap an icy hand around my face, preventing me from
screaming. Panic filled my chest as I struggled to free myself,
but my arms and legs were numb and refused to obey.

Then suddenly the voice stopped calling, and there was a
silence, except for the crackling of a fire and the snapping of
small twigs.

The cold hand released me and I sobbed, my fingers
clutching at the neck of my cloak. I woke then, but not fully.
Drugged and drowsy, I saw the fire with eyes still thick with
sleep. I watched the flames bobbing in their dance and felt
calmed. The warmth of the fire chased away the icy sweat on
my cheeks. Breathing more slowly, I settled once again into a
deep and dreamless sleep.

I awoke groggy, my cloak muffled about my head, dimly
aware that the rain of the day before had returned to join the
dense fog. I peered out from the protective folds of my cloak,
not wishing to expose my face to the clammy air. Something
was different, I thought dully. The fire seemed to have moved

away. I was sure we had been sleeping by the middle tree and
yet, from where I lay, I could see its nobby trunk. I tried with
the vagueness of sleep to make sense of it, and with painful
slowness it dawned on me that I had moved, or had been
moved in the night. I put a searching hand behind me and felt
for Severin. He wasn't there. I turned over quickly, and, raising up on my arms, peered frantically through the mist. I still
couldn't see Severin, nor was there any sound that might have
told me he was nearby.

I was alone and the realization was like cold water dashed
across my face. No! He'd not abandon me, I told myself.
Something's happened. I scrambled to my feet and turned
around, searching for signs of Severin. I ignored my cloak as
it slipped from my shoulders and dropped onto the muddied
ground. The cold fog swarmed over me and swept the warmth
from my skin, but I hardly noticed it, for terror had numbed
all sensations except for the urgency of finding Severin.

I heard a noise, a small snorting sound, and I called out in
the mist. "Severin?" I whispered, holding my body rigid, my
ears straining to catch the sound more clearly. "Severin, is that
you?"

There was no reply. Slowly my feet moved in the direction
of the sound. Circling the ashes of our fire, I crept through the
fog until I was near the middle tree. Heaped in a careless pile,
I saw Severin's clothes. His boots, trousers, shirt, and cloak
lay discarded, as if the owner had stripped suddenly, giving no
thought for how they remained jumbled on the wet ground. I
stopped, perplexed and afraid to move, but again I heard the
shuffling noise and moved, as if compelled, toward it.

I nearly collided with him in the fog. I would have done so
had the mist not swirled and parted like the opening of a
curtain. He was there and I stopped, drawing myself up short
before he could take fright and bound away into the forest. I
saw his head first, the huge rack of antlers with twelve sharp
tines above the crown gleaming a velvety brown in the wet
air. His ears flicked nervously and he stared at me down the
length of a slender nose.

He was a large, magnificent stag. My head barely reached
the top of his rust-colored shoulder. His broad, powerful neck
loomed above me, holding aloft his long head in a graceful
arch.

"Severin?" I whispered in amazement to the stag. I approached, moving slowly, my arms resting at my sides.

The stag gazed at me warily. His eyes were black and glistening, rimmed with a circle of white hair. The antlers dipped lightly as he inclined his heavy head toward me. I sensed confusion and puzzlement in his eyes as he regarded my face. I stood motionless, my blood running cold, as I knew with awful certainty that it was Severin. How like Father to shape Severin in the form of an animal that he hunted for sport. It was the sort of cruel humor that he enjoyed. I panicked, remembering the last hunt I had seen, the stag mauled and gutted, and Father feeding his hounds with bits of meat.

"Severin," I cried softly in despair. The stag made to walk toward me. He stumbled, his legs as shaky as those of a newborn colt that has not learned to balance its large body on delicate hooves. The stag halted suddenly, one obsidian hoof poised in the air. He raised his head in warning and the antlers cut a path through the mist. His breath steamed and he snorted as an unfamiliar smell caught his attention. He forgot about me, absorbed by the animal instinct that alerted him to unseen danger.

"No!" shouted a warning in my head. "Don't let him flee or he will be lost forever!" I forced away my despair and panic as I grappled with what I should do. I had to act quickly. If I stood doing nothing, he would be lost. Like Gest, I thought, and recalled Severin's voice recounting Mara's desperate courage. I reached for the soulstring at my wrist.

"Severin," I whispered again, trying to call the human part of him before the animal fled into the woods. The stag turned to me, hesitating. His body trembled, as if the human in him struggled to oppose the animal's desire to flee. Speaking calmly, my gaze never leaving his, I loosened the soulstring from my wrist, keeping my movements smooth and quiet. I wished it to a length of rope, and when I felt it changing in my hand, I walked slowly toward the stag.

I murmured gentle words as his head inclined to sniff my hand. His eyes stared wildly, but he remained, stilled by a command from within. I slipped the soulstring around his powerful neck and knotted it with the lover's knot Severin had taught me. Tight and true, he had said of it, and I hoped with all my heart that he was right. Standing close to the stag, seeing the rippling muscles of his neck, I realized there was little I could do if he fought against me.

As the soulstring tightened around his neck, his head reared up and he let out a long, mournful bellow. He tossed his head from side to side, as if to shake the rack of antlers rising from his brow. Then he reared back on his haunches and his sharp hooves crashed down on the ground dangerously near my feet. I clung to the soulstring tightly, my arms jerked painfully from their sockets as he raised his body up high and brought it down with a fury. I ducked my head, afraid of the antlers that swung back and forth and threatened to gore me. The tines caught in the branches and he snapped them with a twist of his head. Frantically I wished the soulstring longer. Then I stepped back out of the way of the rearing stag and falling branches.

The rope cut into my palms, burning the skin already chafed from riding. But I held the rope fast and tried to call to Severin. Though the stag bucked and tossed his head furiously, he made no attempt to break free of my grip and run. It was Severin's rage that tormented the stag, the terror of waking to a strange body, to a mouth without words, helpless to free himself.

"Severin, it's Magda! Please, let me help you, please!" I implored him. Wrapping the soulstring around my hand, I tried again to approach him, all the while beseeching him to be calm. Gradually his violent outburst quieted, though he stamped his hooves and swayed restlessly. Then he shuddered as if defeated, and his head dipped, exhausted, the sharp horns digging trails in the trampled ground. His breath came in clouds of white steam as he panted, and the muscles of his chest heaved with the effort of his breathing. I reached him and tentatively laid the flat of my hand against his slick hide. He didn't shy away but stood, head bowed and resigned. I circled my arms tightly around his neck and rested my face against his rusty hide.

SEVEN

"SEVERIN, MY LOVE," I whispered. I clutched his neck and
cried, the tears staining his rust-colored hide a dark brown. As
I sobbed, my face pressed against his neck, I felt a damp nose
nuzzling my ear and hair. The stag huffed warm air on my
neck and butted my head gently. I stopped crying then and
turned to look at him.

There was resignation in the bowed posture of his head,
but not despair. The stag stared serenely, and in his gaze I
sensed an intelligence not native to the animal, Severin's eyes
speaking soundlessly to me. I spoke to the stag lovingly, ca-
ressing the white patch that bloomed like a star above his
black nose and holding his cheek close to mine.

I shivered in the rainy cold. My wet hair clung to my neck
in a draggled mess, and fine red hairs from the stag's hide
scratched my cheeks. I wiped my face with the edge of my
skirt and twisted my hair in a wet knot. I was shaking with
cold, my lips turning a berry blue. I had forgotten about my
cloak lying on the ground and my clothes were already soaked
by the constant drizzle.

"Come," I said to the stag, "let me get my cloak and we

can sit—" I stopped myself short. "I'll sit and think about
what to do now."

Holding him tight about the neck we walked, the stag
moving delicately on his slim legs to where my cloak was
lying in a wet, muddy heap by the campfire. I let go of him
and bent to put it on. The wool, though wet and smelling of
mud, warmed me a little. I felt the pot of salve bump against
my thigh. I took it out and smeared salve on my palms. The
throbbing sting of the rope burns abated and I found I could
bend my fingers again without pain. I huddled by the old fire,
now a collection of wet, gray ashes, and wondered what I
should do next. I looked up at the sky and the rain tumbled
into my eyes, blinding me with sooty tears. I looked down
again and saw the rivulets of rainwater etching lines in the
mud. There was no sound but for the steady drip, drip of rain.

Well, I thought, there'll be no using the night sky to guide
me. The dragon may be there, gleaming with all his fiery
breath, but there's no chance that I'll see it. That leaves following an enchanted trail that shifts and weaves and perhaps
leads nowhere. Some choice, I thought gloomily. How long a
journey was it to Thall? Even Severin hadn't been sure of that.
How long could I survive alone? I had very few supplies left,
enough perhaps for a few days. I could stretch them out longer
if I rationed the food carefully. The stag would forage for
himself. I watched him, already browsing absently on the
bushes near the campfire, stripping leaves off the branches
and gazing at me seriously while he chewed. I wondered how
soon a diet of leaves and grass would effect Severin, trapped
in the stag.

I sat staring at my dreary campsite and felt my desolation
like a dream. The thought of being alone in the woods, my
new husband transformed into a stag and wandering aimlessly
to an unknown destination, was overwhelming. Not too long
ago I had been unhappy, locked within my father's castle
walls. There I had longed for freedom. But not like this, I
thought, shaking my head. Frowning sourly at the pile of
soggy ashes, I rested my forehead on the back of my hand. I
had no other choice but to go on. I couldn't return home.
There, death was a certainty. Out here in the wilderness of the
Moravian forests, there was still a chance. I felt Severin's
leather kit where it lay resting on my chest. I picked it up and
stared bleakly at it, wishing it capable of advice. I tried to

recall exactly how Severin had used the flint. Could I do that? I asked myself. You'll have to, won't you? I answered. I looked at the stag again and sorrow wrenched my heart. I promised I'd try, I reminded myself.

The stag followed close beside me as I retrieved Severin's clothing. In the pocket of his cloak I found the pouch of tea. It felt nearly full and I was grateful for that. Severin had said it could keep one alive when there was nothing else. I would need it when I ran out of food. I also found the remainder of a round of hard cheese and some dried fruit at the bottom of his pocket. Not much, I realized, but I'd make it enough.

I took off my wet cloak and put on Severin's, which was drier, having lain between other clothing, protected from the rain and mud. I decided to wear his trousers under my riding skirts as well. They would provide extra warmth and protect my thighs from the saddle sores I was getting. They were hopelessly big and bagged foolishly around my waist. I undid the laces from his leather jerkin to use as a belt to tie the trousers on. I debated whether or not to wear his sword. I decided against it, as I knew very little about carrying weapons and would probably have stabbed myself before I made decent use of it. I didn't need his jerkin but I didn't want to leave it behind; too beautiful to discard, I thought. But I knew the real reason I kept it. The intertwining patterns of vines and leaves worked on its front reminded me of the first time I had seen Severin in the woods, smiling and dappled with sunlight.

Into my own cloak I rolled what few supplies I had: the rest of Severin's clothes, his short sword, the black pot and mugs, and the remainder of our food. I tied the bundle securely and then, leaning back on my heels, surveyed our camp sadly. Despite Father, despite the terror of fleeing, last night had been a night of joy. The soulstring on my wrist tugged as the stag leaned out to take a few leaves from a bush.

"We are tied by the soulstring, like Gest and Mara," I said to the patient stag. He answered me with a snort and a gentle dipping of his head.

"I'll take us to Thall, Severin," I said firmly. "Once we're there, I'll find someone to lift this spell and change you back." I swung the rolled bundle over my shoulder and prepared to leave. The stag came close and breathed warm air into the hollow of my neck. I caught his face gently, holding it between my hands, and kissed the long, bony nose. "I'll not let you go,", I whispered fiercely to him. "The soulstring binds us and, stag or no, I'll not release you, my husband."

Leading the stag away from the campsite, I walked back through the underbrush to the path, looking for the horses. I spotted the overhanging branch that I had tied them to the night before, but they were nowhere to be seen. I went closer, noting the hoofprints in the soft mud. Peering through the fog, I whistled for them and clucked my tongue as I'd heard the stableboys do at home. I listened intently, hoping to hear the high nickering of my mare. But the horses didn't answer.

"They're gone. The horses are gone," I said angrily. I swore at Father, staring with frustration at the overhanging branch. I resisted the urge to scream and stamp my feet like an angry child. Don't get discouraged so soon, Magda, I ordered myself, you've only just begun your journey. "I'll walk, then," I said to the stag, who continued to browse on nearby shrubs. I hoisted the bundle higher on my shoulder, not wanting to think about how heavy it already seemed. I looked down the path, the fog clinging like a fine gray sea about us. "Which way?" I asked. "Which way lies Thall?"

Behind me the stag stopped chewing and gazed quizzically. I recalled Severin's advice and looked down at my feet. True enough, the path appeared off to my left. Lips pressed firmly together in a determined scowl, I started in that direction, pushing through the mist. The stag followed gracefully at my side, his legs stepping delicately so as to keep pace with my slower stride.

What a strange mirage we formed to any who might have seen us: a young woman, damp and bedraggled, tied about the wrist by a fine rope to a huge stag that moved dutifully at her side. I knew what Father thought. I was sure that somewhere he was laughing at what he supposed to be my humiliation. No, I thought stubbornly, I won't give him the satisfaction. This was my task, my challenge, and I would meet it with courage and confidence. In defiance of the wet, sticky fog, I lifted my chin and sang with a raucous voice a bawdy song that I had learned listening to the stableboys. Let that be my answer to you, Father, I thought indignantly. At my side the stag started, surprised by my noise, and turned to stare, his eyes rolling to show the whites.

My enthusiasm waned as the day wore on. It seemed as if

the forest conspired to make our passage almost impossible. I
tripped and stumbled over roots that rose abruptly across the
path. Brambles snatched my skirts, tangling and tearing the
fabric. Branches with whips of wet leaves stung my face.
Even the stag had difficulty pressing through the crush of
trees, the tines of his antlers getting trapped in nests of low-
hanging branches.

Sometimes, when I looked up from the path, I was certain I
perceived an easier way through the forest; a path that opened
up just to the left or right of where I was traveling. Forgetting
Severin's warning, I would start toward it. But the stag would
resist, tugging at the soulstring, and heading instead in the
direction of the thickets and most impenetrable-looking mass
of brush and bramble. Once I protested loudly, arguing with
the stag, who made no reply except to hold fast. All four legs
locked firmly in the soil, he refused to move in the direction
of the more attractive path. I tried pulling and then pleading,
but the stag jerked his head toward the brambled path and I
was forced to relent. Grumbling angrily as I shoved the thick
bramble out of my way, I remembered the enchanted paths
Father wove for suitors, designed to keep them wandering lost
through the forest. Severin had been able to see through the
illusion to the true path. Though he had instructed me how to
see through the enchantment for myself, I was glad of the
stag's presence, for I believed it was Severin who guided the
stag through the woods.

My first night alone in the woods was the worst and the
most miserable night of my life. The rain and fog, which had
started my day, accompanied me like a curse, soaking me to
the marrow. I found—or rather I should say the stag found,
for I could not see even my hand before my face in the heavy
rain—a low rock overhang that offered us a little shelter. Sitting there, my back pressed against the hard stone, I stared
hollow eyed at the rain, shivering with fatigue and cold.

Although the stone of my shelter was cold and unyielding,
the floor was fairly dry and soft, cluttered with a collection of
forest debris: dried pine leaves, acorn caps, and the abandoned
fragments of a mouse's nest. On the lip of the rock over my
head, staghorn moss bloomed emerald green, the long fruiting
stamens collecting beads of water. The stag nibbled on these
and occasionally took a step outside of the shelter to snatch
the leaves off the nearby bushes. The soulstring lengthened of

its own accord to allow him to reach these branches without jerking my arm up in the movement. Had I not been so tired, I would have marveled at the soulstring's pliancy, the ease with which it accommodated our needs, lengthening when distance was required and shortening when we were close. But at that moment all I wanted was a mug of Severin's hot tea and a fire to warm my chilled bones.

There wasn't much dry matter to be used for tinder under the sheltered rock and certainly not much wood that was dry enough to burn without smoking. I gathered what I could and tried to copy the movements Severin had shown me. The stag watched with great interest, his head cocked to one side as I tried striking the flint. Click. Nothing happened. Click, click, click. I repeated my attempts, growing more frustrated as each time the flint remained cold. I leaned back wearily in the shelter and gritted my teeth to stop them from chattering. I have to have a fire, I thought desperately. Determined, I bowed my head over my hands and tried once more. Click! A tiny blue spark jumped to the tinder. I struck again and more sparks followed. The tinder burst into a tiny flame with a puff of smoke and I blew on it gently, terrified it would go out.

My fire was pathetically small and the flames sputtered weakly. The wood hissed and steamed, throwing off an acrid smoke that stung my eyes and made me sneeze. But it was enough to heat the water and I was able to make a mug of tea. I ate a piece of dry cake, made soggy by the dampness of my cloak. I also chewed a bit of dried apple that tasted sweet even though it felt like leather in my mouth and had flecks of wool stuck to it.

My meager supply of barely dry wood was exhausted quickly and I watched helplessly as the wind shifted, dashing rain in the shelter and gutting the fire. It died with a curl of gray smoke, and no amount of blowing, fanning, or stirring it, trying to find some coals still not quenched, succeeded. I huddled in the dark shelter and started crying, feeling sorry for myself, lost in the forest, wet, cold, hungry, and very much alone. Bravery and courage were fine for those who had a warm fire, a dry suit of clothes, and a pack horse loaded with supplies. But I was so unprepared for anything and felt at the moment undone by my circumstances. The stag leaned down and licked the salty tears from my face. I only cried harder, thinking of Severin and feeling even more sorry for myself that I had lost my husband. The stag stood near the entrance of our shelter, folded his legs carefully beneath his broad body, and lay down next to me. I was sheltered from the blowing rain, squeezed between the stone wall and the stag. His hide was steaming, pungent with the smell of musk. But he was warm in the dank cold. Wrapping myself in both cloaks, I huddled miserably next to the stag. With my head resting against his flank, I cried myself to sleep.

The next morning I woke still rolled into a tight knot. Stiff and creaking, I uncurled my legs and tried to straighten out. It was quiet and I suddenly realized that I no longer heard the sound of the rain pattering through the leaves. I sat up and the stag greeted me with a generous lick across my cheek that made me splutter As I looked out over the stag's back, I saw that not only had the rain stopped, but the mist had cleared.

The forest had lost its dreary, gray mantle. Looking up through the tops of the trees I caught a glimpse of blue sky, like a shard from a robin's egg, peeking out between drifting clouds. I could hear the sounds of the forest coming to life: the rustle of small animals digging through the leaves and the chitterings of birds calling in the threes. I saw a chickadee, its yellow throat and black cap bright against the green pine, as it flitted between the branches, eating little bugs and watching me with a wary eye.

I stood up and stretched, my whole body aching from sleeping on the ground. My mouth was dry and chalky and my eyes were red and swollen from weeping. I took a little water from the skin and splashed it across my face. Using the corner of my torn skirt, I tried to scrub away some of the smoke and grit. Then I rinsed out the stale taste from my mouth. The stag volunteered to help me by licking my ear but I pulled away, grimacing. "That's all right," I said rubbing the spot that his smooth tongue had tickled. "I'll do this alone." The stag eyed me dolefully and then turned away to begin browsing on the bushes.

I looked down at my ragged and torn skirt and decided it would only hamper me further in the woods. I ripped the skirt from the bodice and then tore off the lower half of my shift. The upper half I tucked into Severin's trousers and retied the belt. Then, thinking on it again, I took off the bodice and put on Severin's shirt and then my bodice again, the laces helping to hold the large shirt in place against my body. The too-long sleeves I rolled up to my wrist. The shirt still smelled of Severin, and, when I put it on, I felt the ache of loneliness. My hair was hopeless, matted and snarled with bits of leaves and twigs. I couldn't remember when I had last used a comb. I tried running my fingers through it but that didn't help much. I tore a thin strip of cloth from my old shift and used that to tie it out of my face. I put on Severin's cloak and rolled up my few possessions, including the remnants of my shift, in my black cloak again. My skirt I left behind. It was too bulky to pack and I saw no further use for it.

All the while I had been preparing to leave, I continued to talk to the stag as if he were still Severin. I talked about what we should do on the journey and how I would see to it that he was freed from Father's spell in Thall. The stag seemed to listen and I convinced myself that he understood. I hummed the stableboys' bawdy song under my breath as I secured my bundle. Last night I had thought I was finished, but today I felt differently. They sky was clearing and the forest no longer seemed threatening. I was hopeful and confident.

We started to leave and I stopped suddenly, struck by an idea. I looked at the stag, appraising the height of his withers and broad bony back. I wondered briefly if he would object to carrying me. It was worth a try, I thought. We'd make better time if I could ride.

I had enough trouble just getting on a horse, even with a hand up. The stag stood a good bit taller than my mare. Cautiously, I laid my hands on his withers. He shifted his weight uneasily. I took a deep breath and jumped, trying to hoist myself on his back. I didn't succeed in getting high enough to pull my leg over his back. The stag pranced nervously as my legs kicked against his side. I lost my grip and slipped down to the ground. I tried again. This time, as I jumped, my chin collided with his backbone and I bit my tongue. I shrieked in pain and slipped down again. Furious, I lay on the ground staring up at the stag. He stretched his neck and shook his head. "That's what I think, too," I answered.

Then I noticed a flat boulder jutting out near the rock overhang that had served as our shelter. "Here, let's try that," I said. I scampered on top of it and drew the stag alongside. The boulder's height gave me extra leverage and, when I placed my hands on the stag's withers and jumped, I was more successful. Unfortunately, I was too successful and, instead of landing across the stag's back, I continued tumbling off the other side of the stag into the bushes. The stag gazed at me in surprise and then snorted. I cursed loudly like the stableboys, trying to pull myself out of the bushes and picking out bits of twigs and brambles that had gotten under my shirt. Hands on my hips, I glared at the stag and then shook my finger at him.

"You did that on purpose!" I shouted, trying to regain my wounded dignity. The stag merely gazed at me, disinterested. He turned his head away as a shrub of green leaves snagged his attention. I climbed the rock again and this time was more careful in hoisting myself onto his back.

As soon as he felt my weight on his back the stag's head reared up in alarm. The antlers swept dangerously close to my head and I ducked to one side. "Whoa!" I called. "Easy, it's all right. There now, it's all right." I spoke in a soothing voice and stroked his powerful neck. The stag settled down, but I could sense his unease in small restive movements. "There now, not so bad, is it? Shall we go?" I asked the stag, and touched his flanks lightly with my heels. The stag jumped and began running with a swift, loping gait.

It wasn't the same as riding a horse with a saddle. For one thing the stag's spine was a hard ridge of bone. Try as I might to adjust my posture, with every step he took I bounced up and slammed down hard on the bony ridge. The stag's girth was also much wider than a horse's and I felt like a child, my legs astride too large an animal, unable to grasp my thighs around his sides.

"Wait! Wait!" I called, gasping as air huffed out of my chest with every bounce. The stag halted abruptly, head jerked up in puzzlement, and I lurched forward onto his neck, just managing to grasp it with both arms so I wouldn't fall off again. "I can't ride like this," I explained. "I think I have a better idea." I slid off and untied the rolled-up cloak that I carried over my shoulder. I took out Severin's leather jerkin and laid it open across the stag's back. The leather was soft and I knew that riding on it would eventually ruin it, but I couldn't spend the day banging my backside with every step the stag took. Eyeing me, the stag nodded his head and snorted. He stood patiently as I tried over and over to jump up on his broad back again.

When I finally succeeded, my face was red and sweaty from my labors but I was feeling very proud of myself. Sitting upright on his back I shouted to the stag, "Lead on!" and was nearly jolted off as he took the path at a brisk pace. I clung to his neck and concentrated on keeping my seat firmly placed on his back. But as we rode through the woods, I jostled and bounced from side to side, remaining on his back only by clinging desperately like a burr to the soulstring tied around his neck.

The journey through the Moravian forest became easier as my existence was ordered and refined by a series of routine activities. Setting up camp, making a fire, and brewing tea became a ritual. I found solace in the repetition of these simple but basic tasks and pride in my growing skill. I became proficient at using Severin's flint, and the evening fire and hot tea gave me confidence in myself. During the day, the forest opened up to us and the path was more accessible. I grew accustomed to my awkward mount and it seemed the stag altered his gait slightly so that I rode more firmly on his back.

When the last of Cook's food was gone, I concentrated on finding food from the woods. I blessed Cook daily for her teachings and wished that I had been a more attentive pupil. I found edible plants that had not yet disappeared in the early fall. A patch of wineberries, a little shriveled but still sweet, filled my pockets one day. I found a dying tree strangled by a luxurious vine thick with fox grapes. On another day I spied the leaves of something that I knew was familiar. I stopped the stag and slid off his back, kneeling to look closely at the broad shiny leaves and the clusters of little yellow flowers. Now what had Cook said about them? I asked myself, and then remembered. "Fairy buds," she had called the plant. I found a stick and eagerly dug under the soil to bring up the tiny rounded roots. I brushed off the dirt and smiled at the little buds. I ate one and it had a pleasant crunch, though it was more bitter than the ones Cook had collected in the early spring. I dug a few more, reluctantly leaving a patch unmolested. "Always leave some behind," Cook had said sternly. "Never take them all or someone may get mad."

"Who?" I had asked her, curious that anyone else in Moravia besides Cook should even know the little tubers existed.

"Never you mind!" she'd answered, tweaking my nose hard. "Just remember what I said. Always do well by the

woods and they'll reward you. That's what my dad told me
and that's what I tell you."

Later she had sliced the tubers and fried them with butter,
garlic, and some of the wild mint we had found that day.

"It's good!" I had told her, my mouth stuffed with the food.

"Of course it's good. I made it, didn't I?" And she'd
smiled hugely at me. "I may not have been much of a forester's daughter but I can cook and that's a magic all to itself,
my girl." She had turned her back to me and gone back to her
kettles and pots steaming on the stove. For a moment she had
seemed to me more of a sorcerer than Father, the steam swirling about her as she muttered little phrases to herself, added
bits of this and that herb to the pots to transform the most
ordinary of vegetables into meals that humbled the palate.

I was lucky that day, for after finding the fairy buds, I also
discovered, growing in a little stream, a bush of winter cress,
a smaller version of the summer plant. It, too, had the sharp,
tart taste of its cousin, though the leaves were smaller and the
stems stringier. I was delighted by the find. Not far from the
edges of the stream wild onions grew in abundance on the
bank. I picked many, braiding the tops to tie them into the belt
at my waist. That night I ate heartily, though it was just as
well I was alone with the stag, given the pungent and enduring
smell that accumulated on my breath from the onions. The
stag's eyes watered as he tried to nibble on a few. He gave up,
preferring the green tips of the shrubs and grass near our
campsite, and left the onions to me.

I marked time at night by what I could see of the moon.
The Mother's Moon of our first night in the forest had waned,
followed by the white sliver that Severin had called "Hag's
Moon." Then it, too, was gone and the dark clear sky was the
time of "Maiden's Moon," when lovers met secretly under the
black sky. Somewhere, I thought, people in Thall were having
harvest dances, listening to music, and watching plays. I felt a
rush of loneliness, missing the sounds of human voices and
laughter. Then I would talk to the stag, pointing out to him the
starred plow under which I knew lay Thall. "There, see?" I
would point to it, and the stag would stop chewing his endless
meal of leaves and regard me curiously. "The star, it's winking
at us. It knows we're coming and it's telling everyone in Thall
to watch for us." Feeling more comforted, I would sing, not

because I had a lovely voice, but because in the dark night of the forest the high, reedy sound of my songs put me to sleep.

We were moving north. Our progress, though more pleasant, was slow; the journey seemed endless. Fall had arrived in earnest and the nights were colder. In the morning patches of dew clung in silvery webs to the grass and the bushes. As we walked we stirred up brittle pine needles on the path, their fragrance rising to greet us like a dusty perfume.

Then the forest began to change. The dense pines thinned and, between them, in emerald green, rust, and brown, were growing oaks and maples. They held their summer color, though the leaves had lost the luster of summer and were no longer glossy. Here and there a maple was turning orange and red like a fiery torch amidst the remaining green. And though I was certain we moved northward, it seemed I had traveled a wide circle only to return to the outer edges of my father's forest. I was afraid to continue, fearful that any moment I would see the gray towers of Moravia Castle rising above the treetops, the pennants waving a mocking welcome.

"Have we come the right way?" I asked the stag. "What's happened to all the pines?" I looked around worriedly.

I slid down off the stag, turning this way and that as I stared at the changed forest. The stag continued walking, unconcerned.

"Wait!" I cried, trying to pull him back. The stag shook his head in irritation at the delay. He snorted, pawing at the path as he waited impatiently for me. I remained indecisive. The stag started walking again, determined to go forward.

"All right, all right!" I answered, and followed alongside. "I hope you're right about this." The stag gave no answer other than to pluck a mouthful of leaves from a bush and chew contentedly as he strolled.

I was nervous and yet delighted by the different colors and textures of the various trees. After days of solid green, everything different seemed new and interesting. I heard water running, gurgling pleasantly. The path crossed a narrow stream that flowed with clear, sweet water. I bent over the slippery stones to drink and saw river crabs scuttle under a rock. I sat there for a while trying to catch them, my clumsy attempts muddying the water. Finally, I succeeded in capturing two of them, their front claws taking little bites out of my fingers as I lifted them out of the water. Just as I shall do to you, my little friends, I thought hungrily. I made camp right there and started the black pot boiling with water from the stream. When it was steaming I tossed in my catch, adding to the pot some wild onions, mint, and a few tough leaves of sheep sorrel that I found that morning. Well, it may not be as good as Cook's, I thought later, as I labored to peel off the gray shells and pick at the tiny portions of meat inside, but it'll do! And I munched happily like the dragon in my sister's tapestry.

The next morning we rose early and started on our way. I was feeling well rested and well fed from my meal of river crabs. The stream continued to crisscross the path and, throughout the day, I had a good supply of fresh water. As we traveled I saw other animals as they scurried to and fro, preparing for the winter months. A squirrel chattered angrily at me after I robbed it of a portion of the acorns it had just carefully stored. I saw the rust-colored streak of a fox as it slipped quickly beneath the underbrush, stopping once to regard me, ears pricked forward. I no longer shied away from the animals, fearing them to be my father's spies, but watched for them, enjoying their company when I spotted them. At night, lying huddled beside the stag, I listened to the hollow cry of wood doves. In the early morning I heard the trilling of finches, their songs high and clear as they darted through the trees.

It was later, after Mother's Moon had returned in the sky, that I was struck by the first signs of a fever. I woke, feeling exhausted. Even the simple morning routine was tiring. I wanted to curl up somewhere dark and quiet and sleep like an animal in the winter. My face felt hot and flushed. On the pathway, riding, the constant swaying motion of the stag's gait made me nauseous. "What have you eaten, Magda?" I asked myself. There were some mushrooms the stag had rooted for me to eat, but surely he wouldn't have let me eat them if they were poisonous. There were some blackcap berries. I had hesitated before picking them. "Look for these with the round heads of berries," Cook had warned, and she had held up a drooping stalk, the umbels laden with blue-black berries, for me to see. "There's some that may look like it, but those grow in small clusters along the stem. Those'll make you sick, girl, so look sharp!"

I cooled my face with water from the stream and told myself to ignore the fever and continue riding. The morning passed slowly as I grew more listless with the fever. All I could think about was, when would we reached Thall? When would we reach Arlensdale? There I'll sleep, I promised myself, there I'll get well.

It was midday when we reached the grassy clearing, which appeared suddenly between the trees. After journeying so long through dense woods the clearing seemed spacious and airy. The stag trotted eagerly toward it, as if, like me, he couldn't wait to stand and bask in the open air. He stopped in the middle of the clearing, where the ground rose to a small knoll. I slid from his back and landed thigh deep in the tall grass. The sun shone brightly in a clear blue sky and the grass smelled sweet. I plucked a stalk and sucked the end thoughtfully, lifting my face toward the sun's warmth. A gentle breeze blew on my hot cheeks. The stag was ripping up mouthfuls of grass from the ground and chewing noisily, his jaw grinding back and forth. I smiled at him and stroked his cheek. "Soon, Severin," I whispered. "Soon we'll be in Thall, and it won't be this bony nose I'll be kissing." The stag snorted and went on chewing gravely.

And then it was quiet, as if the world had stopped, as if there were nothing living but the stag and me standing alone on the grassy knoll. The air was deathly still, the usual whisper of the trees hushed. The stag stopped chewing and lifted his head, sniffing the air nervously. My skin prickled and I felt the hairs lift on the back of my neck.

"What is it?" I breathed to the stag. The stag began circling, running with short jerky steps, his eyes alert for danger. Twice he lowered his head as if to strike the air with his antlers. The feeling of dread gathered about me like a thick cloud. A dull ache began to throb at my temples and my mouth went dry. My heart drummed loudly in my chest as I waited for something to happen. And from deep inside me, the wildness bristled and snarled with warning.

I gasped sharply as the breath was sucked from my throat. Father struck, his power exploding above the stag in a ball of yellow fire. The terrified stag reared back on his hind legs, standing upright. His head and neck were enclosed within the sorcerer's flame and held aloft. I heard him bellow, a cry that altered to a howl. I stared, horrified, as the stag's form wavered in the fire. Surrounded by the flames of Father's power, Severin's head and shoulders emerged struggling from the torso of the stag. His head was thrown back, his mouth open and twisted with agony.

"Severin!" I screamed, and reached up.

But he was gone, the stag's form whole as he fell from the fire back to the ground on his forelegs.

"No!" I cried. "No!"

Again the stag reared up and, for another instant, suspended in the sorcerer's fire. I saw Severin's face contorted with pain.

"Stop!" I screamed to Father. Thunder rumbled and growled, though the sky remained empty of clouds. "Stop, you bastard!" The thunder rattled violently, growing louder and louder until I was forced to cover my ears with my hands, deaf even to the sounds of my own screams.

And then it snapped. The wildness, my power and my fury, was released. My arms thrust skyward, fingers splayed, and the wildness galloped through them, erupting from my hands with a blue flame to meet the thunder. Lightning cracked in the sky and streaked toward me like a sapphire dagger. I caught it and it shattered into millions of tiny white sparks that scattered in a veil of light. The soulstring arced with a white-hot flash and shaped a net of shimmering blue light around the stag.

Father's fire disappeared like the flame of a snuffed candle and the thunder ceased its pounding. The sound of it lingered, ringing in my ears. I squinted against the daylight, my head throbbing with pain. The air was thick with the smell of smoke and tallow. The stag's head bent low, his antlers caught in the sweep of grass. His legs trembled and his chest heaved with the effort of breathing. I went to touch him and he darted back, afraid, his antlers raised in warning. His black eyes rolled to the white rims with pain and terror.

"Severin," I called softly, never taking my eyes from the frightened animal. "Severin," I whispered again, and he hesitated. I whispered his name over and over as if it were a spell to call the man back from the stag. Slowly the stag calmed, soothed by the gentle sound of Severin's name.

I approached him and he let me take his head between my hands and stroke his cheek. On my wrist, the soulstring hummed and warmed.

I looked at it, amazed. It had saved Severin's life. Father would have killed him before my eyes but for the soulstring.

The soulstring was a bridge between Severin and me. My power had come to life, summoned by fear and rage, and had flowed through the soulstring in a stream of light to protect him. I shared my power still with Father and, as long as I held the soulstring, Father could no more kill Severin with magic than he could kill me. Not yet, anyway.

I continued to rub the stag's cheek, looking about nervously. The air was too quiet. Father's presence clung ominously and I waited, sensing another attack.

It came with brutal swiftness. Wrenched from the stag's side, I was cast like a doll to the ground. I slammed against the earth and pain coiled me into a knot. Stars leaped across my vision and a shrill ringing battered my head. I groaned and spit blood from a cut inside my cheek. I shook my head to clear away the stars. Pain flared anew and I thought I would vomit. I saw the stag above me, his antlers etching a black pattern against the blue sky.

And then the antlers disappeared. Dazed, I watched as the stag's form shifted. There was a menacing hiss and a huge viper towered above me where the stag had been. A scream tore from my lips and I backed away, terrified, clawing at the ground. Its head followed me, weaving back and forth, its black eyes glittering like polished jet. As I crawled along the ground, the soulstring dragged him closer to me. The tongue flicked out, nearly catching my face. I screamed again and frantically tore at the soulstring on my wrist.

I was nearly freed of it when an inner voice shouted, "No!" The soulstring hissed with blue fire and clung like a tendril to my wrist. "No," came the cry again, and I obeyed. I looked up at the viper. It hissed, venom dripping from two fangs. It lunged, mouth open and fangs directed toward my head. There was no chance to scream, but my body arched in terror.

The viper passed through me like the shadow of a nightmare. I shuddered violently and, with a rush of sudden realization, knew why it hadn't touched me. It wasn't real. An illusion sent to terrify me into letting go of the soulstring. Father must know, I thought wildly, that it's the soulstring that prevents him from harming Severin further. He'll try to frighten me, to goad me into letting go of it.

The viper's form faded and another took its place. An enormous raven cawed harshly. He raised his wings and the black feathers blotted out the clear blue sky. He beat his wings fiercely and the wind gathered around him in a wild tempest. The soulstring tugged violently as the raven tried to pull it free from my wrist, but I wrapped it tighter around my hand. His sharp talons raked the air and he lifted his beak, prepared to strike. I didn't move. He drove his beak into the ground and deep gashes appeared in the soil. I couldn't stop myself then but screamed and twisted away as his beak sliced the air above my head. *It's not real!* I clutched at the knowledge like a drowning man to a branch. Another gash appeared in the soil beside me. I faced the raven and yanked down hard on the soulstring where it was tied to his taloned foot. He stumbled back, cawing angrily. He beat his wings as if for flight but I fought back, crouching close to the ground and holding him down. I jerked the soulstring savagely and watched, satisfied, as the raven lost his balance and toppled sideways.

He faded before he touched the ground. In his place a tree of fire sprang from the soil, flames scorching the yellow grass black. I was blinded by the thick, black smoke billowing out from the blazing tree. I coughed as I swallowed smoke and it burned my throat and chest. "Not real!" I cried, willing myself to remain strong. Flames licked along the soulstring, turning it into a rope of fire. Through eyes streaming with tears from the smoke I watched the flame eat away at the soulstring. In its wake the flame left a thread of ash that threatened to crumble into black dust.

"Severin!" I called out in despair as the soulstring disintegrated. Flames touched my hand, bloomed suddenly on the edges of my shirt, and singed my hair. "Severin!" I cried with a long wailing scream.

I could no longer see the soulstring for the raging fire, but I could feel it. It was there, just beneath the surface of the flames. In my mind I clenched a fist around it, refusing to feel the heat of the flames, refusing to accept the vision of the soulstring's destruction. Arms crossed tightly over my chest, I willed Father's illusion away. Pain surged in my head and snapped along my spine, arching it in a taut curve. I felt like a warp thread being wound ever tighter on its loom. My breath rattled in my chest. Father's power struck at me over and over, like a smith's hammer to the anvil. And, like the anvil, I refused to be shaped or bent by his hatred. As it crashed against me, I gathered it and cast his power echoing back.

I heard my father's cry as my pain engulfed him. Withdrawing his power, he released me suddenly. Freed from the flames, I dropped, senseless, into the yellow grass.

When I opened my eyes next it was twilight. I peered up through half-closed lids at the fading pink light that was stained with the blue black of approaching night. The grass hummed with the droning chant of insects. A breeze blew cool night air across my face. As I stared, blinking, I saw his antlers first, crosshatched against the dusky pink sky. Two pointed ears flicked worriedly on either side. I reached up a tentative hand and saw the sparkle of gold thread glowing on my wrist. It was the soulstring radiating with life.

The stag bent his head and his cold, wet nose touched my cheek carefully. I shivered and then smiled weakly. "I'm all right," I answered, surprised by the raspy sound. The stag began to thoroughly lick my face and I couldn't help but laugh softly. Twinges of pain throbbed at my temple but I didn't mind it. "Let me up now," I protested, "really, I'm all right." And I brushed his head away.

I sat up slowly, but even sitting, I knew I wasn't all right. Nausea swept over me in waves, gripping my stomach, and I doubled over, groaning. I rested my head on my knees as saliva flooded my mouth with a queer metallic taste. After a few moments, the nausea ebbed and my shoulders drooped, exhausted. I stood wearily and leaned against the stag's shoulder.

"I need some tea," I croaked. We walked slowly toward the edge of the woods, stopping every few steps while I waited until each new wave of nausea subsided and I could walk without doubling over. At the forest's edge I sat down heavily and rested. It took every bit of cajoling and fighting with myself to stand again and collect the wood for a fire. I would rather have curled up and slept forever. The stag seemed to understand and when I went too slowly, or stood too long staring blankly at the forest floor, he nudged me smartly between the shoulder blades with his bony nose. Once I got angry, and swung my arm around to drive him away. I stopped abruptly, arm raised above my head, when I looked into the stag's knowing eyes and remembered the vision of Severin's agonized face.

I brought my arm down, suddenly ashamed. I embraced the stag and whispered fevered apologies, stroking his hide.

Severin had willingly linked his fate with mine. He had fought for me and tried to free me from the grip of Father's power. Now he was changed, and it was my duty to free him. If I chose not to fight, he was lost forever. My eyes lowered to the soulstring on my wrist and I remembered my promise to Severin.

I would take him home to Thall and there the curse would be lifted. I closed my eyes and concentrated hard on the soulstring, trying to give it my love and what strength and courage I had. That's what Mara wove in her soulstring, I told myself; that's what will keep it strong.

I opened my eyes and patted the stag's nose. He licked my palm and snorted, bumping his nose against my chest. I laughed and stepped back quickly. "All right, I'm going!" I said to him and went to work on starting the fire. I took the flint from Severin's kit and prepared to strike it against a stone. I stopped a moment, wondering, and put the flint down in my lap. My magic had returned, shaped to the unpredictable wildness. It had come today when I called; it had fought and beaten Father back. Would it come for something so simple as starting a fire?

I looked at the pile of tinder and tried to concentrate on a flame. I tried to think only of the flame, shaping it yellow and orange, filled with heat. But my concentration kept slipping away into a dozen other little thoughts. I couldn't help but think of the cold I was feeling, of the gnawing hunger that continued in spite of the nausea, of the itch on my nose and the pebble poking underneath my knee. I shifted my position and tried again with no more success. It seemed impossible to concentrate long enough to do anything, and the tinder and I remained cold. At last, sighing with resignation, I took up the flint and in no time had made a fire in the usual way.

I shook the pouch, weighing how light it felt. There was only a little of the tea left. I calculated that even being careful, it would be gone soon. Since I had become ill with the fever, the tea was the only thing I had been able to stomach. If Father didn't kill me first, I thought grimly, the fever would, once the tea was gone. As I made the tea, I considered Father's attack. Why had he waited so long? Why had he let Severin and me travel so far unmolested? That bothered me. Cat-and-mouse game again? I wondered. Is he enjoying letting me think I've nearly made it before he attacks me? No, I decided, shaking my head over the mug of tea. Today had surprised him, I was sure of that. He didn't know about the soulstring and he didn't know that I could resist him.

I set my mug of tea down near my food and fed more wood to the fire. I stared at the dancing flame and was chilled by another idea. The sorcery dormant in me was now awake. Nothing wrong with that, but what came next? I was certain that the key to the separation of our shared sorcery lay in my resistance. When my talent was strong enough to fight against Father, then it was strong enough to stand alone. Soon now, Father would have me where he wanted me. And if I knew it, he surely must know it, too.

I lay down, curled up beside the fire, unable to fall asleep but too exhausted to think of staying awake. I prayed silently that the border to Thall was close, that there would be enough time to escape before my father tried to kill me. I would rest this night, I decided, but at first light the stag and I would flee and not stop until we crossed into Thall.

EIGHT

I DIDN'T WAIT for dawn's light but left while it was still dark. I tried to sleep but kept waking, feeling tense and restless. Finally, disgusted, I sat up and stirred the coals of my fire into life. If I couldn't sleep enough to make it worth the effort, I thought, I'd ride instead. I made another cup of very weak tea and drank it quickly, glancing often over my shoulder at the dark shadows of the forest. The stag was eating as usual. His cheeks bulged with leaves he had stripped from nearby bushes and his jaw ground back and forth. It made me angry to see him so complacent while I jumped at every noise.

I drained the remaining drops of the tea from my mug and repacked it, along with the black pot. On impulse, I withdrew Severin's sword from the rolled bundle and tucked it through my belt. Raising my arms to adjust Severin's cloak, I could not help but smell myself. I wrinkled my nose at the rank odor of sweat and smoke. I examined my hands and saw the fingernails, cracked and bleeding, grime trapped under them. The backs of my hands were stained dark brown, lined with little scratches and dirt. Where I had once soft white palms, there were now raw blisters and a few thick, yellow calluses. I touched my face and then quickly drew my hand away. No time for vanity, I said sharply to myself, and kicked dirt on the fire, gutting it.

In the dark I laid the remnants of Severin's leather jerkin across the stag's back. I held his neck and swung my legs in a smooth practiced motion over the top of his back. Settling myself on his back, I felt the muscles in my thighs and knees, which had strengthened in the weeks of riding. I touched his flanks lightly to let him know I was ready. He started forward with his loping gait and I braced myself for the unsteady ride. I may never be much of a horseback rider, I consoled myself, but there was none better than I on a stag.

The forest at night was quiet except for the snapping of twigs beneath the stag's hooves. Though I had been edgy at the start, I soon grew drowsy, rocked by the stag's swaying back and the gentle brushing of trees against my thighs as we slipped through the forest. Twice I woke with a start, my head jerked up, as I caught myself leaning too far over the stag's side.

Day approached almost reluctantly and in the early morning, the sun hid behind a bank of clouds. Through half-closed eyes I saw the gray mist swirl wraithlike through the trees, blanketing the forest once again in fog. The stag snorted nervously and from time to time stopped and raised his head in alarm. A portion of me responded, sensing the danger in the fog. But there was something else in the air, as pervasive as the mist, that obscured my awareness. Try as I might, I couldn't think clearly. I was confused, aware only of a vague and mounting sense of sorrow.

The mist wrapped around me with icy fingers that snaked beneath my cloak and stole my warmth. My hair became soaked and droplets clung to my eyelashes. I shivered, and sweat from my fever chilled on my brow. My eyes burned as if sand scraped against the lids. My mouth was dry and I swallowed hard, trying to rid it of a stale taste.

The forest thickened, trees and bushes knotted together in a tangled web. Small streams of brackish water trickled on either side of the path. The path became wet and slippery, gradually turning into black mud that sucked at the stag's hooves. Leaves disappeared from the trees, exposing branches bent like crooked limbs. The mist hung as an ill-fitting garment on the lifeless forest. I passed two trees, their trunks crippled with burls. In the whorls of gnarled wood were faces, their features contorted with grief. The branches reached for me, begging me to take pity.

The stag stumbled in the mud, his narrow hooves struggling in the deepening mire. I gripped the soulstring so as not to fall and cried out as it scraped the blisters on my palms. Pain throbbed at my temples and down the back of my neck and shoulders. I rode hunched over the stag's neck, scarcely noting where we were traveling. Dazed with fatigue and hunger, I stared bleakly at the sea of gray mist. I frowned, suddenly distracted, as the thought entered me that I was no longer solid flesh. Traveling in the forest had changed me. I stared at my hands, seeing them pale and gray as the fog. I was fading, I thought, becoming transparent, and soon I would have no more substance than the tiny drops of water that formed the mist.

I started to cry big tears that rolled down my cheeks and were swept away by the mist. I didn't want to disappear. I was afraid of fading into the mist. A finger of fog pulled at the soulstring tighter, pain from the torn blisters sharpened my muddled senses. I shook my head as if to clear away the fog and stared wide-eyed. I could see nothing at all but the gray fog. I panicked and my pulse quickened with growing fear. With every beat, my head jumped with new pain. My vision blurred and I was blinded by the stabbing pain. The fog caressed me with a cold breeze and whispered in a sad, lonely voice: "Don't leave us, Magda, we need you. We'll care for you and take away your pain." It drew a hand across my neck, my cheek, and my fevered brow. I shivered violently at its touch, but the pain ceased in my head.

I took a shallow breath between clenched teeth and nudged the stag forward with my knees. The pain returned, throbbing as if in warning. I stopped the stag and held my head between my hands. Again the voice called out to me, changing with every pleading. "Stay, Magda, don't hurt us," Vooris seemed to speak to me. "Stay youngin',"—now it was Cook who called. "Help us, Magda," the thin cry of my sister Ilena. I looked up through the mist, the sense of sorrow overwhelming me. "I can't stay," I tried to say, but my lips only shaped the words and there was no sound.

Father had sent despair to follow me in the mist, and now when I weakened, it cast a shroud over me, wrapping me in desolation. I struggled, but every movement drew it tighter like a vise. "You will stay," the voice hissed. "You will join us at last." My strength was drained and resignation settled like a stone slab across my shoulders. My muscles went slack and my grasp on the soulstring halter became limp. I fell slowly to the muddy ground and surrendered to the nightmare sadness of the mist. The stag lowered his head and butted frantically against my lifeless shoulder. Again and again he tried to rouse me, but I didn't respond. I was fading, joining the mist, and the stag seemed a distant memory. I laid my head on the ground, not feeling the cold or the damp. I drew my knees up tight and numbly waited to disappear forever in the mist.

From afar came the eerie baying of Moravian hounds. I watched through unblinking eyes as the hounds appeared like ghostly demons stepping through the fog. They circled us, waiting impatiently, hackles raised and their eyes alive with yellow flames. Their lips curled back, and they snapped their jaws. In a remote corner of my being, the wildness awoke and prowled restlessly. It called to me to rise and flee. But the shroud of despair held me, and, though I heard the voice, I didn't heed its warning.

I was dimly aware of the stag, his front hooves planted over my curled body and his head down, ready for the attack. He stamped his hooves, and snorted defiantly at the hounds. One hound broke from the line and leaped at the stag's throat. The points of his antlers lifted, catching the hound and ripping a gash in its shoulder. The hound was thrown back. It yelped shrilly and disappeared into the fog. Another snarling hound attacked the stag. The stag reared up on his hindquarters and lashed out with a savage kick at the springing hound. It howled as the obsidian hooves crushed its chest. Blood splattered across my face and I blinked furiously as it stung my eyes. The hound collapsed on the muddy ground and turned its head to me. I stared into its eyes, the yellow flame still burning brightly. I could sense its broken body as if it were my own; feel the pain and terror of its dying. I groaned as its agony cut deep to my heart, tearing at the shroud that imprisoned me.

I used the pain to free myself and the shroud ripped apart, unable to contain the clamoring awareness. Clarity, sharp as the edge of a sword, returned to my senses. I knew the hardness of the wet ground beneath me, felt the coldness of the air, and sensed Father's hatred, palpable as the surrounding mist.

So Father, I thought, it's now. No more running away. The wildness clamored within me and I released it. The air crackled and exploded with blue light. It cast a circle of opalescent flames and the hounds drew back. Flames licked out, trying to catch the hounds. I heard them yelp and growl and smelled the odor of singed fur. I rolled out from under the stag's belly, and stood, trembling, as the wildness flooded me with power.

"Father," I screamed to the mist, "I'm waiting!"

Father's power seized me by the neck. My head snapped back and I was lifted by my throat off my feet; the breath was choked from me. The wildness shrieked in defiance. It raised my flailing arms and my hands blazed with silver talons. I raked and clawed at the sorcery gripping my throat. The talons lashed out with silver flames and I felt Father's power falter and weaken. I fell forward to the ground as the hands released me.

Back bent and kneeling on all fours, I sucked in jagged breaths. My chest burned with a searing pain and I held a hand to my bruised throat. I screamed as Father grabbed my hair and wrenched my neck. Then he slammed me into the ground and pressed his weight against my back. He pushed my face into the wet, yielding soil and I gagged as decayed leaves and mud were forced into my mouth. With angry desperation I fought back, pushing furiously against his weight. I succeeded in twisting my head a small ways to one side and spat out the dirt.

"I'll kill you, Father," I cried in a hoarse voice.

He answered me with mocking laughter and yanked my head back by the hair for an instant before he drove it into the mud again. Power gathered and multiplied within me, fed by hatred and rage. As I thrashed, the wildness roared and bared its fangs. It hungered for vengeance, and for destruction. It knew where to seek both. It burst forth, running in a streak of sapphire light on the cast threads of Father's sorcery, until it found the sorcerer's tower. I rolled in the mud and gasped as I felt it leap, smashing through the glass windows and landing on all fours before Father's startled figure. He drew back, shielding his eyes from the brightness, and conjured a wall of yellow flame to hide him.

I saw the room that had been hidden from me. Father's tower, the source of his learning, the heart of his power. I stalked the room, growling, as he hid within the curtain of fire. The room held nothing for me but the stale scent of withered leaves and the dust of ancient bones. Father stepped through his wall of yellow flames. Fire wreathed his head like autumn leaves and his face was white as chalk. He raised his hands and began to chant a spell. I turned and leaped through the jagged glass to the ground below. Looking up at the tower, my magic shifted. It moved like water, slipping over the surface of the stones, dipping into the cracks and crannies of the tower wall. Lying on the forest ground, I reached up and clenched my hand into a fist. The walls of the sorcerer's tower trembled. I tightened my fist harder and the mortar burst into tiny fragments. The stones crumbled and the walls peeled away like the skin of some delicate fruit. I heard Father's harsh scream as the walls swept him down amid their ruin. The wildness stepped back, roaring, and then fled from the tower, streaking back to me on Father's fading lines of power.

It found me in the forest and lifted me upright from the mud. I stumbled, feeling suddenly weak. The circle of opalescent flame dimmed. I looked out and saw the hounds back away, confused by the loss of Father's command. I cursed and reached for the stag's neck. Even before I had finished swinging my legs over his back, he was running, crashing through the dying forest. Father must still be alive, for his hounds remained.

The hounds bayed as they saw their quarry escape. They didn't need Father to command them now, they knew what was expected of them. Incited by the scent of prey in flight, eager for the hunt, they formed a pack and pursued us. They bayed loud and shrill and drove themselves like arrows through the thick underbrush. I flattened my body against the stag's back, trying to avoid the branches that cracked and splintered as the stag battered through the narrow openings between the misshapen trees.

I glanced up quickly and saw where the stag was heading. There, not far before us, the dense forest cleared into a wide, grassy glade. Beyond it, through the mist, I could see the sun shining. A flash of burnt orange passed me and the hounds ringed us on either side, trying to force the stag to change direction and retreat into the forest. The stag ignored them, and beneath my thighs, the muscles bunched as he increased his speed. Hooves drumming on the clearing soil, we careened toward the glade.

Close at his side the hounds leaped, jaws snapping at his haunches. Their attacks broke his stride, and he slowed to kick them back. As he bucked and kicked, I twisted my hand around the soulstring and fought to stay on his back. A hound charged from behind and attacked my leg, its black nose wrinkled back. I screamed at the yellow fangs about to bite my leg. I screamed again and tried to kick it away. The jaws snapped on Severin's trousers, narrowly missing the flesh of my calf. The hound crouched, growling and shaking his head savagely, to pull me down. The stag, hearing my screams, twisted his neck around and gored the hound. He lifted the shrieking hound, impaled on the tines, and flung it away. The stag bucked again, driving back the rest of the pack. His hind flanks coiled like a spring and then he bound away from the attacking hounds.

All I could hear was the baying of the hounds and the wind as it rushed past my bent head. I clenched my teeth, my muscles taut, anticipating an attack. Ahead I could clearly see where the forest ended, and beyond it lay an open field of yellowed grass. No one need have told me, for I knew. We had reached the Moravian border and on the other side was Thall. Father's hounds would not be able to follow us across the border.

"Come on," I shouted to the stag in encouragement. "We can make it! We're almost there! Come on, Severin!" The stag was panting, his head bobbing up and down as he ran. His neck and flanks were dark with sweat as he poured the last reserves of his strength into our flight.

As the stag reached the border, a hound attacked, throwing its body against the stag's withers and sinking its fangs into the muscled flesh. It clung tenaciously, its back paws raking against the soft underbelly as the stag lifted up on his hindquarters in rage. The stag bellowed and tossed his head wildly, trying to gore the hound with his antlers. Behind us I could hear more hounds coming. In a matter of moments we would be surrounded again.

I pulled Severin's sword free with one hand and brought it down on the hound. The flat of the blade smashed against the hound's skull but still it clung, snarling, to the stag's shoulder. I swung again, this time catching the hound across the neck with the edge of the sword. The blade cut deeply and blood sprayed over the stag's withers. The stag reared back, terrified by the scent of the hound's blood. I lurched sideways and dropped the sword as I grabbed the soulstring to keep from falling. The dying hound fell beneath the stag's hooves. The stag reared back once more and, as he came down, kicked out his hind legs and sprang forward.

At the edge of the forest's shadow, the stag leaped into the air. Severin had said there was a wall at the border between Moravia and Thall, but he didn't say it was invisible. As we entered it felt thin but resilient, like the inner skin of the pomegranate separating layers of ruby-red seeds. It resisted our passage, slowing the stag even in the midst of his leap. Then I felt it tear open along a seam and we passed through, tumbling downward into sunlit fields. The stag landed heavily on his forelegs and his head pitched forward. The sudden jolt made me loose my grip on the soulstring and I flew over his neck, landing in the grass, the wind knocked from my chest.

I sat up, stunned. Yellow stars danced in my eyes; my side ached where I had fallen. I coughed painfully as the air seemed to refuse to enter my lungs. Exhaling harshly first, I was able then to draw in deep breaths. I stared at Moravia's shadowy border, edged with fading yellow stars. The hounds had disappeared and I saw only the leafless trees, their branches shaking tremulously. I sat in the grassy fields of Thall, whole and alive.

"Free," I whispered hoarsely, "free." Though I said it, I couldn't imagine what it meant for me. Bewildered, I turned to the stag and saw him standing in the field, legs trembling and the wound in his shoulder bleeding badly. He raised his head, sniffing the air, and then, exhausted, he dropped his head again. Fear for the stag's life made me forget about myself and I rushed to his side.

I took down the rolled cloak from my back and unfolded it. Using the ragged scraps of my shift and a little water from the skin, I began to gently wipe away blood from the wound. The stag allowed me to cleanse the wound but his shoulder muscles twitched and rippled and he shifted uneasily at my touch. The wound was a ring of angry red marks where the hound's fangs had punctured the flesh. Alongside of the ring the hound's claws had left long, ugly gashes. They were nasty looking, but shallow, and I knew they would heal quickly. I worried about the deeper wounds, fearing disease carried in the hound's bite. After washing the wound I pressed firmly against it until it stopped bleeding. Then I smeared generous amounts of the healing salve, hoping it would soothe the pain and aid the wound.

When I finished doing what little I could, I lifted the stag's bowed head between my hands. He breathed warm air down my shirt and the fine hairs of his muzzle tickled my chest. I stroked his nose and cheek and his pink tongue flicked out and wet my chin, cheeks and forehead. I squeezed my eyes shut to this friendly cleaning, but continued to smile. He stopped then and cocked his head to one side. Deep brown eyes gazed steadily into mine. Suddenly, I was seized with longing as I stared back, seeing Severin's eyes and imagining Severin's face. I swallowed at a lump in my throat, trying not to think of how much I wanted to see Severin's smile, to hold him, and hear him speak again to me. I sighed and looked away, unable to meet the stag's gaze anymore.

"Can you travel or should we rest here?" I asked the stag, looking out at the rolling fields of Thall.

As if to answer he began to walk, limping slightly on the injured side. I hesitated, but he looked back at me as if to say, "Aren't you coming?" I laughed and, rolling up the cloak with our supplies, followed after him.

We walked slowly through the fields, our legs cutting a swath through the long grass. It was peaceful after our frantic escape. The wind rustled through the grass with a pleasant, reedy sound and the afternoon sun was warm. It seemed the land greeted us like lost children and my spirit lightened as we traveled. I felt as a child might who, when waking from a nightmare, finds comfort in her mother's arms, the terrifying images diminished by a loving embrace. I had awoken at last from Moravia's dark dreams and found hope in Thall's bright sun.

The fields gradually gave way to a gentle slope covered with yellow gorse and dark green heather crowned with purple and magenta blossoms. At the top of the slope, the land turned down into a small ravine in which a stream trickled with fresh water. We hobbled down and then up the other side. Under my feet pebbles broke free and skittered down the ravine. At the top of the ridge I was able to see across a broad stretch of land. I groaned loudly when I saw that all of Thall appeared broken and seamed by hills and ravines. The landscape rolled up and down like the waves of a green ocean. My thighs and calves were already aching from our short climb. The stag nudged my shoulder, impatient to be off. I took a deep breath and followed, trying to fool myself into thinking the land was flat.

We stopped walking in the late afternoon. We came upon a rare stand of trees huddled together like crones gossiping on the crest of a hill. Below was a little stream that babbled cheerfully over the stones. I sat down heavily at the base of the trees, closed my eyes, and rested. Where I sat the roots of the trees protruded like bony feet through the soil. It wasn't comfortable but I didn't care. I pulled the water skin from my shoulder to drink and cursed as I discovered it was nearly empty. I'd have to get up again, walk down the ravine, fetch water, and then climb back up again. It seemed so much work for just a little water. I sat there awhile, tired and thirsty, waiting until I had gathered enough strength to stand. With a weary sigh I got up at last and headed down the ravine.

Moving gingerly down the stony descent into the ravine, the stag joined me to collect water. His hooves scraped the rocks, which were slippery with moss and wet from the spray of the stream. At the stream I plunged my face into the water. It was cold and clean and I opened my mouth to feel it moving deliciously across my tongue, taking away the stale taste. I pulled my head out and shook the water off my face and wiped my cheeks with my hands. The stream cleared and I saw my reflection in the rippling water.

I stared at it, surprised, as if it were a stranger, and was tempted to look over my shoulder to see if someone else stood behind me. Surely, I thought confused, that can't be me. I was dirty and ragged. My hair, once a curly, light auburn, hung n dark matted coils tied back by a filthy strip of rag. There was black soot smeared across my cheeks and under my eyes, like a raccoon startled by daylight. Blood speckled my chin and neck, and my skin was creased with grime.

I took a handful of sand and began to scrub away the grime. I itched, suddenly aware of my filthy clothes and un-washed body. I longed for a bath and a clean shift. Even scrubbed, my face was changed, different. I was no longer moon faced and round, but thin and peaked. My cheekbones curved into high arches and my chin drew to a sharp point. My skin was sallow, the freckles a faded brown, and the dark circles remained beneath my eyes. I leaned closer to stare at the image, curious as the strange apparition in the water did the same. I felt bewildered, uncertain of myself, and touched my face and neck, fascinated as the reflection copied my movements.

I stripped off my bodice and Severin's shirt, moving the soulstring from one wrist to the other as I did so, and washed my torso with the sand. I scrubbed my neck and arms and tried to remove the dirt trapped beneath my jagged fingernails. The cold water made me shiver, but I felt better for being cleaner. As the muddy water cleared, I was surprised again by the reflection of my body. My shoulders were thin and bony, the collarbones prominent ridges at the base of my throat. My skin was tight over ribs that stuck out along my sides, and my belly above the navel was shrunken. My arms, though thin, were not spindly but knotted with long, firm muscles that flexed as I moved. My breasts, which had always been rather small, suddenly seemed fuller and in the fading twilight, I saw blue veins that snaked across the pale skin. How odd, I thought; how could I have changed so much? I continued to touch and stroke myself, my hands dipping in the hollow of my stomach and then rising to rest on a little bulge beneath my navel.

So absorbed was I discovering this new self that I forgot about the stag. I jumped with a shriek when he put his cold, wet muzzle to the back of my neck and licked my shoulder.

I turned sharply, one arm draped protectively over my breasts and smacked him lightly on the nose.

"Stop that!" I cried. "You scared the life out of me!"

The stag snorted and drew back, alarmed at the angry tone of my voice.

I flushed red, realizing that I was embarrassed by my nudity, even in front of the stag. It had been so long since I had last undressed, that it seemed a perversely shameful act. I reached out and rubbed the stag's cheek with my free arm. He gave me a chaste lick on the cheek and then turned away in search of something to eat. I looked at him, daintily tearing moss from the rocks, and sighed deeply. I dressed again, tying up the laces of my bodice over Severin's dirty shirt.

"Come on," I said to the browsing stag, "let's finish making camp and get some rest. I am so tired I could sleep for days." We climbed up the ravine heading toward the trees, their strange silhouettes black against a deep blue sky. Stars sparkled between the branches like the opening of spring blossoms.

Later that night, my back leaning against the stag as we curled by the fire, I thought of my father and our last confrontation. My magic was my own again, though I had no control over when and how it chose to appear. But, did I trust my power? No, not at all. I shook my head, hearing again Father's cry as the tower crumbled over him. It was power summoned by rage, fed on violence, and capable only of destruction. That was the nature of Moravian sorcery, and, like a river flowing in one direction, I would never have been able to change that. I didn't want the power to use me as it had used Father and all my ancestors before me. It was, I admitted, seductive, as all power must be. Tearing down the tower had filled me with cruel pleasure. It was not a feeling I wished to become accustomed to. Staring at the clear night sky of Thall I felt relieved, believing that, like Father's sorcery, mine wouldn't work in Thall. It was a part of Moravia and the past, and I hoped fervently that it remained there.

Dry and warm, huddled in Severin's cloak, I stared absently at the moon, Hag's Moon again, hanging like a tooth in the sky. Beside it was the long shape of the plow, and I rested just beneath the bright twinkle of the blade's star. I heard a killdeer rise and call out to its mate in the distance. Crickets hummed in the grass, the last song of summer before the weather turned cold. I settled into a peaceful sleep, and if I dreamed at all, I don't remember. When I woke, the sun was lighting my face, and in the early dew, I smelled the sweet, salty air of Thall. I sat up slowly, feeling truly rested for the first time since I had left Moravia Castle. I threw off my cloak, stretched my arms high above my head, and yawned widely.

But when I rose to my haunches and stirred the coals of my fire, I was gripped by nausea and a sour taste flooded my mouth. I doubled over, unable to hold back the violent retching. So, I thought wearily when the retching finally ceased, I've not left everything behind in Moravia. I steadied myself with effort and brewed the last mug of tea. As always the tea soothed the gnawing in my stomach. It washed away the bitter taste in my mouth and eased the ache in my muscles. From the water skin, I poured a handful of water and splashed it on my flushed face.

It was time to leave. I repacked the few items I had left and stopped to examine the stag's wound. The blood had dried around the gashes and this I carefully washed off. I probed the wound gently, looking for signs of swelling. The wound had reddened in the night and the flesh around it felt very warm. I cursed under my breath. The warm flesh and the redness were the early signs of disease. I didn't know how long the stag could endure before the wound proved fatal, but I knew we were weak from our journey and that chances were, it wouldn't be long. I added a new coat of salve to the wound, hoping that it would at least keep the gashes from reopening as the stag moved.

"Severin, are we far from Arlensdale?" I asked. The stag raised his head to the morning breeze as if tasting the odors of home.

I sighed heavily. We needed help soon; we needed to be in Arlensdale. Images of Teren and Nar flashed briefly and I worried if they had returned. And Theda, Severin's mother? asked a voice. I wondered how this woman might regard me if I came to her, two of her sons dead and the third transformed into a stag. Severin said she was tough, selfish, perhaps like Father. Would I be welcomed there? I shrugged the question away as best I could. Welcomed or not, I had to go to Arlensdale. Severin's life depended on it. What Theda might think of me, or I of her, was not important at the moment.

Suddenly, my stomach grumbled, and despite the nausea, I wanted a piece of bread, newly baked and hot from the oven. I drooled as I thought of it, its taste almost real on my tongue. I imagined cutting slices of the bread and spreading it thickly with butter and strawberry jam. I was assailed then by memories of the smells and tastes of Cook's kitchen. They settled on my tongue like a feast of delicacies: bilberry tarts that dribbled blue stains down my chin, milky-sweet custards, soups with cream, and apples with slices of sharp, white cheese.

As we continued traveling up and down the heather-covered hills, I let my imagination run wild, thinking only of food. My palate was curiously unpredictable. Some dishes I imagined, even those that had once been my favorites, seemed suddenly unappetizing. Racks of lamb and fowls in brown sauce were unpalatable to my fickle imagination, and thinking of the smell of roast beef with garlic and braised onions brought a queasy fluttering to my stomach. Surrounded by images of delirious feasting, I forgot to worry about Arlensdale and Theda. Throughout the day, trudging through heather and gorse, I made a list of all the foods I promised myself I would eat as soon as I arrived at Severin's home.

NINE

THROUGHOUT THE DAY we traveled alone across peaceful and rugged countryside. I began to worry about finding Arlensdale. Severin had given me no instructions beyond reaching Thall and I hadn't met anyone or even found a homestead where I might ask directions. The stag, however, appeared to have no doubts whatsoever about where he was headed. He led with determination, climbing up and down over the heather-covered hills. We wandered through fallow fields overrun with green grass and crowned with purple vetch and yellow daisies. I startled a killdeer nesting in the grass. She flew up with a noisy shriek, the fluttering black-and-white bands of her feathers drawing my attention away from her nest. By a small stream I saw a red snake resting in the sun on a flat stone. High up above, drifting in the wind, was a kestrel. He followed us awhile, and then I saw him dive after prey and disappear to eat, his curiosity forgotten.

Sometimes we stumbled over the remains of old farms, the stone fences broken and scattered in the thick grass. I could just make out the cornerstones and outline of the house. They formed little circles of stones that held the sun's warmth and cradled us from the wind when we stopped to rest. Though the stone was heavy, the houses seemed fragile, like the cracked shell of an egg.

I grew tired quickly and needed to rest often, sometimes dozing off even as I sat talking to the stag. How long has it been since you've eaten? I asked myself as I started falling asleep for the third or fourth time that day. Had it been two days or three? I could only remember drinking Severin's tea. The fever was still with me—that I knew from my hot, sticky face and the nausea that gripped me from time to time. Soon you must find something to eat, I scolded myself; soon, answered a sleepy voice, and I thought no more about it as I napped.

We spent another night camped in the remains of a farmhouse. There I found an old herb garden run to seed amidst the stones and managed to pick a handful of useful plants. The lamb's quarters and sorrel were tough and astringent, and the day lily roots had a musty taste. I tried to eat the garlic, but after one bite abandoned it, repulsed by the pungent smell. I picked a handful of mint and the scrubby leaves of a wild thyme plant and made tea. I wouldn't have called the meal satisfying. I ate out of a sense of duty. But I was sick of foraging, sick of eating green things with stringy textures, and the whole meal rested uncomfortably in my queasy stomach, floating, I imagined, like a patch of bog plants.

In the morning, I began vomiting again. I felt weak and shaky but better for having rid myself of the night's meal. Had I poisoned myself in the forest, or was this Father's doing after all? I wondered desperately. I reached for the pouch hoping for one more cup of Severin's tea, and found only a few dry flakes remaining. I drank a little water, but the few sips I took flowed like lead in my gullet and increased the feeling of nausea. I stood awkwardly, unable to find my balance. Beneath my feet, the ground pitched and rolled like a rough sea in a storm. I clung to the soulstring for support as the hills dipped and swayed. I waited, eyes closed, until the ground steadied itself. Then I opened my eyes slowly, relieved to find the land calm again.

I checked the wound on the stag's shoulder and groaned when I saw how swollen it had become. Green puss was oozing from the ring of puncture marks and I had to brush away flies that buzzed excitedly about the wound. The stag twisted his neck to look at me. His eyes were cloudly, a white film forming at the corners and his nose, usually black and glistening, was dry. I felt angry and frustrated, and wished there was something else I could do to heal the stag. I washed the wound gently, wincing as the stag's head bobbed up and down nervously. I smeared it with another coating of salve, and prayed silently that we'd reach Arlensdale soon. Another day and night on the trail, and what my father had attempted to do to us in Moravia would succeed in Thall.

We started climbing across the hills, the stag limping heavily. I stumbled after him, lurching through the heather, blinking furiously each time the ground appeared to sway and threatened to rise up before my face. We stopped often, the stag just standing amidst the heather and I drinking sips of water and trying not to vomit. The fall sun was warm and our shadows long with the last days of summer. Around us, a gentle breeze caressed our faces, bringing with it the salt air of the sea.

I was staring glumly at my legs lifting heavily through the heather when I heard the bleating of sheep and the sharp bark of a dog. The stag and I stopped, our heads raised warily, as over the crest of a hill a small herd of wooly sheep came bounding toward us. They were followed by two black dogs, running behind and nipping at their heels to keep them together in a tight pack. The stag stamped his hooves and snorted in alarm. The sheep saw us and, bleating wildly, ran off in several different directions. As soon as the dogs saw the stag, they ignored the sheep and began barking at us, taking care to stay just beyond the range of the stag's antlers.

Someone whistled three short blasts and the dogs streaked back up the hill. A shepherd waiting on the hill, one hand resting on his crooked staff, the other shielding his eyes from the bright sun as he stared at us.

"Quiet, dogs!" he commanded as his dogs continued to bark. He said nothing else, just stood there, staring.

I walked up the hill slowly, the stag stepping cautiously at my side. I stopped within talking distance, trying to catch my breath.

"Good day," I said.

He nodded back at me. The dogs barked again and he shushed them with a hand. They sat near his heels and growled softly to each other. He was an old man, with a wrinkled face, grizzled with a stubby gray beard. But his eyes

were a clear blue and his glance darted keenly back and forth
between the stag and me.

"Could you tell me where I might find Arlensdale?" I
asked.

One bushy eyebrow lifted in surprise and he pointed to a
hill that swept down toward a copse of trees.

"Down yonder, that way, then. Through those trees and
over t' hill."

"Is it far?" I looked where he pointed, seeing only more
fields and hills.

"Nay, won't take long."

"Thank you, thank you very much," I replied excitedly.

He shrugged, staring intently at us. I started to feel uncomfortable and then annoyed. I straightened my bodice and
brushed off some of the little bits of heather that clung to
Severin's trousers. The shepherd watched as if fascinated by
my every movement.

"Well, I guess we'll be going now," I said evenly. "Good
day, then."

"Aye, good day, to *you*," he answered.

"Come on," I said to the stag, and we trudged up the hill
past the shepherd and his growling dogs. At the top of the hill,
I sneaked a glance behind me and saw him, still staring at us.
Furious, I turned back and concentrated on reaching the copse
of trees. "Strange place, this," I muttered, though I knew full
well it was I who must have seemed strange.

We reached the trees, a gnarled clutch of scrub oaks, and I
had to sit and rest. I was hot and sticky, and heather blossoms
trapped inside my shirt prickled. I tried to get them out but
couldn't, and settled for scratching instead. I lay back on the
grass, looking up at the gentle swaying of the trees. I closed
my eyes wearily and dozed. A fly buzzed in my ear and
landed on my cheek. I wanted to shoo it away but my arm felt
too heavy to lift, and soon I didn't care as I was fast asleep.

The stag woke me, licking my face, and refused to stop
even when I tried to wave him away with my arm. I didn't
want to wake just then. Please, I begged silently to him, just
let me sleep a little more. But he was insistent and at last I was
forced to sit up and open my eyes before he would stop.

"There, I'm awake. Are you happy?" I snapped angrily.

The stag looked at me with dull eyes, a sticky fluid drain-

ing at the corners. He huffed a breath of moist air and docilely
licked my hand.

I regretted my harsh words. "I'm sorry," I said, shaking my
head and rubbing his cheek to apologize. "I don't know what's
come over me. I'm so bad-tempered now. You're right," I
sighed, "it's time to be going." I stood wearily, stretched my
aching back, and then started the long climb up another hill.

When we reached the crest of the hill I stopped, amazed at
the beauty of the valley spreading out below. There were
many small fields, pieced like a peasant's quilt and seamed
together at the edges with stone fences. Some fields were the
faded green of pastureland dotted with white sheep grazing in
the afternoon sun. Others were brown and yellow where the
remains of the year's harvest were being raked and stacked. I
squinted in the sunlight and saw two men working, one bending with a rake to collect the drying hay, tossing it up to where
another waited atop a wagon. Beside me, the stag lifted his
head to the air and bellowed. Then, to my astonishment, he
bolted, running toward the haymakers. I had no choice but to
follow, running as fast as I could, so as not to fall too far
behind him.

We weren't far from the hay field, me slipping and tumbling down the slope of the hillside, when I realized I knew
the men. My heart jumped and, like the excited stag, I tried to
run even faster to reach them. I was sure I recognized Teren's
broad back as he bent over and pulled together a large armful
of the golden hay. When he stood to toss the hay up to the
wagon with his rake I was certain. I couldn't mistake the
square cut of his bearded face or the portly shape of his belly.
On top of the wagon I heard a familiar voice cursing as the
hay landed on him. Standing amidst the piled hay, Nar
brushed it off his head, spitting out dust and chaff.

"Can you be more careful, then, passing that hay up?" he
shouted to his older brother.

"Can't you work any faster?" Teren retorted. "I don't want
to be all night loading this hay. There's better things I'd be
doing with my time."

"Such as spending it with that red-haired lass with the
big—" Nar started to say and was stopped by a sheaf of hay
that flew up and landed squarely in his face.

"Teren! Nar!" I shouted from the next field, frantically
waving my arms over my head to get their attention. They

stopped their arguing and looked around, clearly puzzled. "Teren!" I repeated, breathless, for the stag was dragging me faster than I could run and I was trying not to trip and fall. Teren turned all the way around and when he caught sight of me, arms waving over my head as I stumbled down the hill dragged by a stag, he stopped short, unable to comprehend the spectacle.

"Teren, it's me, Magda!" I croaked out, realizing that I was an unexpected sight and that he might not recognize me. When he heard me call my name, he threw down his rake and ran to meet me. I stopped running then and dropped to the ground, my limbs too weak to carry me farther, my breath coming in hard, short gasps. The stag also stopped, his big chest heaving as if this run had cost him the last of his strength.

Teren reached me at last, huffing with the effort of his uphill run.

"Gods, Magda, are you all right, then? You look awful!" he blurted out.

Happy as I was to see him alive and well, it wasn't the greeting I had anticipated and I flared up angrily. "No, I'm not all right!" I said between broken breaths. "I'm sick with fever, I haven't been able to eat anything for days, and I'm exhausted." I was shouting the words before I had finished speaking.

Nar came up close behind but Teren yelled to him over his shoulder. "Fetch Mother—and Grandda! Tell them Magda's here and be quick about it!"

Nar didn't hesitate, but pivoted and continued running in the opposite direction to the other side of the field. Teren approached me slowly, eyeing the stag and the pointed tines of his antlers.

"Magda, forgive me. It was a stupid thing to say. It's just I was surprised to see you, and with that—that stag. Would you like something to eat, then?"

I must have glared at him like a starving wolf because he backed away quickly, not waiting for my answer.

"Wait here and I'll get you something to eat and drink." He went to the wagon and fetched a bundle off the buckboard.

I sat on the grass, not wanting to cry, but so weary that it seemed the only thing worth doing. Teren reappeared and handed me a chunk of fresh bread. I took it, holding it like a rare and precious jewel, and marveled at its golden crust, dusted with flour. Then I held it to my nose and sniffed its yeasty perfume. I took a small bite and, as I chewed it, tears brimmed in my eyes. They spilled over and ran down my cheeks in dirty tracks and off my chin. I sat there, crying and clutching the piece of bread to my chest.

"There, there, don't cry, then," Teren said, patting me on the shoulder. "It's all right. Go on now, eat," he urged.

But I couldn't, for once the tears had started, they were quickly followed by choking sobs that grew into loud anguished cries. My shoulders shook and my ears ached with the sound of my crying. Teren sat back on his heels, unable to console me or stop the flood of emotion.

After a time, I quieted myself, and little by little regained control of my emotions. I shuddered and gulped in air like a child settling down after a hard cry. Teren spoke in a low voice.

"Magda, I'm sorry for what we did to you, Nar and I, in the forest. I don't know how we let ourselves be fooled so. When we realized our mistake, we circled back and tried to find you and Severin. We searched everywhere, calling, but it was useless. As it was, it took us several days to find the trail leading back to Thall. We took it, hoping that we'd meet up with you."

I was staring at my lap, my eyes swollen from weeping, but I could hear the contrition in his voice and knew that he blamed himself for abandoning us. I was about to answer when a woman's voice stopped me.

"Now's not the time to ask for forgiveness, Teren. Can't you see she's ill?"

I looked up and saw a woman standing with Nar and an old man who carried a small leather bag tied with a beaded cord at his waist. She had a broad face, deep brown from the sun, and her white hair was pulled back into a long, simple braid. In her earlobes winked silver earrings; the bright blue of their stones matched the eyes that were staring steadily at me. Like the men she wore trousers and a light leather jerkin for riding, though her white shirt was embroidered about the collar and cuffs. The stag edged closer to sniff her shoulder and hair. She waited patiently, letting him smell her, and even opened her palm to let the stag lick its surface.

"Give me a cloth and some water," she said in a husky voice.

Nar gave her one and she knelt and poured water over the cloth. Then she handed it to me. I took it, murmuring thank-yous, and wiped away the dirty tearstains on my face. When I was done she offered her hand to help me up and I grasped it. I was pained by the familiar feel of the large hand, dry with the rough surface of calluses. Severin's hands, I thought, and Severin's face, as I looked at the strong, clean jawline and straight nose. But she had none of Severin's warmth and I saw resentment and mistrust in her appraising stare.

I wasn't much to look at, pale and worn, eyes red with weeping. Glancing over at Teren, I could imagine what he had told her about me. But I stared back, head tilted upward to meet her gaze.

"I am Theda, clan mistress of Arlensdale, and Severin's mother."

She said the words importantly, as if laying claim to a noble title. My back stiffened.

"Magda, of Moravia," I answered, and waited for her to continue.

"The farseer dreamed of your coming. We've sent people to the border every day in the hopes of finding you." She gave the stag a puzzled frown. Obviously the farseer hadn't said anything about him. She motioned the old man to draw near. He was hobbled and bent looking but his movements were spry and quick. "Sefert is a healer," she said. "Let him hold your hands and he'll draw the fever out."

I thought it strange that she didn't ask about Severin. Perhaps she was being practical and considerate, by offering me assistance first, but something in her manner galled me. She treated me as if I were a child and I found it insulting.

"No, not me first," I spoke quickly. "The stag—"

"Of course we'll heal the stag, but in due time. We must see to you first," she answered, "and then you can tell us the news of Severin."

"You don't understand. The stag is Severin!" The words rushed out. "My father transformed him while we were in the woods. I brought him here to Arlensdale so that you could break the spell. He was bitten by hounds and badly posioned. Don't worry about me. It's Severin who needs your healing!"

Theda's brown face blanched at my words.

"How long," she asked in a tight voice, "has he been a stag?"

I thought back quickly to the changes in the moon I had seen, and answered, "At least a month, maybe more."

She swore softly and drew a hand across her face. "Too late," she murmured. "It is too late to save him."

"No!" I blurted, thinking she had misunderstood me, "he was only bitten a few days ago. Surely it's not too late to stop the poison?"

Sefert moved to the stag and touched him lightly on his long nose and cheek. The stag lifted his head and weakly licked the gnarled hand in response. Sefert looked at Theda silently, grief etching the old face. He turned back to the stag and rubbed a hand along the graceful arched neck. He stopped his hand above the wound to examine it. He touched the salve curiously, tasting it with a fingertip, and turned to me, a question on his face. I pulled the little pot from my pocket and showed him. He nodded in recognition and a sad, knowing smile appeared briefly. Then his hands fluttered before him but his voice remained silent.

At my elbow Theda explained, "Sefert doesn't speak words. But his hands say that you did well to use the salve. It has saved the stag's life."

The stag shifted restively and the muscles of his flank rippled with Sefert's light touch. I watched, fascinated, as Sefert rubbed his hands along the stag's neck and then the withers, willing the stag in a kind of trance. I had never seen a healer before; there were none in Moravia. Sefert laid his hands gently on the open wound and the stag stood quietly, almost unaware. Sefert closed his eyes and bent his head in concentration. Only the wind rustling the dry hay and the far-off bleats of sheep interrupted the silence.

Sefert's eyes suddenly snapped open and he gasped like a fish breaking the surface of the water. He drew his hands away from the wound with effort, as if they had become flesh of the stag and breaking contact caused him great pain. Nar steadied the old man, a hand cradling his elbow, and gave him a drink from a small leather flask. I looked at the wound, and was awed to see only pink streaks of clean, healthy scar tissue remaining.

"The wound is nearly gone!" I said, amazed. "You've

made him well again. Please," I asked Sefert, my hand clasped on his arm, "change him back now to Severin."

The old man looked at me with a sad expression and spread his hands wide in an empty gesture.

"That's impossible," Theda answered. "He's been a stag too long."

"No!" I protested, but she continued.

"It's not safe to be in animal form very long. The shape-shifters say that two instincts, animal and human, are balanced for a short time. The longer Severin stayed in the stag's form, the more the stag's instincts took over in order that the stag would survive in the woods. If he were to be changed back now, he would be an animal transformed into a human body, unable to understand what had happened to him. The stag in the human body would die of terror. He must be freed and allowed to live as he is, a stag."

"No!" I shouted, knowing in my heart that she had to be mistaken about Severin. "You are wrong! Severin is there, I know it. I can feel it. I could never have found my way out of Moravia without him. He led me here—isn't that proof enough?"

Theda stared, stony-eyed and unconvinced. Teren looked away, his lips pressed in a frown. Nar blinked rapidly, and chewed at the edges of his mustache. His hands opened and closed in tight fists. I became furious with them.

"You're condemning Severin to the life of an animal while he is still human enough to understand his imprisonment. You can't do that! I won't let you!" I turned quickly to jump on the stag's back and flee from Severin's family.

Theda moved swiftly, catching my arm and hauling me back. Her grip was fierce, digging into the flesh of my upper arm. She glared at me. "Do you think it's easy for me?" The blue eyes glittered like polished steel. "He was my son! He left here a man and now that man is dead." I twisted free of her grasp but froze when she drew a knife that she wore at her waist. She turned sharply from me and started to cut the soulstring that had bound Severin and me together during our journey.

I leaped at her, but Teren grabbed me and held me back. As I struggled, kicking and bucking against his grip, rage gathered and flowed like hot metal along the soulstring. Theda grasped the rope at the stag's neck to hold it steady while she cut, but the soulstring, burning with my anger, seared her hand and she snatched it away with a startled cry. She stepped back, waving the burned hand in the air, and turned to stare at me in bewilderment.

"A soulstring?" she asked, shocked. "Is this a soulstring?"

"Yes," I snarled in reply, twisting like a snake to free myself from Teren's hold.

"Oh, for Mara's sake, Teren!" Theda said and stamped her foot. "Let her go!" Teren released me and jumped back, arm over his head as I whirled around swinging my arms, hands curled into fists.

"Magda, wait, listen to me!" demanded Theda. Angrily I turned to face her. "When did Severin give you the soulstring?"

"The night before he was transformed. He showed me how to use it. Then he tied it to my wrist and said we were married. I used the soulstring to halter the stag because it was all I had. I didn't want to lose Severin in the forest."

Hope sprung suddenly into her eyes. "There's a chance, then. Through the soulstring Severin might have shared your thoughts, your feelings. If he did, then it's possible that he has remained human in spite of being shaped to a stag."

"I know he's there," I said firmly. "Please help him."

Then Theda regarded me gravely. "No one in Thall can change what was done in Moravia."

A coldness touched my spine and stabbed my heart.

"The power to undo this spell must lie with someone of Moravia. Teren has told me that you have magic but can't use it. Is that true, then?"

"Yes," I answered, "I've a talent for sorcery but I can't summon it. It comes when it will."

Theda lowered her gaze, frowning. "Maybe we can help with that part."

"My father's magic doesn't work in Thall. The hounds chasing us couldn't cross the border. How can you be sure that I will have any more success?"

Theda turned questioningly to Sefert. The old man answered at length with his hands.

"Sefert says that he thinks the soulstring has wedded your magic with Severin's," she told me. "Your talent is yours by birth, but the ability to use it here is yours by love. Severin offered you the soulstring and you accepted it. The land has to honor that commitment. It must accept you—even with Moravian magic."

"My magic answers only to rage. And when it comes it's violent and destructive," I whispered. "Would you have me summon something I can't control? Something that may destroy Severin, not save him?"

"And won't you at least fight for control of your power? When Severin's life depends on it?"

"I don't know how."

"Severin imprisoned within a beast, and a beast dwelling within you. Are you not both condemned already, then?" Theda said bitterly.

I didn't know what to say. She was right and yet I was afraid of the wildness, afraid to call it.

"You'll not do it alone, Magda," Teren said in a gentle voice. "We'll be here, to help any way we can."

I looked at the stag, thinking of Severin. Then I looked at the solemn faces of Severin's kin, and knew that no matter how frightened I was, I couldn't refuse. Sefert stared silently at the stag, and his face spoke of a terrible sadness: a healer unable to heal. "I'll try," I said in a small voice. "How should I begin?"

Theda nodded, her mouth a thin line. "First, let Sefert help you with the fever. The magic will take much of your strength."

Sefert came to me and I gave him my hands, resting them in his upturned palms. He smiled reassuringly, the faded brown eyes momentarily studying the edges of my face. Then he closed his eyes and concentrated. I felt his touch, feather soft on my skin, and then I was washed by a cool breeze. A moment later the buzzing in my ears faded and the nausea was gone. But I was disappointed when Sefert withdrew his hands. I still didn't feel right, as if the fever lingered, aching in my joints and lower back. Sefert opened his eyes and his smile split into a wide grin.

He turned to Theda and his hands moved rapidly, darting like birds in the air. As I watched, Theda's expression changed suddenly, her lips parting with surprise. Teren and Nar crowded closer, eagerly following the movement of Sefert's hands. I looked from one to the other with growing puzzlement.

"What is it? What's wrong?" I demanded.

Theda turned to me and I saw the hard lines of her face had softened. "You are well, Magda. You have a fever that most welcome with happiness. You are with child. Sefert says he has felt the life in you and that it's healthy and strong. With proper food and rest you'll feel better."

I stared back at her, speechless. It had never occurred to me that I might have been pregnant. I had thought only of dying, not of birth. My hands went to the rounded bulge beneath my navel, to hold it, curious at this unlooked-for sharing of my body.

"Magda, is it well with you?" Theda asked, concerned by my silence.

"Yes," I answered, and smiled. Though I was still weak from the journey, I felt strengthened by wonderment. I carried a child and that act seemed more powerful to me than all the sorcery in Moravia, than all the wildness within me. My heart beat faster and I felt my cheeks flush with impatience. My body was a tower of living stone, walls of flesh and sinew that sheltered new life. It was invincible and miraculous. That tower held my child and my heart and I knew that it was strong enough to contain my power. Within its walls, I would tame the wildness.

"Help me call the magic," I said to Theda.

She nodded and pressed my hands firmly between her palms.

We stood silently, the sun casting a long shadow over Theda's shoulder. Then I saw the fields of Thall spin slowly at first and then faster, the rolling hills stretching into threads of light. I drew a long, slow breath and my back arched. The threads of light lengthened and thinned until at last they vanished and, around us, I felt the web of Thall pulled away.

Before me, Theda changed. Her silvery hair unwound itself from the braid and swept across my face like the beating of wings. Blackness spilled over the flowing white hair, and spread a stain over her face. She turned her head to the side and her profile stretched impossibly long.

Strong hands held mine but still I was lost, frightened in the unfamiliar landscape that settled around us, changing even as Theda continued to change. As in a dream, I had no sense of my physical self and yet I was everywhere in the odd forest to which we had now come.

A cold, bitter wind touched us. Theda nodded her head

impatiently, and stamped with one black hoof. A mane of blue-black streamed along the arch of her neck as she began to gallop. The path was dark and thick with trees. I could smell the dank, musty soil, see the clods of dirt tossed behind us as she ran. The path twisted like a labyrinth and I heard the steady pulse of her hooves as she ran, undaunted by its dark turns. She wedged her body through tangled briars, trampled yellowed bracken, and leaped over the fallen trees.

She came to a broken tower. I knew the place though I had never seen it. It was the prison Father had built within me to hide my magic. A strip of wall was torn open, exposing the spiral staircase like the interior of a snail's shell. She scrabbled over crumbling stones choked with weeds and powdery dust. Only then did she stop. Her nostrils flared and she snorted, smelling danger. She raised her head and neighed shrilly. From within the ruins came a shrieking cry that ended in a snarl. Her ears pricked forward and she pawed the stones.

I saw the wildness where it hid amidst the fractured tower. It hunched against a gray wall, prowling slowly along the unbroken rim of the tower. As it walked, it gathered power to itself like inhaling deep breaths of air. It bristled at the intrusion and it flexed bright claws that gleamed diamond hard. Its eyes shone with blue flame and its fur crackled in a sapphire light. It perched above her, watching as the horse stepped closer to the broken tower.

It coiled tightly, ears flattened against its skull, and then leaped.

"Theda!" I screamed, and heard the crack of lightning. I tried to pull away but somewhere in distant Thall Theda's hands gripped mine fiercely. In the forest she reared up on her haunches and twirled about to face the wildness.

It snarled, fangs white, and crouched low on the ground. It was ready to spring. I lunged for it, clasping it tightly around the neck to keep it from springing. It twisted its head savagely, the burning eyes blinding me. It roared and hissed but I refused to let go.

At the drumming of hooves its head snapped forward again. The black horse bolted, galloping over the stones and disappearing into the forest. Suddenly the wildness ignored me and began to pursue. I clung to its back like a burr as it hurtled over the stones and into the underbrush.

She ran before us, the black flanks shifting in and out of

the forest shadows. The wildness followed, its fury pushing it
to greater speed. But she was too swift, galloping always
ahead, leading us farther away from the broken tower. The
wildness crisscrossed through the underbrush, hoping to cut
her off as she turned on the winding path. Twice it nearly
caught her, running alongside her hind flank, its body bunched
to leap. But she twisted away sharply, bounded through the
brush, and foiled its attempts.

The horse was tiring, her pace slowing and her breathing
labored. Foam collected at her mouth and her neck shone with
sweat like oiled wood. The wildness sensed her weakening
and surged forward. Back bent, its hind legs meeting its front,
it stretched out its forelegs and tore up the distance between
them. It was close, matching its pace to the tired horse and
waiting until it was ready.

It snarled, victorious; extending its silver claws, it leapt at
her haunch.

"No!" I commanded and shoved Theda away. I heard her
cry out and heard the shrill neighing of the horse as it disappeared from the forest. I clung to the wildness as it hung in the
air, and pulled it down. We landed hard on the ground, locked
in a furious embrace. I screamed at it and it hissed and spat as
we fought. We rolled and crashed through the bracken. I
scrambled over its back and grabbed its neck, forcing the
wildness to stand erect on two legs. It fought me, lunging
forward and slashing the air with clawed hands.

I was breathing hard, grunting with the effort of holding it.
But I tightened my grasp on its neck and shook it fiercely.
"Enough! Be Still!" I shouted. It howled and then ceased
struggling. Warily, I released my hold and it consented grudg-
ingly to remain upright. I swallowed thickly and looked
around, uncertain where to go next. I saw the flickering of a
tiny flame farther down the darkened path. We walked, the
wildness at my side, toward the light.

I stopped when I saw him, waiting beside an overhanging
tree, the small flame flickering in his open palm. He was
much younger and leaner. His hair was black and thick with
curls and his face unbearded. He smiled at me, the light playing on his smooth cheeks as he passed the flame from hand to
hand. I stared at it, mesmerized, unable to look away.

"Better, then," he said, nodding at the wildness standing
erect. It growled at him, indignant and resentful.

"Do you know me?" he asked, and stepped forward, still tossing the flame gently from hand to hand.

"Teren," I answered, surprised at the low rumbling of my voice.

He nodded, pleased. "I've come to fetch you. Will you walk?"

"Yes," I said and stepped beside him, staring at the flame. I saw it wasn't a flame but a light from a long shard of crystal. It glowed, opalescent, casting a circle of colored light. He tossed it aloft and it floated like a lantern above us, lighting the way.

"Is it far?" I asked anxiously.

"Nay. The way grows shorter. Quickly now, Severin waits."

The wildness growled, and flattened its ears again. It bristled, hackles raised along the neck. It lifted its head and sniffed, catching the scent of the border and something else. I smelled it too, a sickly sweet stench like carrion. It turned my stomach and I gagged.

I faltered and my hold weakened. The wildness burst into blue fire. It scorched the trees and blackened the soil. Teren fell back, moaning, an arm drawn over his face, his light diminished in the curling blue flames.

"Flee!" I shouted to him, "flee!"

I didn't see him for the wildness possessed me and began to run. Head thrust forward, its arms slashed the air as it lengthened its stride. I felt the moist leaves beneath my feet and cold mist sweep across my face. We raced to the border and I saw the opening between the trees and the yellow fields beyond. The air hummed loudly with buzzing of insects and the stench grew more powerful.

We catapulted into the fields, the wildness pitching its head forward and tucking its body to somersault in the grass. It cast me out and I fell, tumbling down a hill through yellow grass. I threw an arm out to stop myself falling. I stood angrily. The wildness was there, standing and watching from the crest of the hill where it had tossed me. It gave a deep throaty laugh and sauntered slowly down the slope toward me.

Shimmering in a blue haze, it extended a hand toward me and I took it. I gasped as I beheld its face behind the curtain of light. It was my face, thin and feral, with eyes of lapis lazuli staring into mine. It laughed again and I saw the small fangs that bordered a row of even white teeth.

She tilted her head in the direction of the hill and I looked up, seeing nothing. She pulled me up after her, eyes scanning the crest of the hill eagerly. At the top she stopped and looked at me questioningly, head cocked to one side. It was a challenge and I nodded in reply. She turned back to the hillside and pointed. I hesitated, and then looked out, down the sweep of grass to where the forest's edge touched the field.

We were not alone. Slipping between the trees into the field was a line of men. They stood silently, their shapes waving back and forth with the grass like tall, misshapen reeds. They waited for me to join them. The wildness nudged me forward, a hand pushing firmly between my shoulder blades. I stumbled and, as I caught myself, felt the vague tremors of fear.

Compelled by the wildness, I approached. Agitated flies buzzed in little black clouds, and the stench was overpowering. We stopped close to the men and a strangled cry caught in my throat. I stared wide-eyed, knowing them at last: my suitors, or what remained of the men my father had condemned to death.

As I neared they shook and rocked with anger, as if my presence increased their suffering. They were mutilated, cradling torn limbs, or clutching vainly at their broken bodies; some were without eyes, the sockets bleeding freshly; others with heads that wobbled on throats slit ear to ear in a hideous grin.

The wildness led me to them, bid me to look into the bruised and tortured faces. I shivered with the horror, my hands, which tried to cover my face, remaining locked and immobile at my side. I wanted to flee from these men whose hands reached out at me as I passed with a slow, heavy step. They plucked at my sleeves and tried to grasp my arm.

"Magda," they called in hollow voices—those that could speak; those that could not, wailed.

"No more!" I cried, turning to the wildness. "Please, no more." She stared back at me, face hard and cold as ice, blue flame smoldering in the lapis eyes. This was my heritage, my power, shaped and gifted me by Father, by my ancestors. I would not control the wildness until I had accepted what it was, how it had been used. The shimmering blue face shifted, and the eyes lost their hardness. They gazed at me, blue and gray like the sea, and I saw longing and sadness. I looked away from the pleading eyes and was confronted by my suitors.

They surrounded me, shuffling closer and closer in an ever-tightening circle. I twisted and turned, frantically searching, but the wildness was not there. I was alone with my suitors. I began to tremble as they reached out and touched me with ghostly hands, on the face, the arms, the breast, some crying for mercy, others, retribution. Like a little fish pulled in a net, I thrashed and choked in the close air.

I had denied the wildness rage and so it vanished. I had no other way—knew no other way—to express my magic. I felt trapped, helpless and impotent, by the ghosts that circled me. I was lost and so was Severin. Despair filled me and I heard a long, harsh scream that must have been mine though I was dumbstruck, unable to utter a sound. Then a voice, dry like the creak of an old door not often opened, whispered in my ear.

"Steady, Magda. You're strong yet. Don't turn away from the past. Use your magic to heal it. Give love where none was given and you'll give peace to the wraiths."

I shook my head, unbelieving. The wildness had fled; I had no way to call it.

"No," whispered the voice. "It waits for you, but you must shape it to a different task. Let me help you mold it to the healer's touch."

I felt the soft touch of Sefert's hands on mine and I ceased to fear as a calm like a subtle fragrance enveloped me, replacing the terror. Closing my eyes to the horror, I took in a long, deep breath, holding it until my lungs ached and then released it slowly, letting the panic escape with the air.

Then I opened my eyes and beheld my suitors. I found that I could look at them, not with revulsion, but with pity. They crowded together, pressing me, intimately sharing the anguish and pain of their wounds. They were my father's creations, but they were my ghosts. I understood now that only I could grant the healing that might offer them peace and rest at last. That was the challenge the wildness had offered me.

I reached out and held the bloodied hands of a suitor. His face was torn beyond recognition; vacant sockets stared, sightless. He groaned and bowed his head at my touch. I gasped as

I felt his pain stabbing like a dagger in my breast. I clung to him, the pain bitter and terrifying.

"Call to it, it waits," Sefert said.

Rocked with pain, I summoned it; called the wildness to answer my need. I felt it first, trickling to my hands like a small uncertain stream, blue light reflected on its mirror surface. I could taste it, water that was sweet and cleansing.

It was small but it was enough. Through Sefert's guidance I knitted the bones of the broken skull into a whole. The wildness flowed wider, becoming a river running smooth and swift. The man changed slowly, his mutilated face transforming as the healed features covered the torn openings. He lifted his head and, though his eyes reproached me, he thanked me soundlessly and vanished.

I moved quickly to the next, then the next, and the next. Each suitor brought me pain, but each healing strengthened the flow of my power and shaped it to a new purpose. I felt Sefert's steady hand, his skill sure and certain as he touched each ghost through me and guided my power in the healing. Through him I experienced the healer's joy in flesh made whole again.

But as my power returned, I became impatient. Severin, I thought urgently, I must reach Severin before it's too late. I was becoming ragged from shouldering the pain of my suitors and exhausted from the constant demands on my power. The magic was there but I was weary and threadbare. I wanted to rest. Yet the suitors continued to grasp at me in an endless stream of need.

"Hold on, Magda," Sefert's voice urged. "We're nearly there."

Somewhere I nodded and took the hands of another suitor. I let the image of Severin sustain me. I thought of him, his face dappled by sunlight, his brown eyes gazing earnestly and his smile bright against his skin. I could see the curl of his hair that draped over one ear and the straight line of his nose.

Then suddenly there were no suitors left. The wind lifted the long grass and I saw the black-and-white bands of a killdeer as she settled on her nest. I inhaled the dusty fragrance of heather and heard the soft rustle of leaves from the Moravian forest. I had healed them all and the ghosts returned to Moravia to sleep untroubled. I sensed Sefert's touch withdraw and I called to him before he was gone.

"Thank you. You have healed us."

"No," replied the tiny, dry voice, "you have healed yourself. Go now, Severin needs you."

"How do I change him back? What do I do?"

"Remember him as he was. Shape an image of the man and when you can sense the flesh and blood beneath the image, strip back the stag's form and release Severin." He withdrew then, his warmth lingering on the edge of my senses.

I was alone again on the grassy hillside. The grass rustled a whispered message and the wind played with my hair. I turned around in a slow circle, searching. Then I saw her, coming down the hill to meet me.

Her form shifted lazily, like a cloud that changes in the wind. But I could see her face, round and full, shining like a mirror surrounded by an aura of sapphire light. She came to me, and placed her hands on my shoulders and gazed steadily into my eyes. The blue flame spilt out on my shoulders and wreathed my head. She smiled and then kissed me on the lips.

"Severin," I whispered and she nodded, taking my hand.

The sky whirled past me and the ground beneath me trembled. I wasn't afraid, sensing the firm hold of the wildness. It became dark and I saw nothing. Then I blinked as suddenly the world was lit by pale green light, shot through with yellow rays from the sun. I was in Moravian forest again and I could see Severin from my hiding place beneath the green bushes as he rode past the pond with his brothers. The image was sharp and clear. I studied it, the tilt of his head, the line of his profile. I heard his voice and rejoiced in its timbre, resonant in me like a bell. The forest faded and I was in the courtyard of Moravia Castle. I stood once more among the crowd and watched as Severin called forth the true hound. I could sense his talent now, feel his affinity with animals.

And then my heart ached, for I remembered our night in the forest: the smell of smoke mingled with sweat, the taste of salt on my lips and the light from the full moon falling across Severin's face when we embraced. I could feel the supple contours of his body, the smoothness of his skin, and the warm breath as he lay with his head on my breast. And I felt the soulstring tingle as he tied it to my wrist, its life drawn from the core of Severin's heart.

I started to sculpt, cutting away from a shapeless block the image of Severin standing before me, eyes opened and the mouth smiling. I held the image there, testing it and measuring it against the true and then worked again to correct its faults, adding to it, smoothing out the roughness. When I believed I could do no more, I concentrated on animating the carved form: the sound of his voice and laugh, his scent, and the movements of his body as he walked and rode. His wooden form began to breathe, the eyes stared back at me, and the mouth moved to show white teeth, even and straight. He reached for me, arms stiff as if newly awakened, and I heard the faint murmur of my name on his lips.

"Now," I said to the wildness. "Now it's time."

I heard the crackle of lightning and looked up at a sky overhung with thick gray clouds. The wind whistled in my ears and blew fine speckles of sand across my face. I stood alone on a shore and smelled the salty tang of the sea. I looked out at the blue-gray water, waves rushing with caps of white foam to lap at my feet. Across the water hung a thin blue line, a bridge arcing gracefully into the sea.

I breathed deeply, drawing the last of my strength to me and stepped out on the bridge.

I followed it, a narrow path spun out over water, until it curved and dipped again into the sea. I could see it, spiraling down, and disappearing in the blue-gray water. I hesitated, afraid. I leaned over the edge to look, hoping to see Severin.

The water rose and splashed against the bridge. It bucked and swayed with the motion and with scarcely a splash, I toppled in.

I was pulled downward, twirled gracefully by the current. Beneath the waves the water glowed red as a poppy. I saw something in the water, a spark moving toward me, and I stared transfixed as it swam and pushed itself against the swelling waves. I knew what it was; our child, tiny and small, uncurling like a new fern in my body, its head unrolling from a slender stalk. The little shape grew and wriggled like a silver fish and as I watched, arms and legs began to sprout and the child's head grew round until it looked more human. It kicked its legs and somersaulted like an acrobat. It was growing larger, the movements of its arms and legs becoming more deliberate, the mouth searching for a thumb to suck and the eyes opening to see the red glow of light that filtered into its protective cavern. I could hear the pulse of blood that flowed from me to the child, its rhythm like the steady rocking of

waves against a boat. The baby turned in the womb, the cord
that bound us like our own soulstring floating around it, and I
saw that the child was a boy. A son, whose face and body I
could already see was like mine and at the same time curiously different from me, for I could see his likeness to Severin, too.

I cried to Severin and my voice echoed in the hollow
space. The child turned to me and stared in wonder at the
sound. Again I called to Severin, trying to find him. I heard
him answer, faint and distant. I turned, searching, and I
glimpsed him far away, his arms outstretched to me, the
soulstring tied about his waist. Hand over hand I began to pull
him toward me. But the child between us grew larger, and
suddenly I couldn't see Severin, only hear the faint echo of his
cry. There was no sea, only the tower, and the child filled
every hollow and space within its walls.

I felt awkward and changed, my body grown swollen and
heavy with the child. I gasped as tiny legs kicked beneath my
ribs and each twist of the infant's body rippled the skin of my
belly. Arms wrapped across his chest, the child became quiet,
his head resting between the bones of my hips, unable to
move freely in his shrinking home.

And then it began. The slow squeezing and rolling of muscle that drew the baby down deeper into the hollow of my hips
and pressed him against the hard shell that had locked him
from within. I caught the motion, and followed it as it swelled
like the crest of a wave and then subsided. My breath shallow,
I opened fists clenched tight against the rising pain.

Again and again the waves that rose and dipped drove the
child against the closing of my womb until, at last, I sighed
with relief as a small tear burst the wall and water gushed out,
washing my legs in preparation for the coming child. My
knees buckled with the strain and I started to fall, unable to
stand. I was caught from behind by a pair of arms that locked
beneath my breasts, holding me upright and supporting me as
I labored.

The child's head butted against the cracked shell and it
widened and stretched to provide passage out. As small and
tight an opening as it was, he could not stop his slow movement down and out of my body. My muscles bunched and
pushed him hard, thrusting him out toward a blue and golden
light.

"Severin!" I roared, the sound hoarse and ragged, my lips cracked and dry from my labored breathing. "Severin!" I shouted again to him and reached to pull him from the darkness. The soulstring on my wrist vibrated like a plucked cord and it rang with a clear, piercing note. It filled me with sound, echoing in my head and driving the rhythm of my pounding heart as it resonated louder and louder. I saw Severin then, lying naked and curled, knees to nose in a blood-red hollow. The arms strained to unfold and pull away from his breast, his head twisted up, stretching and pushing at reddened walls that held him prisoner. He freed his hands and began to claw at the band of muscled flesh. The child within me waited, poised, until I could not contain the spasm that arched my body like a bridge and drove the child out in a final burst.

Through the echo of the soulstring's searing note, I heard the stag's bellow and then the tearing and ripping of flesh, bones that groaned and cracked, sundered violently to admit new life into the world. The smell of blood, rich and pulpy, filled my nostrils and throat like damp steam. But I felt no pain, only pleasure, intense and prolonged as I hung suspended by magic that crackled and burned in a profuse blue light about me. And then, slowly, the light faded and released me.

I was standing, arms outstretched, the fingers of my hands splayed wide, reaching to catch something. Severin's family were standing behind me, hushed and expectant. Then I saw the carcass of the stag, lying on its side, split down its belly. The wound gaped, red and steaming in the cooling air. White ribs poked upward around a hollow opening. Severin stood motionless beside the dead stag, eyes closed and arms dangling limp at his sides. He was naked and pale, wet skin slicked with blood, his face like a death mask, thin and gaunt.

A cool breeze touched us and he shuddered suddenly, drawing in air with a broken gasp. Blood flushed pink beneath the sunken cheeks and his face began to lose its deathly pallor. His eyelids fluttered open and I waited, afraid as the eyes stared back at me black and empty. Then he blinked, dazed by the light, and I saw the spark of life return to them. Severin looked at me; his mouth opened and he struggled to speak. He started walking, wobbling on weakened limbs, and a hand reached out to me.

I caught him as he fell into my arms and we toppled back-

wards to the ground. I clasped him close to my breast with one
arm and, with the other, swung the cloak over both of us to
enfold him in my embrace and protect him from the cold. I
held him cradled tight with in my arms and rocked him gently
like an infant. He looked up at me and smiled. His bloodied
fingers touched my cheek in recognition and he breathed my
name in a soft, loving whisper.

The tears began to stream down my face as I answered
him," My love, I've won. I've won."

He nodded lightly and then struggled to say more, his
voice raspy. "The child—did you see our son?" His eyes were
bright and eager.

"Yes, he's beautiful. Like his father."

"Like his mother," he chuckled.

Through the tears, I started to laugh and bent to kiss his
wet hair. Theda knelt on the ground beside me, tears redden-
ing her eyes. Sefert knelt in front and touched Severin's head
in greeting, his cheeks glistening with fallen tears. Severin
looked at him and smiled.

"Grandda, don't cry. I'm well enough. Just to feel the land
again and to see your faces." Severin sighed happily.

He leaned his head back, to glance over my shoulder at
Theda.

"Mother, I'm sorry."

Theda tched and shook her head sternly. "Nay, don't think
on it. I'm only glad to have you back." She wiped away the
tears with the back of her hand and squeezed his hand. She
rested a hand on my shoulder and I turned to look at her.
"Thank you," she whispered.

Then she moved aside to allow Teren and Nar to kneel
beside Severin. Teren's face was pale, his hair and beard
singed black. I touched his shoulder worriedly, but he shook
his head. Turning to look at Severin he began speaking in a
low voice.

"Severin . . . that boar hunt . . . how can I begin—"

Severin stopped. "Are you and Nar still fighting, then,
over whose fault it was? I'm sure you've driven everyone on
the farm mad by now with your quarreling," he teased.

Teren grimaced and exhaled heavily. Nar coughed, embarrassed, and then gave Severin a guilty smile.

"It's enough, then. You're forgiven. It was a spell, it
wasn't your fault." Severin reached out from the cloak to

touch his older brother on the shoulder and smile. Then he
settled into my arms again and shut his eyes. "I'm tired," he
said, "and I want a bath. In fact"—he opened one eye to
squint at me—"I think we both need a bath."

I sighed. "Oh, for a tub of hot water and a clean bed with
sheets!"

Teren helped us to stand and when Severin was on his feet,
gently took him from me wrapped tightly in the cloak. Lifting
him, Teren and Nar supported Severin between them, stepping
carefully through the field so as not to jostle their precious
burden. Theda took me by the waist and I leaned on her for
support as we walked behind.

I stopped and turned back to look for Sefert. He was
kneeling beside the carcass of the dead stag, patting the hide
reverently, honoring the dead beast that had carried Severin
home. He untied my soulstring from around the stag's neck
and came to where Theda and I waited. With deft movements,
he retied it around my wrist. Then he smiled at me and made a
small flowing gesture with two fingers.

"It means 'soulstring,'" Theda said.

I held up two grubby fingers and copied the gesture. He
grinned widely, nodding, and we turned to follow Severin and
his brothers home.

As we entered the circle of houses that made up Arlensdale,
Teren called out to several people who came running to help.
They crossed the central courtyard of the farm and carried
Severin to a small wooden house that was reached by means
of a little path laid with slats of wood. Their clogs clattered
like unshod ponies as they walked across the pathway and into
the small house. Theda led me to another wooden house just
like it that was reached by the same raised pathway. Ferns
grew in a thick stand about the house and the bright blue of
forget-me-nots winked at me like the eyes of little birds. At
the doorway, Theda sent to the main house for towels and
extra linens and food to be prepared for our return. She then
helped me through the door and sat me down on a low bench.

"What is this house?" I asked, curious, for I had never seen
one like it. High up near the ceiling small latticed windows let
in light, but maintained privacy. The wooden bench on which
I sat ran along all four sides of the room. Above the bench
were pegs and hanging on the pegs an assortment of odd

clothes, men's and women's, while below, resting underneath, were wooden clogs with pointed toes and small raised heels. Some had hearts painted on the toes, others birds and flowers. In the center of the room was a large wooden tun, cut in half and squatting like a hen over a clay hearth in which a small fire burned with bright orange coals.

"It's a bathhouse!" Theda replied, surprised, as she pulled off Severin's shirt over my head, undressing me like a child. "For Mara's sake! Don't you have them in Moravia, then?"

I shook my head. "They aren't very interested in bathing, I'm afraid. It's too cold most of the time in the castle, and hot water has to be hauled up from the kitchens." I was almost naked now and goose bumps were prickling the arms that I crossed modestly over my chest.

"Barbaric," sniffed Theda, pulling off my boots and politely ignoring the smell. "Here, let me show you, then, how we bathe in Thall." Naked, I was led over to a separate bench that sat over a grid flooring of wooden slats. I could see below some of the ferns, bravely poking up their heads between the openings. There were several buckets, ladles, and brushes sitting within easy reach of the bench. Lifting a bucket, Theda dipped it into the large tun and withdrew some of the water. Then taking a ladle, she doused me with it.

"First, you get wet," she announced as I sighed with the pleasurable feeling of hot water on my back and shoulders. "Then you scrub." She produced a little pouch of soap that she ran across my back, shoulders, and down my arms. Picking up one of the brushes, she scrubbed me like a floor, the stiff bristles scraping against my tender skin.

She scrubbed me hard with her brush, cleaning away the grime of a month. I felt the outer layer of my skin peel and flake away beneath the rough brush. She rinsed me clean, the gray soapy water draining down to the ferns under my feet. Then she scrubbed again, this time more gently, and I helped, taking a cloth and washing my face, my ears, and my throat.

"I don't know what to do with your hair, it's so matted. It'll need to be cut. Do you mind being short-haired, then?"

"No," I said, "not at all. I've always found long hair a nuisance."

She reached over to the pegs and took down a small pair of silver scissors hung by a leather thong and began to cut. My hair fell away in tangled clumps of twigs, leaves, and knots. It was hard to recognize the muddy color as mine. As she cut, my head grew lighter. It felt as if my head would float away, no longer held down by the weight of hair. When she was done, Theda scrubbed my short hair, rinsed it, and then scrubbed again. When she rinsed it a second time, she combed through the hair and looked for pests. Satisfied that there were none, she washed it once more and then rinsed me off.

I thought I was done and stood, ready to dry myself and leave for I was anxious about Severin and wanted to see him. Theda stopped me with a smile and a gentle shake of her head.

"One thing left. A short soak for you in the tub." She pointed to the little steps that led up to the side of the tub. "Here," she said, grabbing a pair of clogs and slipping them on my feet. "So your feet don't get burned in the tub."

I stared, aghast. "You can't mean it! I'll cook in there!"

"Go on now, it's not that hot, and the soak'll do you good. I'll get you fresh clothes while you're in there. Go on, then," she ordered firmly.

Slowly I walked up the steps and gingerly entered the tub. It was hot, but not unpleasantly so. I was glad of the clogs for the closer to the bottom of the tub, the warmer the water became. The tub was ringed inside with another little bench beneath the surface of the water. Sitting on it, I was submerged up to my neck in hot water. I closed my eyes and sighed as the steam breathed about me in gray swirls. Every ache and stiffness in my body seemed to slip away. My arms floated on the surface and the water trickled between my opened fingers.

Theda smiled, satisfied. "I'll be back shortly, then," she said.

"Mmmm," was all I could muster in reply.

She did return soon, her arms laden with white linen towels and a nightdress for me. "Come on now, time to get out. Sefert's reminding me not to let you soak too long, being that you're with child. As if I didn't know, having birthed three myself." Her strong arms reached to help lift me out of the tub.

I felt as wilted as the sorrel in Cook's soup and did nothing to help as Theda dried me down with towels and threw the nightdress over my head. It was much too large and as I stood it trailed on the floor, my hands disappearing in the sleeves. Theda rolled back the cuffs and then sat me down again as she applied another towel to my short hair and rubbed it vigorously. I looked down at the beautiful nightdress she had given me and was delighted by its crisp whiteness, the collar done in a lacy pattern of cutwork flowers, and around the yoke extra petals of white cloth were stitched like leaves. it smelled of the sun's drying and the tiny lavender pillow that I found tucked in its pocket.

When Theda was done with my hair, I reached up and touched it. It was very short. The damp curls had wound tighter in a boyish fashion about my face. But it was clean and soft, like the nightdress, and I felt completely renewed.

"Come," said Theda, "let's go back to the main house." She wrapped a red woolen shawl over my head and shoulders for warmth and we left the bathhouse. The sun had already set and the sky was streaked with fading orange and pink. Amber lights glowed from the stone windows of the main house, casting squares of light on the ground. I was wearing the bath clogs, tripping at times in the unfamiliar shoes. Theda tucked her hand under my elbow, steadying me as I held the extra length of nightdress bunched in my arms.

When we entered the main house Theda turned to me with a serious expression on her face.

"There's someone here to see you. He's been waiting near on a week now."

I looked back at her, amazed. "Who is it?"

"An actor."

"Where did he come from?"

"Moravia, he says. He arrived with Fanyon's troupe."

"Did he give a name?"

"No, only insisted he was to see you if you arrived before tomorrow."

I hesitated, considering. Moravia again; would I never be free of it?

"Shall I send him away, then?" Theda asked.

"No. No, I'll see him," I answered, curiosity getting the better of me.

Theda led me to a side door, stepping back after she'd opened it for me. I peered around the door, cautious as a cat before entering.

There was someone there, standing with his back to me as he faced the fire. I edged farther into the room. He didn't look very imposing. He'd a small frame, almost like a child, I thought, expecting from Theda's words to see a man. His dark hair was short and stood out, spiky as a hedgehog, around his head. He was dressed in the motley colors of an actor, in a jacket of red and yellow stripes. At his elbows and wrists were sewn little bells.

"Who are you?" I asked, breaking the reverie of the still figure. At the sound of my voice he whirled around and the little bells tinkled and chimed with his movement.

"Magda, you made it! I've been waiting for you!"

The voice was familiar but the face had changed. "Vooris?" I asked, startled. I stared at the rounded face that was no longer pale but a berry brown and freckled over the nose. The dark eyes glittered, catching the reflection of firelight.

"Well, it's not Zuul!" he retorted sharply and the bells tinkled gaily as he cocked his head to one side.

"Vooris, how did you get here?"

He laughed and shrugged his shoulders. "It was easy, actually. Easier than I thought," he answered.

After my own journey, I bridled at his diffident tone. "So tell me, how did it happen, then?"

"I told you, you're starting to sound like Severin. A season here and you'll be talking like a farmer's wife."

"Are you going to tell me what happened?" I asked with irritation.

"Yes, yes. All right. I'm just glad to see you. Aren't you glad to see me?"

"Of course I am."

"You don't sound it. I went to a lot of trouble to get here, you know."

"So did *I!*" I snapped, annoyed.

"Yes, well. Of course you did. Heard about it from one of the farmhands." He scratched his head and looked away, uncomfortable. "Well," he began, "Father was very angry when he discovered you had fled and that he'd slept through it. He flattened the stables and then he destroyed the west tower. You should've seen it! People were running everywhere to avoid being crushed by the falling stones."

"Anyone hurt?" I asked.

He nodded, tight-lipped, and glanced quickly at the fire.

"Cook's dead," he said softly.

"No," I moaned and covered my face with a hand. It's not fair, I thought angrily, it's not fair. I pictured Cook, her face flushed red and white from the heat of her steaming pots and saw her shake a spoon at me. Miserable, I looked up and saw Vooris, his shoulders erect and his chin pointing defiantly. His face was in the shadows, and with his eyes half-lidded, he resembled Father.

"And then?" I asked, a cold hardness in my voice.

"Then, Father locked himself in his tower and that was the last I saw of him."

Vooris's eyes suddenly opened wide, the pupils dark with anger. He grimaced, his expression caught between rage and grief. "I wanted to kill him, you know, but I didn't have the courage."

The coldness drained from me, and I recognized Vooris my brother, not Father, standing before me. "I would never have asked that of you," I said gently.

Vooris stared at me and the tension slipped from his shoulders. He heaved a sigh of relief. "Each day that Father stayed locked in the tower, I celebrated, knowing somewhere you were still free."

I nodded, thinking back on the cold fog, and repressed a shudder.

Vooris continued: "While Father was locked away, Fanyon's troupe came to perform at harvest fair. They were heading south for the winter and it was their final performance of the season. It was an opportunity to make my own escape. I knew that once Father came out of the tower, I'd never have another chance. I stole as much as I could, from Mother, Ilena, and even your dowry, Magda, to bribe Fanyon into taking me."

"Did Father find out?"

"Of course. That cursed Zuul spied on me. The day I left he ran to Father with the news."

"How did you get away?" I asked, astonished.

Vooris gave a dry laugh. "Old Fanyon's a crafty fox. Tends to admire married women a bit too much and more than once he's had to make a quick escape." He gave me a lopsided grin and pulled out a strange amulet from his pocket. It was a green stone, shaped in the figure of a tiny man, bent over a staff. It didn't look like much but I guessed that was on purpose.

"What is it?"

"A dupe-stone. Fanyon's got a box full of them. Won them

gambling with a shape-shifter at Thistledown, a village not far from here."

"How does it work?"

He put it around his neck and as I watched he changed into the figure of an elderly man, bent and clutching his staff. "It shapes the figure to the image of the carving," he croaked in an ancient voice.

"So you left Moravia an old man?" I asked.

"To Father I was. He searched, but as long as I wore the dupe-stone, he couldn't find me."

"Hmm," I said, thinking aloud. "I wondered why Father had left me alone for a while in the woods. He must have been looking for you then."

Vooris had removed the amulet and was now smiling.

"What will you do now?" I asked him.

"I leave tomorrow. We head south by sea to winter quarters."

"So soon? Can't you stay here awhile?"

He shook his head. "I must go. Part of the deal I made with Fanyon was to apprentice myself to the troupe for at least two years. I told you he was crafty. Took all my wealth so I'd have to hire on just to put bread in my mouth." He shrugged. "There were other reasons, too," he said softly. "Fanyon's a hard master but he's fair and I like what I'm learning. Look!" he said excitedly. "Watch!" He grabbed three apples resting in a brown bowl on the table and began to spin them in the air. I started laughing as he ate one of the apples, snatching bites out of it as he kept it spinning with its mates until there was only the core left tumbling in the air.

"What do you think of that, eh?" he sputtered, and bits of unchewed apple sprayed out of his mouth.

"Wonderful!" I shouted back, laughing at his glowing face.

He dropped the apples into his hand and wiped his mouth with the back of his hand. "Well," he shrugged, suddenly embarrassed. "It's a far ways from life in the dungeons." And for a moment his face became rigid, the expression stricken with horror. He shivered and the sound of the tinkling bells brushed it away. When he gazed back at me, I saw the old arrogance, but I didn't mind it anymore.

"A strange way for the house of de'Stain Moravia to end, isn't it?" he said. "You a farmer's wife and me an actor."

"Will you come and see me?"

"Yes, in the summer."

We stared at each other, uncertain what to say, content not to say anything. I glanced at the door, concerned for Severin. Vooris noticed the worried look and abruptly came to the door, preparing to leave.

"Take care, Vooris," I said.

"You too, Magda."

We stared a moment longer, waiting. Then I pulled him to me and hugged him hard. He let me hold him, and then broke away, shyly meeting my eyes. Then his mouth twisted in a smirk.

"Next time I see you, you'll probably be big and fat."

"Come in the early spring and you'll be right!" I retorted without explaining further.

He scowled, puzzled, and then shrugged. Then he darted from the room and only the faint jingle of the silver bells marked his passage out.

Just after he left, Nar's head appeared around the edge of the door. "Sefert thinks you should have some tea before you sleep."

"How's Severin?"

"He's doing well. Sleeping already. Come on, I'll get you the tea." I followed him down a narrow corridor to the kitchens. It was a warm cozy room, copper pots gleaming orange about the wide hearth, and a heavy black teapot hanging over the fire. A long wooden table held bread, fruit, and cheese on a painted blue plate. I sat down on the bench and Nar handed me a mug of tea, sweetened with honey, and a slice of bread, spread thick with butter and cheese. "Eat and drink," he commanded lightly and stood to watch as I gobbled the bread and cheese dutifully and washed it down with the hot tea.

When I was finished, we left the kitchen and climbed the creaky wooden stairway, which opened out to a small hallway. Theda was coming out of one of the rooms, moving quietly, and when she saw me shooed Nar away and led me into the room.

On a big bed at one end of the room, Severin lay sleeping underneath a quilt of blue and yellow wool pieced to resemble the motion of rising and falling waves. His head rested on a clean white pillow and his cheeks shone pink and ruddy from the bath in the glow of firelight. Beside him was an empty place, and the coverlet had been turned down exposing the white sheets. I climbed into the bed next to Severin, trying not to disturb him.

"Are you feeling better, then?" Theda whispered.

"Yes," I whispered back.

"The actor—?"

"My brother," I murmured. I could feel the questioning look she gave me, but the softness of the bed was already making me drowsy. I'll tell her tomorrow, I thought sleepily.

"Good night, then," she whispered, and I heard her withdraw. I inched deeper into the covers, reaching out to touch Severin, when I heard the door creak and open again. I waited, listening, and then turned my face, squinting at the figure hovering in the doorway.

"Feel better, then?" Teren asked. "You look better."

"Yes, thank you, I am doing much better now. I'm just a little tired," I hinted as he stood staring.

"Oh, aye, of course," he stammered, and then turned to leave. "Good night," he called in his hoarse whisper.

"Good night," I whispered back. I settled again in the bed when yet another soft, scratching sound made me sigh deeply and raise my head to the door again. This time it was Nar, his head just poked through the opened crack.

"Are you needing anything else, Magda? More tea?"

"No, thank you, all I need is some sleep," I answered, thinking to myself that it was a good thing that Severin didn't have a large family or I'd be up all night reassuring them.

"Just call if you need anything, then, I'll be glad to fetch it for you."

"Thank you, Nar," I replied, and when he hesitated a moment longer, "Good night," I added more firmly.

"Aye, good night, then." And he was gone.

"At last," I sighed, and at my side Severin opened one eye and winked at me.

"Have they all gone, then?"

I smiled back. "Yes, I think so, unless you have any more relatives who'll come to tuck us in."

He laughed and my skin flushed with pleasure at the sound. I laid my hand against his cheek, now smooth. Under the covers he reached out, pulled me close, and kissed me. I heard the steady pulse of our hearts and felt the warm sweet-

ness of heart's ease. When we parted, Severin leaned his head
away to stare at my shortened hair.

"Your hair? What happened to the curls that used to fall
into your face?"

"I had to cut it, it was too dirty to comb." Then, self-con-
sciously, I touched my hair. "Don't you like it?"

He considered me gravely and then grinned broadly. "Yes!
It becomes you. But then, there's nothing that would not be
made more lovely for being near you." His hands searched
under the fabric of my nightdress.

"For Mara's sake!" I exclaimed, imitating Theda's husky
voice. He stopped short, surprised, and then burst out laughing. "What are you thinking of, then, Severin? We're supposed to be sleeping." But I didn't stop the hands that had
slipped beneath the nightdress and found their way around my
naked waist.

"We've waited a long time for this, Magda. Come my
love, sleep can wait a little longer." His breath was warm and
his lips soft as they brushed against the hollows of my throat,
quieting my protest.

TEN

IT'S A YEAR now since I arrived in Thall. I woke this morning with the sunlight streaming over the stone windowsills of our house and felt too restless to stay abed. I kissed Severin's shoulder lightly as he slept, his back to me. In the sun's light I could see the white scars that raked along his shoulder, a reminder of Father's hound. I touched them gently with a fingertip and he stirred, murmuring something to me in his sleep. I shushed him and curled the covers about his shoulders as I slipped from the bed.

Standing barefoot in my shift, I crossed the room and peeked in the cradle that rested by the fireplace. Our son, Corin, lay there sleeping, his breath coming in soft little snores. I watched him, fascinated as any new mother. His round cheeks were smooth and creamy pink. As I bent to kiss him, I inhaled his baby's smell, sweet like the dusty perfume of harvested wheat.

I dressed quietly, pulling on a deep blue skirt and lacing a blue bodice over my shift. I ignored my shoes but took up a small beaded bag and tied it to my waist. Almost without thinking, I touched the soulstring at my waist, making certain it was there and knowing at the same time that it would be. I left the room, pulling the door closed behind me with a soft click.

It was early yet and few were awake in the cluster of houses that made up Arlensdale. My stomach grumbled pleasantly for food and I set off for the kitchens where I knew I would find someone awake. I poked my head around the door and saw Theda, taking her turn at the bread making. She was kneading the dough, throwing it down vigorously on the marble slab and pounding it with her strong arms. She had rolled back her sleeves and opened her blouse in the heat of the kitchen. I could see the little drops of sweat that dotted her upper lip and streaked her chest.

"Good morning," I called and stepped inside to steal a sticky bun, warm from the fire.

"Good morning, then," she answered, flashing me a wide smile.

"Is Sefert here?" I asked, licking the sweet icing from my fingers.

"No, he's left already. He told me he'd wait for you by the stream. That is, if you didn't sleep too late."

"I'd better hurry," I said, quickly grabbing two more sticky buns. "I don't want to miss him."

As I rushed out the door, Theda called to me. "Magda, as you're going by the stream, can you drive the geese when you go? They're needing to get out from underfoot for a while."

"Yes," I called back. I grabbed a willow switch near the kitchen door and started to round them up. They honked angrily and hissed, their heads snaking out to nip at my naked heels. But I persisted, and soon they had grouped themselves into a indignant gaggle and waddled out toward the stream.

As I walked feeling the warm sun on my back and the soft earth beneath my feet, I started to laugh. Magda de'Stain Moravia, heir to thirteen generations of sorcery, now goosegirl of Thall. I sighed contentedly and took another bite of sticky bun.

It wasn't quite true, of course. I was much more than a simple goosegirl. I was wife to Severin of Thall, mother to Corin, and I was a healer. Sefert was teaching me his art, and I studied the healing properties of plants as I had once studied with Cook.

As we neared the stream, the geese began honking excitedly, smelling the water. I looked up from my daydreaming and saw Sefert, sitting on a stone, his gray head bent over a plant he was inspecting. The geese rushed past him in a flurry of gray and white wings. He looked up, startled, and caught sight of me. Quickly, I gulped down the last bite of sticky bun and, wiping my hands on the folds of my skirt, ran to meet him.

Stories

❖❖ of ❖❖

Swords and Sorcery

❖❖❖❖❖❖❖❖❖❖❖❖❖❖❖❖

**A hero's horrifying quest in a land
dark with magic...**

Twilight of
the Gods

Dennis Schmidt

Vestla Ravenhair, mother to Voden,
spoke of the Well of Mimir
with her dying breath...
So Voden Wanderer set out to
a dread, far-distant land, to seek the Well
and drink of Knowledge there.
But Mimir asks much of those who would
dare taste her waters...